SHIELD HERO

Aneko Yusagi

S'yne's Sister

???

Myne

In her hand there was a simple object,
much like the shield had been for me when I was summoned:
just a box for holding ofuda.

"What is this?"

Table of Contents

Prologue: An Exchange of Otherworldly Information

"That was a pretty easy wave today."

"Indeed. I can only hope that we keep on winning like this," Glass replied. We had been taking on the waves in Kizuna's world and just landed the killing blow on the boss of the latest one.

"Naofumi, kiddo, you and your friends are all super strong. Much stronger than when you returned here," L'Arc commented.

"You guys are quite a lot stronger too," I replied. "I guess it helped to be fighting with my original weapon."

"You're much stronger than when we first met," L'Arc agreed, "so that would make sense."

That was the reason why we had defeated this wave so easily—we had gotten lucky and been matched with the world that my allies and I were originally responsible for. As a result, my weapon had been transformed from the mirror into my shield, with which I was far more proficient. As soon as the wave started, our levels had also taken a huge jump upward. Our levels here in Kizuna's world were added on top of the levels we originally had back at home. As a further bonus, we'd had access to all the magic that we otherwise couldn't use here.

That had allowed us to just cut through the wave and resolve the issue at the source, prior to any damage being caused.

"I think the Bow Hero performed the best during this battle," Raphtalia commented.

"Raph," added Raph-chan, the pair of them praising Itsuki.

"Itsuki, well done!" Rishia said.

"Thank you," he said.

"He gets my vote too. That situation definitely suited Itsuki the best," I said. We'd been able to use our sealed holy weapons again, and from the perspective of levels and numerous other factors, Itsuki definitely had the highest attack power in our party. My own focus was placed on defense, meaning I couldn't really hog the spotlight when we were on the attack. As a result, there was nothing strange at all about Itsuki having the highest attack power in our current group.

"I guess we got lucky that it was your world we collided with," L'Arc said.

"It made for an easy victory, but it's hard to say anything is good about the waves," I replied.

"Naofumi, maybe we shouldn't stand here chatting . . ." Itsuki said.

"I know," I replied, nodding and looking around. We needed to poke our heads into our world, see how things were going, and help out with the fighting over there. Itsuki and I, however, had crossed over using pretty unique means, and so getting back was also going to be a bit of a pain in the ass.

I really wanted to avoid as much hassle as possible.

In the world to which I had originally been summoned, one of two people would likely be leading the charge against the wave: the Sword Hero, Ren Amaki, or the Spear Hero—frankly, total nutcase—Motoyasu Kitamura. Peering into the split caused by the wave, I could see an image of the other side—albeit warped, as though through some kind of lens.

"It'll be a pain if they close the crack from the other side," I said. "We need some people . . . I think Raphtalia and Rishia would be best suited to go over and explain what's going on. If the two of you cross over, you should be able to explain that things are going pretty well for us over here."

"Yes, good idea. It is definitely worth letting them know that we have all met up safely," Raphtalia agreed.

"What about me?" Filo asked.

"You suck at explaining things," I said smartly.

"Hey!" she replied. The Demon Dragon gave a snort upon hearing this exchange. I knew she didn't get along well with Filo, but I wished she would avoid such open hostility.

"What was that noise for? You got a problem with me?" Filo retorted, glaring at the Demon Dragon.

"If you want to fight each other, go do it elsewhere. We don't have time for this," I told them.

"This scale head started it! Bleh!" Filo replied, puffing up her cheeks in rebellion.

"If you are going across to the other world, take this along with you. It's a message for the Dragon Emperor on that side—the one who tried to consume me. It will let him know the situation without any messing about." The Demon Dragon proceeded to spit up what looked like a shard of crystal—a Dragon Emperor fragment—and then gave it to Raphtalia. It looked like a pretty nasty piece of work, and Raphtalia had a really unsure look on her face as she accepted it.

"Okay then, we'll be right back," Raphtalia said.

"We're counting on you, Rishia," Itsuki offered.

"Yes, okay! I'll see you soon, Itsuki!" Rishia replied. Then the two girls jumped into the wave crack.

"A shame we don't have a bit more time," I commented. I might have felt like a cool superhero, having my strength back, even just for a limited period. In fact, it was a complete pain in the ass to not be able to maintain this level of strength at all times. If that was possible, we'd have no trouble wiping out the scum called the Vanguards of the Waves, Bitch, and all of the other annoyances festering in this world.

We waited. After about five minutes, Raphtalia came back through the wave crack. There was someone else tagging along with her, although I wasn't sure why.

"So this is what it's like to cross to another world," said the newcomer.

"Indeed. Quite the experience, but we don't have long, so please make this quick," Raphtalia said.

"Very well," came the reply.

"Eclair. Hi there," I said to her.

"Ah, Master Iwatani," Eclair replied. "Raphtalia has told me what you've faced. You never have things easy, do you?"

"Not really. How are things back there with you?" I asked.

"That's what I'm here to talk about," she responded. "I know we don't have long, so Rishia is discussing things back there."

"Okay," I said. It made sense to leave one person behind while the other brought someone back to report to us. We could confer and align our information later, once there wasn't a time limit. This felt like a suggestion from Trash.

Yomogi and Tsugumi looked over at Eclair and made some noises to show they were interested.

"Three birds of a feather, all flocking together. If we ever have more time, I'd like to have you spar a little," I said. They had similar temperaments and would probably get along well.

"What was that? But no . . . we don't have time to fight here," Eclair said, her brow furrowing, but she kept herself under control. I wasn't sure what was up with her . . . but I also didn't really care.

"What do you think he meant?" Tsugumi asked.

"I mean, there is something about her . . ." Yomogi pondered. "Maybe if we get a chance some time, it might be fun." It definitely sounded like they were feeling something.

"Why did you come, Eclair?" I asked.

"The king selected me to explain things," she replied. Just as I'd expected. Since he came back to his former glory, he didn't waste a single second—the epitome of efficiency. He really was the Wisest King of Wisdom, everyone understanding him and always getting results even though it felt like he was skipping all sorts of steps.

"Where's Trash now?" I inquired.

"He's received the deciphered pages from Rishia and is looking over them—while also placating the Spear Hero and Wyndia's dragon at the same time," Eclair explained. Hearing that, Filo almost bolted. No doubt Motoyasu was raving about Filo just being within reach and how he would break through any barrier to reach her. I had made the right decision leaving the village in Ren's hands.

"Are you sure we should have left her and come back?" Raphtalia asked.

"The king said that we would only keep Master Iwatani waiting if we tried to deal with that ruckus. We didn't have a choice," Eclair said. It sounded like things had been pretty crazy. "The Spear Hero looks like he's paying attention, but then he twists what he hears . . ."

"Maybe we can use Filo as a carrot to control him," I pondered.

"That might work some of the time, but right now he is

completely out of his head. There's no explaining things, no talking him down," Eclair replied. So Trash wasn't going to be able to make it. "Luckily for us, he might not get along with Queen Melty, but he does at least listen to her . . . It's just taking her a while to arrive." If Trash had sortied to fight the wave back home, I could easily imagine that Melty would have hung back to provide support from the rear. Even having awoken again as the Wisest King of Wisdom, Trash would still be fighting on the front lines. Based on his code of conduct, that was the most efficient place for him to be.

"Excuse me . . . but what are you talking about?" Kizuna asked, tilting her head in puzzlement.

"Nothing for you to worry about. Just some issues with a moron on our side," I told her.

"If you say so . . ." she replied.

"And Gaelion is upset about something too?" I asked Eclair.

"Yes. The moment he took that Dragon Emperor fragment or whatever it is Raphtalia brought over with her, he flew into some kind of rage. According to Wyndia, he is desperate to come over to this world, no matter what, and won't listen to reason. Throw the Spear Hero into the mix and there's quite a ruckus going on," Eclair explained.

"Hah . . . that'll teach him." The Demon Dragon gave a crafty smile, as though she'd got one over on Gaelion somehow.

I should have known better than to let her send anything over! Just because he almost scrubbed her from existence, that was no excuse for causing this kind of trouble in retribution! "I let your Dragon Emperor know everything that is going on," the Demon Dragon explained, looking at me intently as she defended herself. "He just lacks control over himself, clearly. Losing his mind to something so minor, honestly. He hardly sounds like an emperor to me." She paused for a moment. "However, it might just be an indication of how involved he is?"

"You'd better be ready to pay the tab for this," I warned her.

"I am more than capable of paying anything it requires! Shield Hero, as punishment I am willing to become your slave," she said.

"Where did that come from!" Raphtalia shouted.

"Boo!" Filo added.

"That would be a reward, not a punishment for you. If you want to try and overcome everything through love, go sleep with Kizuna," I fired back.

"Why are you bringing me into this?! Leave me well alone!" Kizuna exclaimed.

"Gah . . . that's one tab I certainly couldn't pay. Well played, Shield Hero," the Demon Dragon bemoaned. So far, she seemed capable of little other than sexual harassment. She also liked to play favorites, with little explanation of her choices, stirring further unrest. If she hadn't proven so useful during the battle at L'Arc's castle, I would have got rid of her by now.

"Raph . . ." Even Raph-chan looked like she'd already had enough of the dragon's antics.

"Shall we just ignore the Demon Dragon?" Eclair suggested. "We need to wrap things up quickly or all sorts of problems may occur." We didn't have any more time to mess around. We needed to complete the exchange of information—and fast.

"Causing all these additional problems, right when we have the remaining wave time to worry about . . ." I shook my head. They were like unruly children; they really were. Rather than getting worn down by their antics back home, I decided to look upon this trip to another world as a nice break from all that hassle. If someone wanted to call that avoiding reality, I wasn't going to stop them.

I proceeded to quickly give Eclair a breakdown of what had been happening in this world.

"We met up again with Raphtalia pretty quickly after reaching this world and also took out the guy who stole the scythe vassal weapon. Then we saved the Hunting Hero, Kizuna, but got dragged into a whole other mess as a result." I pointed to Kizuna to introduce her, hoping Eclair could keep up.

"I'm Kizuna Kazayama," Kizuna said. "I was summoned

to this world as the Hunting Hero. Can I call you . . . Eclair, was it?"

"Eclair Seaetto, hero from another world. I hope you will give all the aid you can to Master Iwatani, Raphtalia, Rishia, and the others," Eclair responded, and the two of them shook hands.

"I see, I see!" Yomogi said. I wish they'd stop looking at each other. They did have a similar atmosphere around them, but one big difference was that Eclair didn't care about her love life.

"I only got the basics from Raphtalia, but it sounds like you can't use your holy weapons anymore?" Eclair asked.

"That's right. It's got something to do with S'yne's sworn enemies. Even worse, Bitch showed up with them," I replied. I felt a strange pressure coming from S'yne, who was standing close behind me. It was kind of the same as what I'd felt in Q'ten Lo, but this time it felt even more pronounced.

In any case, we had been in some serious trouble until the mirror vassal weapon showed up, and we'd still barely made it through. We had been aided immensely when Bitch, Itsuki's former underling Armor, and the former holder of the musical instrument vassal weapon Miyaji all got into an argument that had played more like a bad comedy routine. After that . . . we'd faced so many more struggles that I felt sick even trying to recall them.

We saved Kizuna, but she had been forcibly attached to a weapon cursed with sloth and then turned to stone. Even once we'd turned her back to normal, she had basically become a NEET. This had led to us heading out to a dungeon called the Ancient Labyrinth Library, which was managed by Ethnobalt, in order to find a way to destroy the cursed accessory. The contents of a small, mysterious vial of liquid we had found there had been able to break the curse on Kizuna.

Meanwhile, the power-up method for the mirror had turned out to be eating, and so I'd been cooking up a storm. With all the powerful enemies we'd been facing, we needed to get as strong as possible. As a result, however, Kizuna and her allies had been getting distressed at having to eat so much. As a compromise, I decided to look into whether there was more efficient food that wouldn't require such large servings. This led us to a place called Seya's Restaurant, but that resulted in a bizarre cooking battle. Seya, the owner of the restaurant, was also a Vanguard of the Waves. After winning the battle, we saved the town that was under Seya's control and obtained all sorts of rare ingredients. When we tried to extract information from Seya, however, his head—and his soul—proceeded to explode.

Next, we decided to revive the Demon Dragon, hoping to obtain a means to combat the nullification of support magic that the enemy was sure to use against us. We managed to obtain the collaboration of the dragon, but at the cost of what amounted to her endlessly sexually harassing me.

That was when S'yne's sister got some more Vanguards of the Waves together and came to attack L'Arc's castle, sneaking close in the guise of volunteer fighters. They even unleashed a twisted beast into the battle, having taken a monster from this world and given it the powers of a corrupted holy weapon. Some good things came out of that attack too, though—we managed to eradicate one of Bitch's allies, known only to me as "Woman B," alongside another Vanguard of the Waves.

When I laid all the facts out for Eclair, it really struck me again just how much shit I've had to go through.

"Now to the big news, Mr. Naofumi. Everyone in our world already knew that the former princess has crossed to this world. They seem to have discovered it after we departed," Raphtalia reported.

"What does that mean?" I asked. It sounded like they already knew that Bitch was here in this world—like something happened after we left. Trash was still over there, after all. I wouldn't put it past him to find out something like that. Eclair nodded and opened her mouth.

"It appears that the former queen ordered certain individuals on a special mission to search for and spy on the former princess. However, things took a turn before the information they discovered could reach her majesty . . ." Eclair trailed off.

Getting attacked by Takt was certainly "taking a turn." After that, Trash had taken over the duties of the queen.

"So what did they find?" I prompted her.

"A letter left by the spy who obtained the best information indicated that they were about to cross to another world with the former princess. Even though they would be unlikely to be able to report again, they swore to continue their duty to get revenge and give the former princess a taste of hell," Eclair continued. That was some spicy language.

"I don't know who wrote it, but it sounds like they have their own stuff going on with Bitch," I commented.

"I haven't been told all the details either, but apparently many of the spies were selected from among those with personal issues with that particular princess," Eclair confirmed. So now it looked like we'd had spies among Bitch's forces all this time—spies with grudges against Bitch—and the final information from one of them had let everyone at home know that Bitch had crossed to another world. Of course, we had encountered her before acquiring this information, so it didn't really do us much good now.

"Understood, anyway. Anything else to report from your side?" I asked.

"Nothing in particular. We aren't facing any major problems at the moment. As Ren said, we just have to pray that nothing untoward happens," Eclair replied.

"Okay," I said.

"It sounds like you have been making considerable progress here, Master Iwatani," Eclair commented.

"Yes, we have. We've discovered the truth behind these ones who call themselves the Vanguards of the Waves and also determined some good information on the one ultimately behind the waves," I told her.

"Tell me more," Eclair said.

"These Vanguards of the Waves—people like Takt—it turns out, are also here from Japan, just like me, Itsuki, Ren, and Motoyasu. We've been able to theorize that they died once back in Japan and obtained illicit access to these other worlds by being reincarnated here. All of them have been selected due to having personalities just like Takt, so there's no way we can have a reasonable discussion with them," I told her. Everyone had surely read stories about this kind of fantasy situation. The protagonist dies, but their death was a mistake by God; unable to bring them back to life in their original world, they get reborn somewhere else. All the trouble these guys were now stirring up was part of the invasion by the one who was really behind the waves.

"I'm not sure what you mean by 'reincarnation,' exactly . . . but I understand the gist of it. We have been aware for a while that we're facing some unpleasant enemies. Uncovering the truth about them is certainly progress. What about the one leading them, then?" Eclair asked.

"The one who assumes the name of God . . . that's all we've really got on them. It sounds like they've got someone pretty powerful in their corner," I said.

"Hmmm . . . I'll share this with the king, Ren, and the others later and align our information with them," Eclair said.

"It might help if Trash came here to discuss it," I pondered. He could often come up with some pretty crazy ideas that we would never think of ourselves. I cursed at Motoyasu for screwing things up again.

"The king is still conflicted about doing harm to the former princess. He has little confidence he will be much help in this matter. He told me that you should end her if you get the chance, however," Eclair reported.

"Understood," I replied. She had fallen so far but was still the daughter he had once doted on, and that was likely to affect his thinking—even as the Wisest King of Wisdom. He was unable to provide any advice because he had to remain impartial. That said, his understanding of the human mind allowed him to preempt his enemies. So it was a mixture of the good and bad. In any case, it would definitely be a bad idea to have Trash fight her.

"Master Iwatani, do you require any reinforcements?" Eclair asked.

"Hmmm," I pondered. A good question. This situation would allow us to bring over anyone else we needed. A few more of the seven star heroes might not be a bad idea. There was Fohl and Trash over there. Rishia was already here with us . . . This line of thought made me realize that S'yne's sworn enemies had quite a few of the seven star weapons. It was probably best to consider the ones that were unaccounted for to have been taken . . . so the axe, hammer, claws, and whip were likely in their hands. To be honest about it, I would have liked it if both of them could come over, but that would also leave our world too exposed. Ren and Motoyasu could probably handle it, but removing both Trash and Fohl was going to greatly increase the risks, making me worried about security at home. There was no guarantee that they would use all their stolen seven star weapons in this world, after all.

Mulling it over, I decided it would be too hard to bring Trash and Fohl over. It sounded like a good idea right now, but it would make things much harder on us if our home then got attacked. We wouldn't be having these problems if there was a video game guidebook telling us what was coming next. In reality, any hints of such information had almost always turned out to be nothing but a trap.

All of this really was such a pain.

"Is there anyone who actually wants to come over?" I finally asked.

"Many would do so if you ordered it," Eclair replied. "The king and Queen Melty are the only two who said they would have to decline." That made sense. They both understood the situation.

"It's likely that S'yne's sworn enemies are also active over there. Keep on searching for them," I instructed.

"As you command, Master Iwatani," Eclair replied. At that moment, two shadowy figures emerged from the crack.

"So this is another world?" one of them said.

"It doesn't look all that different," the other one commented. "Eclair, they said that you'd better wrap things up." It looked like the newcomers were . . . the old Hengen Muso lady and a strange-looking Raph species—one that was all fluffy and looked more like a therianthrope. It wasn't a bad look. The fact that it could talk, like Filo and Gaelion, wasn't something I was overjoyed about, but appearance-wise . . . top marks.

"I've got it covered," Eclair replied, calm and collected. "What about Rishia?"

"She said she'd be right here," the Raph said. I recognized that voice though. As I looked intently at the Raph-chan with the therianthrope-like voice, the old lady talked to me.

"Saint. I have heard of your progress," the old lady said.

"Okay," I replied.

"I wish to see this new world along with you!" she exclaimed.

"What about your son?!" I shot back. This old Hengen Muso lady had trained Raphtalia, Eclair, and Rishia. She continued to train my forces in my village, teaching the Hengen Muso

Style that allowed even non-heroes to become much stronger. We'd faced hardship together when Takt attacked, but that incident had also made the old lady's son finally get serious about his training, and I'd thought the old lady had given up on travel between worlds in order to focus on that.

"How lucky I am!" she said with a laugh.

"You can't just shut me down like that. Tell me why you're here!" I replied.

"Actually . . ." Eclair stepped in, rather than the old lady. "It was her son who noticed that she wished to come along with you, Master Iwatani. He has been training with Fohl and me, even when his mother isn't around, and will still have plenty of chances to get stronger. So he told her to come and experience this new world."

"Okay . . . fair enough," I said. It sounded like this was her son's doing. If she wanted to come along, she could have just spoken up the first time. But if the situation had changed, then there was no need to turn her away. "Whatever you like. You should know that you won't be able to understand the language here unless Therese casts some magic on you."

"Saint, words are unnecessary if you can speak with your fists," the old lady said.

"Just keep your mouth shut then," I warned her. Violent conversations were the last thing we needed.

"Hurrah!" the old lady crowed. "New techniques and new

students await me in this world!" She seemed pretty positive about this entire experience.

"On to the next thing . . ." I turned my gaze to the Raph-chan therianthrope.

"Shield Hero! Look what I can turn into now!" That clinched it.

"Yes! I knew it was you, Ruft!" I exclaimed. From his voice and his appearance, I had been pretty sure that's who it was.

"That's right! After I performed the Raph-chan-type class-up, now I can turn into this!" he said excitedly. I was definitely excited too. I reached over and stroked Ruft's face.

"Yay! The Shield Hero stroked me!" Ruft said happily. He felt a lot like Raph-chan . . . definitely not a bad sensation.

"Mr. Naofumi? I'm seeing something I really need to ask all sorts of questions about. Maybe you can explain it to me later?" Raphtalia said.

"Raph?" quizzed Raph-chan.

"Can you fight?" I asked him.

"I'm more sensitive to magic than when I'm demi-human! I think I get a strength boost too!" Ruft said. I really couldn't have been happier.

"Can't you do this too, Raphtalia?" I asked. "It might boost your combat power, like the killer whale sisters . . . I mean, it's fine if you just end up looking cute."

"You are really scaring me right now! Mr. Naofumi! I'm a vassal weapon holder, so I can't have a class-up!"

"Right, of course . . . but there has to be some way to make it happen!" I exclaimed.

"Please don't look for one!" Raphtalia exclaimed back.

"If you could turn into a Raph-chan, Raphtalia, I would lavish all of my attention upon you. Ah, so many versions of Raphtalia to enjoy!" I rejoiced.

"Saying that isn't going to get you anywhere. Am I meant to be excited by such a prospect?" Raphtalia could be stubborn too! As we talked, Ruft looked over at Shildina. Shildina looked uncomfortable, averting her gaze and standing woodenly still.

"I was surprised when you suddenly vanished like that," Ruft finally said to her.

"Oh my. I was surprised too," Shildina replied.

"Yes. Both of us surprised," Ruft said.

"You've changed, Ruft," Shildina replied.

"Good, isn't it?" he responded. Shildina didn't reply to that for some reason. I couldn't be happier with the results myself.

"Does this mean I have to go back?" Shildina asked Ruft and me, looking a little displeased at the idea. Shildina hadn't originally been among the team planned to come to this world, but some kind of accident had brought her here. Sending her back was definitely an option. Ocean-dwelling monsters gave better experience, so she was suited to helping boost the levels of everyone in the village and prepare them for the waves. That was the job I had actually given her before we left.

"About that. The king suggested that it wasn't some kind of accident, but that Shildina got dragged into things intentionally, perhaps by the vassal weapons. If that's the case, he said there was no need to rush her back," Eclair said. Ruft also nodded at that explanation.

"That means maybe Shildina has some kind of big role to play!" Ruft added.

"I mean, you guys are the ones defending our world. If you think it's fine, I guess Shildina can stay here . . ." I said.

"I would very much like to fight alongside you, sweet Naofumi," Shildina replied, making a clear statement of intent.

"Good luck, Shildina. I'm going to try my best too, so tell me all your stories once you get back," Ruft said.

"Yes. I'll talk your ear right off," Shildina replied.

"Queen Melty and her father are both so incredible. Spending time with them shows me how much further I have to go. I've got so much more I need to learn," Ruft said. I was impressed by him taking this so seriously.

It was also true that we really shouldn't be calling Trash "Trash" anymore after his awakening. I saw now why the departed queen had been unable to let him go.

I took a moment to look at L'Arc. I didn't get mad at him like I had at Trash, but he also didn't really feel like a king to me. L'Arc was more like . . . a general, I guess. Or a Nobunaga-type, declaring he would unify the world just to be betrayed by one of his underlings and burnt alive. Maybe that was a bit too specific. For the sake of Ruft's education, anyway, I decided it was best not to reveal that L'Arc was a king.

"Naofumi, kiddo, stop looking at me like that. You're thinking something rude, right?" L'Arc said.

"Why is it that everyone around me appears to acquire the ability to read minds?" I pondered. I really needed to spend some time in front of my mirror, working on my poker face.

"The way you picked that moment to look at me, how could I not have some idea what you are thinking?" L'Arc retorted. Sure, that was a good point.

"Sounds like we're done here," I stated. "If you can, try and find a way to resist the nullification of support magic."

"Very well. We will need to make some minor adjustments, but defeating the waves as quickly as possible is our common goal . . . Ah, Master Iwatani, the people from your village were also asking when you think you will be returning," Eclair asked.

"Honestly, I can't say at the moment . . . I'll do my best to get us back as quickly as possible," I replied.

"I will let them know. See you later."

"Shield Hero, see you soon!" Then both Ruft and Eclair were gone—leaving just as Rishia came back through.

"It was all go for a moment there," Kizuna said.

"I've got lots of friends now," I replied dryly. Kizuna proceeded to take her Hunting Tool 0, which had been obtained

from the red liquid we found in the Ancient Labyrinth Library, and perform an experimental slash across the wave crack. Of course, everyone on the other side had been told that we were going to do this. The wave crack started to make a noise and then close.

"Oh?!" I exclaimed. It looked like the whole thing was sparking and crackling. The wave ended, and the sky returned to the normal color.

I immediately looked at the time before the next wave.

"Huh. I thought the cycle of waves reaching this world was pretty short?" I said.

"Yes, it should be," Kizuna confirmed. The cycle had been short, maybe because three of the four holy heroes were dead. Waves were happening between every two and two and a half weeks. That had now been extended, however, to a month and two weeks. That was pretty much the same as back home.

"Do you think attacking the cracks with Hunting Weapon 0 has the effect of slowing the next wave down?" I asked.

"That would be amazing! However, it also places more of a burden on Lady Kizuna," L'Arc commented.

"I can handle it. It's more than worth it, honestly, if it means we can slow down the next wave," Kizuna responded. She was right. This endeavor had paid off.

Our exchange of information complete, we retreated away from where the crack had been.

Chapter One: A Visit to the Head Temple

It was a few days later.

The old lady, new to this world, had been joining us in leveling up and had made some decent progress. Visitors from the other world could level up just by clutching some earth crystals, so it wasn't all that hard to make significant gains. She had also performed a limit-break class-up in our world, so she was the kind of person who would just keep on leveling regardless of what we did.

With Raphtalia, I headed to the castle dining hall and chatted with Kizuna and Glass. Raph-chan and Chris were playing happily together. I still wasn't sure what Filo, Sadeena, and the others were doing. Probably just getting into some kind of mischief. S'yne was sitting on a chair a short distance away, sleeping with her eyes open. Her familiar was putting a cape over her. She was resting up while she could, from the look of it, so she should be ready to move when needed. If I left the dining hall, I was pretty sure she would get up and follow me, so I decided to chat and cook here for a while for her sake.

S'yne had been this way a lot recently. Her vassal weapon was finally, truly breaking down. It was reaching the point where it could hardly translate anything she said at all. I could tell when she was trying to say something, but she just couldn't get it across. Her familiar would try and help out, but even that was becoming difficult. She had managed to get a few things across—something about me and something about the holy weapons, but none of the key points. I was also starting to think she might just suck at explaining things.

Eventually I'd asked her to just write it down, but then she'd said she wasn't good at reading or writing. As I looked over at S'yne . . .

"That old lady is incredibly nimble on her feet," Glass was saying at my side, clearly very impressed. "I guess she would be impressive, being your master, Raphtalia."

"She is quite something," Kizuna agreed. "But . . . I'm not quite sure how to say this . . . The way she shouts like that . . ."

"The fact she's so noisy is definitely one of her shortcomings," I finished for her. All the retro kung fu movie noises were really annoying, but she could leap around like a cat when she had to. I wished I could just get over it, but it also gave away her position every time. It seemed like she could shut up if she ever needed to attack quietly, but her movements were so exaggerated too. Just being quiet wouldn't stop her from bothering me, to be honest.

"It seems to me like she's moving like that for our benefit, making sure we can see her every movement," Raphtalia countered. "I always feel like I'm getting stronger just watching her."

"I'm not sure it's worth it . . ." I replied. "She's gone off with Ethnobalt to train the library rabbits, anyway. She looked like the cat that got the cream. Seriously, that look on her face really pissed me off!" Seeing her in the open space in front of the library, instructing all the library rabbits together, had been like a scene from some kung fu temple in the mountains. The library rabbits held a position here much like the filolials did back in our world. But clearly a different world could mean a very different approach. Seeing the library rabbits were more serious, I had to say I preferred them over the filolials. It might even be worth putting together a library rabbit unit, placing Ethnobalt at their head and setting them loose on the waves.

"I've no idea why you would get upset by such a thing," Kizuna said.

"I find it very motivational," Glass agreed. "Yomogi and the others are keen to keep training, and I think things are going in a good direction." I wasn't going to disagree. Having more, better-trained fighters was a good thing. Not to mention, there was something else. The old lady and Yomogi and the others couldn't really talk to each other, so their level of communication was pretty impressive too—even if I felt somewhat conflicted about her "talk with fists" style actually working.

Anyway, while keeping an eye on the old lady as she started to collect students in this world, we were on the move toward the head temple of the combat style that Glass used—or at least, we were in the middle of having a mirror registered to my mirror vassal weapon. That mirror would be sent to the head temple of the combat style that Glass used. We'd put a rush on it, and the mirror was scheduled to arrive within the next few days.

During their most recent attack, when S'yne's sister raided L'Arc's castle, they had overwhelmed us with their support magic nullification. It was now vital for us to find a means to resist this support magic nullification, and according to the Demon Dragon—who used similar magic capable of nullifying support magic—the founder of Glass's style had employed some kind of counter to it in the past. So that's who we were heading toward.

"Still . . . not sure about going back there," Glass said, her face clouded.

"Is there anything that we should be worried about?" I asked her.

"There were some issues, but we handled them before the waves started," Kizuna commented.

"Indeed . . . I'm sure it will be fine," Glass said. "I just don't have many happy memories of that place."

"Glass was picked on by some other students, because she was the one selected by the fan vassal weapon," Kizuna explained.

"Those problem students were all kicked out of the school

eventually, but still . . ." Glass added. I vaguely recalled Kizuna saying something about all this—honestly, who kept track of all these backstories? Something about Kizuna and her merry band going on an adventure to defeat the Demon Dragon, prior to the waves even starting, and solving all sorts of problems along the way. L'Arc had also faced some kind of issue with his succession to the throne. Glass had probably faced some hardships too. From the basic outline I kind of recalled, Glass had taken part in fighting the Demon Dragon too.

It seemed to be coming back to me. The students had all taken turns, in order of seniority, at attempting to be selected by the fan vassal weapon. But Glass had ended up being the one selected. As a result, the other disgruntled students had shunned her, hoping perhaps she would die in battle and give them another chance at being chosen by the fan vassal weapon. I took a moment to ponder what worthless wastes of space these students must have been, something like . . . Trash II. With the new knowledge we now had, I even wondered if maybe they were among the resurrected.

"Sounds like they might hold a grudge against you," I said. "Think they might group up with Bitch and her goons to attack us?"

"They wouldn't have the backbone for something like that," Glass replied.

"They were just trying to have things easy . . . like the

worthless nobles you see in other nations . . . something like that," Kizuna added. It sounded like she was making light of the situation, but maybe I was just getting too suspicious.

"Anyway, if they aren't going to show up and cause trouble, I don't need to comment," I said. That seemed like the best idea. If they did appear, of course, we'd give them suitable treatment. "Then we have the issue of Glass's birth." This was all supposition on my part, but I thought there was the possibility of her being the bloodline of the pacifier for this world, like Raphtalia was back on ours. I was basing this on the fact that a crest that looked a lot like a sakura lumina tree had responded to Glass when we were in the Ancient Labyrinth Library. I'd only heard it secondhand from Kizuna, but issues with her family had also meant she was ranked low in her style.

"I haven't really talked about it, have I?" Glass said. "Not that there's much to say."

"Still, it might provide us with some hints," I pressed her.

"Maybe . . ." Glass still seemed unsure.

"The master fixed his eye on Glass because she was just a complete natural, absorbing things even without being taught, and so he brought her officially into the style," Kizuna said.

"That's right . . . Even if you want to know more about my bloodline, I don't have any documents that can provide such information," Glass confirmed.

"Hmmm . . . so a different situation from Raphtalia, but maybe just as annoying," I said.

"You make it sound like that's my fault. The causes seem to be Mr. Naofumi and L'Arc, respectively," Raphtalia rebuked. In her case, me putting her in that miko outfit that only royals were allowed to wear had caused our village to be attacked from so far away. It hadn't been Ruft in command either. Raphtalia's parents had basically fled the country with Sadeena. Unlike that whole situation, Glass didn't seem to have any kind of family line we could trace.

"You think the fan selected you because of your blood-line?" I pondered.

"You were already stronger than the other students before you set out on your journey, right? Am I wrong?" Kizuna asked.

"I mean . . . you're not wrong," Glass responded. She wasn't very forthcoming when it came to this topic. There was probably some unpleasant stuff that she didn't really want to talk about.

"We just need to head over there," I said. "What do you want to do once we arrive?"

"Searching for the key to stop the nullification sounds the most important," Kizuna said.

"Yeah," I agreed.

"We'll have to ask the master about that," Glass said.

"You got some problems with him too?" I asked.

"No . . . but after his students caused all these problems, he got pretty depressed and rarely comes out of the dojo anymore . . ." Glass replied. The total opposite of the old lady—that old bag was packed with energy. Even if she did open a dojo to try and attract students, she probably wouldn't spend very long there.

"We tried to cheer him up a bit, but she hasn't really been to see him that often," Kizuna added.

"I see," I said. So Kizuna and her allies had been working through their own issues but hadn't quite reached the end of that process yet. Thinking about it, I was in a similar situation myself. From what they had just told me, it also didn't sound like we were going to get much out of this meeting.

"Shield Hero." The Demon Dragon chose that moment to flap over.

"What now?" I said, irritated already.

"I have a place in my former territory that might be worth inviting you to. Prepare a mirror," the dragon demanded.

"Your former territory, huh?" Kizuna quipped.

"If this goes as I hope, you may be able to recover all manner of treasures and other items that I hoarded," the dragon revealed. She was trying to hook me with bait that would catch my interest, probably hoping to make me like her.

"What kind of items?" Raphtalia asked.

"The continent where your castle was located, Demon Dragon . . ." Kizuna started.

"Right. After the Demon Dragon was gone but before the waves started, all the surrounding nations were bickering over who it belonged to," Glass confirmed.

"There's no helping people, is there?" I said. Same greed, different world. "Did that settle down once the waves started?"

"A little . . . now they're hoping to use this chaos to take over other countries, rather than some out-of-the-way land. So they are fighting each other. But with the damage from the waves themselves and then the issues caused by the Vanguards of the Waves, those conflicts are calming down . . ." That sounded like the work of Trash II, Kyo, the guy who stole the scythe, and Miyaji—morons like that. Kizuna and her gang had taken all of them out, of course. Anyone who was left was probably gathered with the holder of the harpoon vassal weapon.

"How shamefully pathetic. Shield Hero, you can put all concerns aside; having investigated the place with my magic, I determined that everything I concealed there still seems to be in place. A visit will definitely prove worthwhile for you," the Demon Dragon said. She was currently training hard and had hit around level 70 already. Her food enhancement was at the same level as Filo . . . In fact, she probably ate even more than her and was developing quickly.

She also had unique magic of her own, and I was getting a little worried about whether it was safe to allow that. She had the worst possible personality, but she was deadly serious when it came to combat, so she made great progress. She was always boasting about dragon stamina and going out hunting all night. I often wondered when—if—she was getting any sleep.

"You just need to send me to the closest possible country and then come meet me at the appointed time. Simple. If I take a mirror with me, you can come anywhere, correct?" the dragon said.

"That's true . . ." I admitted. There was no controlling the Demon Dragon; that was the issue. She was basically still doing what she had promised to do. She was playing along with us . . . for now.

"Are you going to trust her?" Raphtalia asked.

"Should we really let the Demon Dragon just go off on her own?" Glass added. They both made good points, I had to admit. Right now, she just looked like a small, talking, baby purple dragon. But once she started becoming a proper "Demon Dragon," it was going to make things a lot more complicated. If having broken the seal became a political issue, that could cause all sorts of trouble too.

"I'm ready for the worst—but I still don't really want it to come out that the Demon Dragon has been revived," I said.

"Hah! All you need to say is that this foolish fighting has caused me to revive in all my glory. That will prove a worthy lesson to these imbeciles who have fought over my lands since I was defeated," the dragon suggested.

"That might not be a bad cover story. We could say that the pointless fighting has caused a number of dragon cores to collect together and revive the Demon Dragon," I pondered out loud.

"But if the Demon Dragon comes back, the humans—" Kizuna started.

"I don't care about that. Who's better? Who should be on top and who should be below? I don't care," I said.

"Well said, Shield Hero!" the dragon cheered. "I am ready to become your—"

"Enough of that. Just stop it!" I grabbed the persistent dragon's head with one hand and tossed her away.

"This is a problem like those seen in Melromarc and Silt-velt," Raphtalia commented.

"I don't see the harm in letting her do what she can to help out, at least for now," I replied. I looked at the dragon. "Go ahead."

"Very well, Shield Hero. I will provide you with whatever it takes to catch your interest," she replied. I wasn't sure what that meant and didn't like the sound of it. "Just as a side note, Shield Hero, I'm aware that your tastes favor girls who look young but are very generous! And that you don't care how pretty they are."

"Sure, whatever," I replied. I was getting accustomed to blowing off her attacks now. Thinking of her as a combination of Atla and Gaelion made it easier to handle, perhaps—and also kept me from really disliking her.

I pondered for a moment on how much I had changed. That was thanks to Atla too.

"Then I shall depart at once!" the dragon said with a laugh.

"I will make you like me. You'll see!" The Demon Dragon headed away.

"What a . . . unique individual," Raphtalia said. She probably hadn't expected the dragon to be quite so aggressive in putting the moves on me. I wasn't so bothered by it anymore. I was even starting to think she had a cute side to her. Having come this far, I almost wanted to see how hard she would work to get my attention.

"Can you believe that's the king of the monsters? The terrible creature that plunged the world into terror?" I said.

"Not an easy thing, is it?" Glass agreed. I could understand Kizuna's mixed feelings at being summoned to defeat such a creature.

"Do your best to make peace with her," I told them.

"You think that's possible?" Kizuna asked.

"Try explaining things to her—without bringing me into it. I think she's softening up already," I said. We were definitely sharing more of a dialogue now than we had when we first fought the Demon Dragon. However, I still wasn't sure if being corrupted by my rage had made the dragon go crazy or if that had been Gaelion's fault.

"I guess so. She was more arrogant, colder before. We'll do our best to keep the peace, even when the promised time comes," Kizuna said. She was trying, at least.

These were the kinds of things we talked about as we saw

off the Demon Dragon with a mirror. After that, we trained in the castle and researched accessories. I also made the time to greet some people Kizuna was friendly with. There was a magic user that looked like a ninja and made a big impression. I almost thought he was a Shadow.

It was a few days later.

"Is the town here close to the head temple of your style?" I asked.

"That's right," Glass replied. The mirror was close to its destination, and so I'd put a party together—Kizuna, Glass, Raphtalia, Raph-chan, Sadeena, Shildina, S'yne, the old lady, and myself—and we made our way out. Itsuki, Rishia, and Ethnobalt were off raising their levels. Itsuki, in particular, had gone off to listen to musical instrument magic from each region, seeking to increase his own variety of musical magic. L'Arc and Therese were attending collaboration meetings in each nation with Yomogi and Tsugumi while also acquiring monster parts in the vicinity.

As for Filo, she had been here with us yesterday, but after taking a look at Glass's nation, she'd left. She had been put on display before and wasn't keen on the Japan-style nations in this world. As a result, she was now off with Itsuki due to their shared interest in music.

As expected, the country Glass originated from was a

Japan-style nation. It made sense, because Glass loved to wear a kimono. The town looked like something from a Japanese period drama. It had an atmosphere like Q'ten Lo, and the people looked . . . a bit like ghosts, if I was being honest. They had a bit of a spooky feeling to them, giving the whole place a kind of haunted-house feeling.

They had big red Shinto gates in the city and also big wooden buildings that looked like old-timey brothels. Women who looked like those feudal courtesans were walking the streets. There was a lot of room for variety even within the range of "Japan style," clearly.

"This place . . . looks like there would be some kind of eldritch sword lying around," I said. It was an ominous and yet glittery, gaudy place. I thought the night scenery would be quite the sight. Ninja running across the rooftops or something like that might be fun.

"Yeah, I think I get what you mean," Kizuna replied.

"Although I can't quite put my finger on it, it's a bit different from Q'ten Lo," Raphtalia added.

"True. I did feel for a moment there like I was in Q'ten Lo too," Sadeena agreed.

"There's no sakura lumina, the clothes are more flashy, and there are so many spirits," Shildina finished for the three of them, each providing their own comparison between Q'ten Lo and Glass's nation. "It's the middle of the afternoon and yet it feels like night. Is this because of all the wooden construction?" Shildina was getting a little excited, perhaps interested in our surroundings. Since she hooked up with us, she'd been taken out to all sorts of new places, so the whole thing was a string of new experiences for her.

"They do like the color black," Sadeena commented.

"A lot of the plants and ores that originate from this region are black," Glass explained. "That naturally leads to black constructions, which they offset with lamps to make them brighter or illuminate with magic. There are also many rich veins of gold here, far more than in other nations, and so they feature a lot of goldwork."

"I see," I pondered. The timber did have quite the luster to it. It looked more like charcoal, and I was surprised to learn that wasn't the case.

"Let's keep moving," Glass suggested.

"Okay, after you," I told her. After making our way through the town, we found ourselves looking up at a mountain with a long stone stairway cut into it. Perhaps because the soil, ores, and trees were all black, the lanterns that took over the streetlamps alongside the stairway were lit with a blue-white flame. The whole thing was making me think I might be in some kind of survival horror game.

"Saint, you've shown me again how worthwhile it is to live a long life. An opportunity to witness the culture rooted in such a place as this . . . if I was half my age, I'd be raring to get up there and fight some monsters," the old lady croaked.

"Don't stop at monsters," I told her. "I bet you could fight off some evil spirits too." My otaku knowledge was packed with kung fu action movies involving specters and spooks. The old lady looked just like the kind of hand-to-hand ghostbusting specialist who showed up in such fare. Now that I thought about it . . . Raphtalia, Sadeena, and Shildina also all blended in nicely with this Japanese esthetic.

"Raph," said Raph-chan. That little cutie could play the perfect tanuki spirit in a place like this. Give her a teapot and she'd be just like something out of one particular old Japanese story.

On the other hand, S'yne looked pretty out of place. I decided not to say anything. She was pretty good at reading the room, and if I made a comment, she'd probably go ahead and transform her familiar into a wooden doll or change into some kind of eldritch puppet master.

We continued up the interminably long steps and eventually reached what looked like what could be called a temple or shrine. It was also made from black materials, so it all looked pretty shady. Perhaps a cultural thing. At a glance, it seemed pretty rundown. But on closer inspection, it was actually well cared for.

"Master! Master!" Glass was quick to step into the temple grounds and start shouting her head off.

"Saint!" the old lady warned me with a grunt. I raised my guard immediately at her warning, and in the next moment the shapes of around ten people appeared, coming directly at Glass and the rest of us. They were all shouting and moving at what they probably considered top speed. For us, that still made them pretty slow though.

The fastest-moving one of them charged directly for Glass. He was using a fan, just like Glass herself. Glass matched the speed of her opponent, attacking and defending as though dancing. It looked like sparks were grating out from their battle, and I was a bit nervous for her safety.

"Not exactly the warm welcome I was expecting," I quipped, throwing up a Stardust Mirror and letting the incoming attackers bounce off it. They grunted pleasingly in surprise at this unexpected impediment.

"I should have mentioned this," Glass said. "Please be careful not to hurt them too badly."

"They do this every time. You get pretty sick of it after about your third visit," Kizuna groaned. They did seem to have rules. Those who had attacked or defended put their weapons away and went to sit along the wall. I wasn't keen on them making us fight like this.

Raphtalia and Raph-chan both gave shouts as they worked together to drive off another attacker. The poor guy must have been shocked out of his wits when Raphtalia and Raph-chan vanished into smoke just as his attack was about to hit. Then, after reappearing next to him, Raphtalia proceeded to knock him out with her sword hilt.

"You lack conviction!" the old lady shouted as she grabbed the weapon hand of another attacker and casually tossed him to the side. The poor guy screamed in surprise as he flew through the air. Now that was going too far.

"We need to get in on this action," Sadeena said.

"You said it," Shildina agreed with a nod.

"No need—" S'yne started.

"Lady S—says there—no need to wo—about that," her familiar relayed, with a worrying amount of static mixed in. Even as the killer whale sisters readied their weapons, S'yne proceeded to wrap up all the attackers in thread, binding them together on the spot.

"Oh my," said Sadeena.

"Oh dear," added Shildina. That instantly resolved the issue, but the two whales looked less than pleased. S'yne could have let them have a little fun.

Glass was still fighting. Her opponent looked like . . . an old man. He was the lean but muscular type, with priestly-looking clothing . . . like the clothing Ruft used to wear. He looked kind of blurred and semitransparent, meaning he was definitely a spirit.

Then I took a moment to identify the attackers we had

driven off. There were five spirits, three jewels, one grass person, and one human. They seemed to have accepted defeat and lined up along the wall.

"Circle Dance . . . Breeze Blizzard!" The old man attacking Glass shouted a skill, spreading his fan wide and swiping it upward hard. That was all it took to unleash a raging gust of wind that assaulted Glass. She gave a shout in return, spreading her own fan and sweeping it toward the sky to blast the wind away. After it rose upward, it turned into snow and floated back down. I was impressed by the theatricality of it.

"Circle Dance Cutting Formation: Instant!" was Glass's reply, one of her fastest attacks. It involved circling around behind the target in an instant and attacking five times in quick succession. Glass blurred and attacked with her fan—but all of her strikes were deflected, reflected, or avoided. Her opponent continued the dance, thrusting his fan in front of Glass. But unwilling to back down, Glass responded by thrusting right back.

"Hmmm. I'm glad to see your skills are intact," her opponent said.

"You too, Master," Glass responded.

"I've also received word of the obstacles you have faced. Things haven't been easy for you, have they?" her master said.

"No, they haven't," Glass replied. Having completed this fight-as-a-greeting between martial artists, Glass turned to us to introduce her attacker.

"This is my master, the teacher of my style," Glass told us.

"Welcome to the dojo of the Freegem Style. Lady Kazayama, and . . ." The master looked over us all, and for some reason his eyes stopped on the old lady. I saw something spark in the air between them, I was sure of it. Both of them immediately adopted a fighting stance.

"Can you please let us complete the introductions?" I asked her. "Why are you so keen to kick off round two?"

"Why do you think, Saint? A powerful fighter stands before me. What other reason do I need?" the old lady retorted.

"Enough!" I said sharply.

"Master, please calm down," Glass said, also trying to prevent another clash. "You can do that later."

"Now would be better! I would very much like to fight her . . . but I guess it can't be helped," the old man said. Both of them dropped their fighting stances and reached out to shake hands.

"Right! When the talking is done, we fight!" they both said.

"How are you doing that?" I asked. "You can't even understand him, right?"

"Saint, when you talk with your fists, your intent can be imparted!" the old lady replied. I shook my head. Just what did she think we were here for! Certainly not to watch an old couple beat each other up.

"Getting back to the introductions," Kizuna stepped in, "we have the Shield Hero from another world, Naofumi

Iwatani, and Raphtalia, who was selected as the katana vassal weapon holder for this world. We also have S'yne, the sewing kit vassal weapon holder from another world, and then some companions of Naofumi's." She really only bothered with the holy weapon and vassal weapon holders. "Naofumi is also pulling double-duty at the moment as the Mirror Hero, chosen by the mirror vassal weapon of our world."

"Indeed . . . I've heard these rumors too. One with the capacity to turn peril into victory, so I hear . . . and you do seem to have quite a unique combat style," the old man muttered, looking me over—and not looking all that impressed. "So, Lady Kazayama. Tell me what brings you here."

"Well . . . we've got a bit of a complicated situation . . ." Kizuna proceeded to explain everything that brought us here, the enemy we were about to face, as well as information on the magic that they were sure to use against us.

"I see. It sounds like someone has been whispering of the hidden secrets of Freegem Style, now doesn't it?" he finally responded.

"You have hidden secrets, Master?" Glass asked.

"You might call them that . . . There are techniques that have only been passed down to the true successors to our style. They aren't something to be taught lightly, even to one worthy of their acquisition," the old man revealed.

"Sounds like some kind of annoying trial or test is coming up," I muttered.

"Naofumi!" Kizuna shushed me, even as the old man shot a glare in my direction before turning back to Glass with his brow furrowed.

"I normally wouldn't be teaching you them, at least at this point in time, but given the circumstances . . . Glass, you've been selected as the holder of the fan vassal weapon. This tells me that you are worthy of this honor. However . . ."

"However?" Glass prompted.

"Regrettably, while the fact that such techniques exist has continued to be known, the actual techniques themselves were mostly lost in faction conflict within our style. As of right now, only a few techniques remain in our possession," the old man revealed.

"I've heard this story before!" I complained, shooting a glance at the old lady. A similar-sounding conflict within the Hengen Muso Style had reduced their numbers and caused all sorts of techniques to not be passed down to subsequent generations. I wondered for a moment if this was also an attack orchestrated by the one who assumed the name of God.

"Furthermore, the technique to repel support magic had issues with how often it could be used, practically speaking. The technique to repel drops in status was lost a few generations before mine," the old man revealed.

"So this was a complete waste of time?" I asked, almost phrasing it as a statement.

"No . . . I'm still interested in these hidden techniques that remain. Master . . . will you please instruct me in their ways?" Glass asked.

"Very well," the old man said.

"Hey, one other thing, just as an afterthought—do you know anything about Glass's parentage?" I asked. "It seems her ancestors were positioned to prevent misuse of the holy and vassal weapons." It seemed worth a try to ask. Then the old man tilted his head as though he did indeed have some idea.

"There is one thing . . . a story of one of the former fan vassal weapon holders stopping one of the holy weapon heroes who went on a rampage," the old man revealed. "Maybe that's what you're talking about." It certainly sounded like a hint of some sort. "They were said to come from the same country as the founder of our style too."

"Which is where?" I asked.

"The lost nation of Amachiha," he replied. It sounded a bit like Q'ten Lo, but also like it had already been destroyed. However, looking for a fairytale country and actually finding it also sounded like something that could very much happen in this world. Maybe it was like Atlantis or the continent of Mu. Actually getting into Q'ten Lo had been a pain too.

"That's the continent once ruled by the Demon Dragon, said to have existed long ago, right?" Kizuna asked. So it was ruined! But that piece of information really gave a further boost to the idea that we needed to go to the Demon Dragon's nation. I wasn't sure I liked that. If she provided us with something invaluable at this juncture, I could see her getting totally carried away and continuing to harass me sexually until I finally got to return to our world.

Then I had another thought: what was the deal with such a country being in the Demon Dragon's territory anyway? Couldn't she have saved us from wasting all the time coming out here?

"So we need to go and search the Demon Dragon's continent?" I said, shaking my head.

"Well, this might provide another opportunity . . ." the old man pondered. "I think we should attempt to clear the area known as the Holy Tool Grotto, which is located deep inside this dojo."

"What's in there?" I asked.

"I don't know," he replied, with a totally straight face. I felt like slapping him. *Bring out the kung fu master who does know, then!* It sounded like he had more to say, so I resisted the urge to poke fun and let the moment pass. "It is a place sealed away by past successors to our style and vassal weapon holders, to be entered again at the appointed time. There is a chance that the techniques you desire slumber within." Okay then. It was a sealed place that even those training here didn't know much about. We might find something that suits our purposes, and might get nothing from it at all, but it was still worth taking a look.

"Ah, of course. I concur. If there's anything useful here, that will be the place it's located in," Glass said. So she knew about it too. Even better.

Led by the old man, we proceeded inside the head temple. It looked like a supersized temple, basically. Deep inside . . . in a cave, there was another temple. The illumination looked like floating human souls, and the whole place felt perfect for driving out evil spirits.

"This is a place where higher-ranking members of our style train and live," Glass explained.

"You are divided up, even within the same dojo?" I asked.

"Yes. Before I departed, I lived with those outside but came here to train," Glass replied.

"Maybe that's why the other students had some funny ideas about you," I commented. Places cut off from the outside world could get some warped ideas about what was going on outside. If the fan vassal weapon chose someone from the lower outside building, rather than higher students living in here, that could have made them dislike Glass.

At my comment, both Glass and the old man made sour-looking faces.

"This has been our custom for many generations. It is my fault in the end for failing to see the arrogance that it created in them." The old man looked like a deflating balloon as he spoke.

"Naofumi! No need to be so blunt!" Kizuna jibed, giving me a prod.

"Huh? Not sure what the problem is," I responded. "Forget that rotten lot, take some more students, and change the old rules if you have to," I said. Of course, this kind of old guy tended to be pretty stubborn. He would probably choose to be depressed and do nothing rather than change things. "The old lady might be able to give you some advice. She's experienced her own internal conflicts," I went on. The two styles had a pretty similar backstory.

"Mr. Naofumi, can you please be more gentle . . ." Raphtalia started, always quick to admonish me.

"You're right," the old lady cut her off, mysteriously agreeing with me. "I experienced a similar kind of conflict when I was young." She could understand what the heroes were saying, perhaps, but surely not what the old guy was saying. "We have a long and bloody history of eradicating those who possessed our style but failed to respect it. That's why I decided to let the style die out. But through the teachings of the saint, I have come to realize that making the effort to find those who are worthy is the true path to take." A well of life force rose from the old lady, and then she pushed it at the old man. Hooked by this, the old man glared back at her just as intently. At least that put some air back in his balloon.

"Hmmm," the old man pondered.

"It's only natural to regret the discovery of fools among your students," the old lady continued. "But letting that hold you back, and doing nothing as a result, is even more foolish. I will beat you back into shape!"

"Hey, don't give him any ideas right now . . ." I said. Maybe they couldn't hear me though, because they stayed in their fighting poses, staring each other down. It felt like the whole thing could explode at any moment.

"Oh my!"

"Oh dear!" The killer whale sisters made a pointless contribution from the sidelines.

". . . Master, would it be better if I guided Kizuna and the others to the Holy Tool Grotto?" Glass asked, sounding like she was giving up on getting much done.

"Yes," he replied at once. He was giving up his duty in order to fight the old lady! This was why half his students were idiots, surely!

"Well then . . . we fight!" the old lady exclaimed, and then they descended into screaming and kung fu shouts. The old lady leapt forward, and the old man intercepted with his fan. The old lady followed up smoothly with a compressed bead of life force and dropped back again. The old man brushed it aside and then plunged after her.

"Hengen Muso Technique Point of Focus!" the old lady shouted. The old man gave a gasp of surprise as he almost ate the defense-rating attack from the old lady, but then he changed his grip on the fan and guided the life force to send it flying back. I'd never seen Glass do anything like that, so it didn't seem like an attack from her style. I looked over, and sure enough, Glass's eyes were wide in surprise.

"He responded to that so quickly! He says he's old, but on a technical level, I still can't compete with him," Glass said.

"Acho! Hengen Muso Secret Technique! First Form! Sun!" The old lady closed in with the old man, light surrounding her as she taunted him. It might have just been my imagination, but I was sure I saw a tiger behind the old lady and a dragon behind the old man.

With a grunt the old lady somehow managed to perform a double jump in the air, coming down with an axe kick from above. A few brief moments saw a flurry of attacks take place. Each life-force-imbued attack the old lady unleashed looked like some kind of crazy fighting game attack. Raphtalia and Glass could sometimes pull them off, but she was mixing normal attacks and ranged ones without any difficulty at all. It was pretty impressive from her and just as impressive from the old man who took them all in stride.

"Are we planning on watching the entire fight?" I asked.

"It's pretty informative, to be honest. I'd like to," Raphtalia replied, somewhat unexpectedly. I went wrong raising her as such a muscle head. Glass was nodding too, clearly in agreement.

S'yne didn't seem so bothered, but then she had taught Atla and me how to defend using life force, so she was a harder audience to please. Not that she was rich in facial expressions at the best of times, but she really didn't seem that interested.

"I understand that, but we've got priorities," I reminded them both.

"No, Naofumi! You really don't want to witness this impressive display of skill? Isn't that a waste?" Kizuna chimed in.

"I get where you're coming from, but don't forget what we're here to do. Glass, Raphtalia, you just need to work hard to reach that kind of level yourselves," I told them.

"I'm not sure I can live up to such expectations! Now I think I really do need to watch all of this!" Raphtalia responded.

"If it really means that much to you, just have them fight again later. The two of them are just talking with their fists, anyway . . . and at a glance, the old lady has the upper hand. The old man will be more impressive once he's worked through this, so let's finish what we're here for first," I replied.

"Oh my, little Naofumi. Very impressive," Sadeena said.

"You're quite something, sweet Naofumi, seeing all that," Shildina added, the two of them praising me while taking in the acrobatics of the two elderly fighters. I was just surprised no one else could see it as easily. The old lady and the old man had wanted to fight, and the old man had something on his mind. They looked like two people who could talk with their fists, so hopefully this would all turn out fine. Until they reached that point, this was all prologue. There would be plenty to see after that happened.

Of course, if things didn't go as I suspected . . . then the old guy would either get pummeled into the ground or the old lady would lose interest and give up fighting him further. The potential for either of them to get seriously hurt wasn't even a consideration. The old lady would never let something like that happen.

"Seeing all of that from such a short snippet of battle . . . even if you hail from another world . . . you are truly a holy weapon hero," Glass said, her eyes wide at my reply. I wanted to tell her that wasn't what was going on—especially as she was looking over at Kizuna.

"Glass, what's that look for? You're not wondering why Naofumi and I are so different, are you?" Kizuna asked, her eyes half closed in exasperation and her arms folded.

"No, never! I would never do such a thing!" Glass defended herself. Kizuna wasn't some combat maniac, after all; she was just a kid who liked fishing. It was unfair to expect too much from her. She wasn't a hero really intended for combat with other humans, and I had been hardened by having to watch my enemies and learn when to defend—she didn't have that requirement either. Kizuna could do different things from me, so there was no need for her to be like me.

"Raph!" said Raph-chan.

"Pen!" said Chris, the two of them watching the fight between the old lady and the old man with their paws in the air—looking as though to say they would stay and watch.

"Okay, you two, we'll leave this with you. If anything untoward happens, or if the fight looks like it's going to get more serious, come and let us know," I told them.

"Raph!" said Raph-chan.

"Hold on . . . what?" Raphtalia still looked a bit puzzled, unsure of what exactly was going on. That actually seemed like the most natural reaction.

"Let's finish what we came to do," Glass suggested. "Before my master is finished with his distraction."

"That's the way!" I told her. "Let's get to the bottom of this, with a bullet!" Glass immediately started to move toward our destination, practically at a run, like a child hurrying to finish her homework so she could watch some TV.

"I'm not sure why, but I'm just getting a feeling that something is really wrong here," Raphtalia said.

"That's odd. I was just feeling the same thing," I agreed.

"Oh, you two! How would that be different from any other time we've gone on a little adventure? I'm quite accustomed to it now," Sadeena said glibly.

"Sadeena, dear sister, I'm not sure that's something you should ever become accustomed to," Shildina quipped.

"I think Naofumi is starting to influence Glass too. I'd better warn her to be careful," Kizuna said. I just ignored the noise from behind and carried on moving.

Chapter Two: Holy Tool Grotto

We arrived in front of the sealed chamber. It was something that looked like a cave closed with a thick door so heavy there simply had to be a hoard of treasure behind it.

"This is where my master was trying to bring us. It has been here since ancient times, but no amount of investigation has ever been able to provide an answer on how to open it. This place is forbidden, even to members of our style," Glass explained.

"Sounds like going inside will get you more than a stern talking to," I said.

"Normally, yes. But my master has given his permission, so the only remaining issue is whether we can open it or not," Glass replied.

"Anyone ever think of checking it out by just smashing their way inside?" I asked.

"There are thick additional barrier walls inside there, apparently," Glass informed me. It was the kind of thing everyone thinks they might try their hand at, but no one can actually break. It occurred to me in that moment that maybe we could have just crashed through the walls in the Ancient Labyrinth Library—however, they had pretty strict rules about no fire, so attempts at reconstruction would probably get you kicked out too.

"Do you think Raphtalia, Raph-chan, and Glass might be able to open it, like at the Ancient Labyrinth Library?" Kizuna asked. I pondered for a moment. We'd left Raph-chan behind to watch the old lady in battle. I was foolish for not realizing that needing her here might be an eventuality.

"If only things were that easy," Glass replied. "My master also told me that there is apparently a legendary holy tool housed inside." From the external décor, I was expecting either a legendary hoe or some torture equipment. That thought originated with a bizarre murder-mystery novel I read once. It was set out in the boonies and a treasure trove like this appeared in the story.

"Enough discussion," I said. "Let's just give it a try."

"We don't have Raph-chan . . ." Raphtalia reminded me.

"We can still see if you and Glass can get in, Raphtalia," I told her.

"Okay," she replied. We started to examine the door to the Holy Tool Grotto. It was plastered with ofuda.

"Check out these ofuda," Shildina said.

"I see them, sister," Sadeena responded.

"I'm interested in what kind of magic these ofuda are comprised of. Sweet Naofumi, can I investigate?" Shildina asked.

"I mean, if you have to . . ." I replied. Having received

my half-hearted permission, Shildina reached out to one of the large ofuda attached to the door.

"Hmmm . . . yes . . . I see . . . okay," Shildina said.

"Did you learn anything?" I asked.

"Hmmm . . . it feels like incredibly complex magic is sealed in here. But it also reminds me of a similar place back in Q'ten Lo," Shildina revealed.

"It does?" I asked.

"It's like the seal on the weapon hall the Past Heavenly Emperor left behind. Ruft broke that seal, allowing us inside . . . but hold on. Could this be residual thoughts too?" Shildina wondered. Even as she was talking, the ofuda on the door suddenly burst into flames, and with a sound of grating stone, the door . . . just opened on its own.

"Oh dear!" said Shildina.

"What did you do?" I asked her.

"I don't know. As soon as I realized there was a kind of residual energy here, it just opened on its own. The door may have actually been created with some kind of self-awareness," Shildina theorized. The old man had said that it would open when the right time came. Maybe that time was now. Maybe it had opened as a reaction to our weapons. That seemed possible.

"Shildina does cause a strange sense of oppression in spirits like me," Glass said. "Maybe she interfered with whatever is going on with this door?"

"That's also possible, but then all you'd have to do is bring a soul eater here and the door would open," I responded.

"Maybe those ofuda were to ward off soul eaters?" Kizuna suggested.

"If they were that specifically targeted, someone would have worked that out by now," I countered. I still had to accept that this whole thing was likely extremely complicated. That sounded like a pain in the ass to me. "Whatever. If it's open, then we get to check inside. We don't need to think about how it happened."

"I guess not! Let's just get to the good stuff!" Kizuna enthused.

"Filo would have loved to check this out," I commented. She loved to explore anything—even just people's houses.

"Indeed, she would. I remember when she explored Melty's house from top to bottom," Raphtalia reminisced. I nodded in reply, checking inside the grotto as we talked. It looked pretty . . . moldy. I took another step inside and looked around. There were shelves lined with all sorts of items and treasure chests sitting around. Far in the back there was a big fan, which definitely stood out. It depicted a large catfish across its surface. It was a pretty dramatic piece of art. It looked ready to start swimming at any moment.

"Is that a fan for . . . suppressing earthquakes?" Raphtalia asked.

"It looks like that old Keystone Fan," Kizuna pondered.

"What's that?" I asked.

"I gave a bunch of materials to Romina, a while back now, and that's the name of the fan she made from them. She used this big catfish I caught," Kizuna explained.

"That was a pretty powerful weapon," Glass recalled. "I used it for quite a while." She proceeded to reach up and touch the fan on the wall, and her own vassal weapon fan flashed. It seemed as if her weapon copy had been activated. Glass proceeded to check the abilities it offered.

"It has an equip effect a lot like the Keystone Fan. I guess it's what you and Kizuna would call a direct upgrade," Glass confirmed.

"Okay. How is it compared to the True Demon Dragon weapons?" I asked.

"It has quite a lot of similar capabilities, so I think picking between choosing one or the other based on circumstances would work quite nicely," Glass confirmed.

"Hey. If it's an upgrade of the Keystone Fan, there's only one thing I want to know it can do!" Kizuna said, obviously thinking Glass would know what she was talking about. Glass nodded, closed her eyes . . . gripped the fan tightly . . . and the fan turned into a sword!

"Do you mean the Wave Sealing Sword?" Glass said.

"Can you use that sword in battle?" I asked.

"Yes. As a special exception, I am able to use this sword," she replied. It seemed like a weapon capable of transforming in accordance with the intent of its wielder. That was a first.

"The name makes it sound pretty suited to our purposes," I commented.

"The waves caused the fusion of the worlds, which means worlds are crashing together, right?" Glass said. "Think of it like a tidal wave coming after an earthquake." She made a good point. They had likely been called the "waves" due to them being a disaster that comes again and again, like waves lapping at the same shore. The monsters spilled out in waves from the cracks too. The tidal waves from which the name likely originated also occurred after an earthquake. That made me think that maybe this was a weapon created to resist the waves by suppressing and sealing their two causal factors.

"What skills and abilities does it have?" I asked.

"Circle Dance Reverse Formation: Lawless Counter and Fan Dance: Snow Plum . . . and then soul sympathy enhancement and soul sympathy maintenance extension," Glass replied.

"They don't mean much to me from just the names," I admitted.

"Indeed. I'll give them a—very careful—trial run outside," Glass said. She proceeded to leave the Holy Tool Grotto and unleash a skill.

"Circle Dance Reverse Formation: Lawless Counter!" The

fan unleashed the skill as though repelling something away . . . but after that, nothing seemed to happen. An uncomfortable silence fell across the group.

"Anything?" I finally asked.

"No . . ." Glass replied.

"The name suggests some kind of counter skill," Kizuna added helpfully.

"Yeah, I thought that too. I mean, it's right there in the name," I replied. Some of the games I played had counters where you stopped an incoming enemy's attacks and then stole their weapon and used it for yourself. "How about someone throws some magic at you, and if you counter it, we'll know we're on the right track," I suggested.

"That's no different from what you normally do in battle," Glass replied with a smooth verbal counter. "If I want to just flick someone's magic back at them, I'm sure I could do it without this skill." Glass had indeed repelled magic with her fan in the past, now that I thought about it. It was a technique from her style, so I had been told.

"Maybe it can repel support and debuff magic then. Let's hope that works," I said.

"You might be right. Can someone use some? Kizuna, do you have any ofuda with you?" Glass asked.

"Hmmm. Yeah, I do," Kizuna replied. She took one out and started to prepare to unleash some magic. The magic in our world was far more convenient than this. We didn't need any ofuda or anything like that. But we were left with little choice but to use them now, due to not being able to use our magic here.

"It's a waste of an ofuda," I said. "I'll use some of my magic; it can recharge if I let the accessory gem take a break. I'll try some light support magic, so try and repel it." I could apply Way of the Dragon Vein, using a gemstone as a medium to artificially recreate the magic of this world.

"Very well. Please wait a moment, though. I can't use it again yet," Glass said. So we sat on our hands, waiting for Glass to be able to use the skill that might reflect magic. Finally, she spoke again. "Okay, I'm ready now. Send it over whenever you are!" I applied Way of the Dragon Vein to the gemstone and launched some of the artificially activated magic at Glass.

"Circle Dance Reverse Formation: Lawless Counter!" Glass shouted. The magic that I had unleashed hit the fan just before it hit Glass, turning into a glowing ball of light and getting knocked away—right back at me. I let it hit me, and the support magic was cast on me instead.

"From the name, then, it does seem to be a magic-reflecting skill . . . Glass has already been able to reflect attack magic, but this means she can reflect support magic too," I surmised.

"That's right. It seems to require quite a lot of time before it can be used again. I won't be able to use it in rapid succession," she reported. Being able to reflect support magic did sound pretty useful, but now we had to worry about a long cool down. That said, we'd basically found exactly what we were looking for almost as soon as we got here.

"This is definitely something we can work with. Now we have a chance to deal with their support magic nullification," I said. There was still the issue of whether she could repel enhanced magic, but we'd cross that bridge when we came to it.

"Next, Fan Dance: Snow Plum. I see. This is how you trigger it," Glass said. She proceeded to spread the fan and then begin dancing while transforming her weapon into the sword. It immediately felt like something shot past me. It was a lot like the Sanctuary from Ritual Magic or a cursed skill.

"It feels a lot like Sanctuary from Ritual Magic," Sadeena said, responding as I had surmised.

"I was thinking the same thing. We need to check exactly what it's doing . . . Glass, are you finished yet?" I asked. The windup for the skill seemed excessively long.

"The explanation I am seeing just tells me to keep doing the same motions. I'll try stopping for a moment," Glass explained. As soon as she stopped dancing, whatever she had been creating went away too.

"A skill that's only active while you are dancing . . ." I pondered out loud.

"I checked my status, and it looked like we were getting a boost," Kizuna said.

"That means everyone around Glass gets a power-up so long as she keeps dancing," I said. Both of these could be useful, but they were going to be murder to use effectively. After all, Glass was primarily an attacker. We didn't need her dancing around in support at the back—that could also be super risky. Still, finding the magic-reflecting skill was definitely a good day's work.

"Quite amazing! Right, little Raphtalia? Little Shildina?" Sadeena enthused.

"Indeed. We practically tripped over the very thing we were looking for," Raphtalia said.

"However, I'm worried about practically applying it," I commented. S'yne's sister had fired off her support magic without so much as a second thought . . . That long cool down was going to be hard to overcome. It wouldn't really help if things descended into a game of tag with buffs and debuffs again. Not just me but anyone who could use life force already had the ability to repel attack magic too. "We need to make it easier to handle, or it isn't going to do us much good."

"Indeed . . . this is the kind of skill that you need to have ready in a moment of crisis," Glass agreed. I wondered for a moment if there was anything we could do.

"I guess we just have to continue the investigation," I said. In that moment, S'yne's stomach gave a serious hunger rumble. She at least had the decency to flush a little.

"I'm feeling—" S'yne started.

"Lady S'yne—food. Naofumi, Naofumi, your food," her familiar managed to impart.

"Who are you, Filo?" I shot back. "We can eat later!" She seemed a little embarrassed to be so hungry, yet she still drew attention to it. I was also less than pleased about her asking for food from me.

"Anyone have any wine?" Sadeena asked.

"I've got some ancient brew right here. It came from a sunken ship in Melromarc," Shildina replied.

"It can't be intact if you found it down there! You drunkards!" I shouted.

"If they are drunkards, you're the super drunkard, Naofumi!" Kizuna quipped.

"I'll remember you said that, Kizuna!" I shot back. I wondered again why Kizuna was so eager to grab onto jokes about that. I was sure she had lots of fun in life, but I'd teach her that a big mouth could lead to disaster.

We continued to explore the Holy Tool Grotto. I came across a hoe covered with various decorations and a blade with something black on it that definitely wasn't rust. That was pretty weird. It almost made me wonder if the ancestors who kicked all this off were influenced by stories from someone summoned from another world.

Putting that aside, we started to pull some gear with really

Japanese-sounding names from the chests—things like Shich-ishito, a sword; Okitsu Kagami, a mirror; and Chikaheshi no Tama, a jewel. Most of them were in bad shape, however, and some were completely busted.

"These are like those sacred treasures from home, don't you think?" Kizuna commented.

"Something is a little different about them. Maybe that's why they weren't out on display," I mused. Kizuna was talk-ing about the Imperial Regalia of Japan and other Japanese treasures from lore, mainly comprising of the Kusanagi no Tsurugi sword, the Yata no Kagami mirror, and the Yasakani no Magatama jewel. If these had been the real thing, it would have made them incredibly powerful weapons . . . but even for knockoffs, they looked pretty decent. If I recalled the lore cor-rectly, the Chikaheshi no Tama had been a jewel that led vengeful spirits and the souls of the departed to the other side—and we were dealing with leading the resurrected, the Vanguards of the Waves, to where their souls were supposed to be. I hoped it was something created with this situation in mind. I then picked it up and took a closer look at it. I was unable to get much data within the range of my appraisal abilities, so I decided it would be faster to just weapon-copy the Okitsu Kagami.

Okitsu Kagami: Hetsu Kagami

<abilities locked> equip bonus: skill: "Release Rebound," curse attack resistance (medium), relay mirror, support magic visual aid (medium)

special effect: magic power increase (medium), curse resistance (medium), magic power consumption reduction (medium), magic incantation (medium), warding, anti-evil spirits, soul vision, SP healing (medium), drain nullified

The effects looked very good when the abilities were unlocked, but as a weapon right now, it was basically an upgrade to the Soul Eater Shield. It couldn't reach the heights of the Spirit Tortoise Carapace Mirror or the True Demon Dragon Mirror. For better or worse, it felt like a weapon closely related to Glass and her abilities.

"It has a skill called Release Rebound on here. I bet that's similar to the skill you were trying out back there, Glass," I said.

"It sounds like we've achieved what we came here to do," Glass said.

"Yeah, but I can't say my mind is at ease. Just to be sure, Raphtalia, you copy this sword too," I instructed.

"Okay . . . here we go. I have a similar skill, Release Evade, if that means anything," she reported. Someone had been collecting gear with skills of a similar type, from the look of it.

"The issue would be we don't have anyone who uses a jewel as a weapon. I guess this one is for Therese," I said. It was a bit degraded, but some careful work and it could make a nice weapon for her. I'd work it into the accessory I was already making for her and create a new weapon entirely.

"That seemed too easy . . ." Raphtalia commented, always looking for the cloud around the silver lining.

"I know what you mean." In this case I agreed with her. "Something is bugging me about all this. We didn't find anything Kizuna can use with her Hunting Tool either."

"I noticed that," Kizuna quipped. "I would have liked some new gear too." I looked over the stuff we had found again as we complained. The most promising—and intact—one was the Seismic Suppression Fan. We'd have to let Romina take a look at them all once we got back.

"They have degraded over the long years they have been abandoned here, but they can still be used as weapons. We should give them to those who don't have vassal weapons," Glass suggested.

"Who here can use fans or swords though?" I pondered, my gaze naturally drifting over to Shildina.

"Oh dear!" she exclaimed.

"Pick it up and give it a practice swing," I suggested. Glass passed over the Seismic Seal Fan that she had copied hers from. Shildina proceeded to turn the fan into a sword, just like Glass had done, and then give it a few swings. She looked pretty competent with a sword. It also looked a little like she was dancing. She'd been the miko in Q'ten Lo, so she must have taken part in festivals and stuff like that.

"You look pretty good with that in your hands, little Shildina. When I was a miko in Q'ten Lo, all that dancing was nothing but a pain in my sweet butt," Sadeena bemoaned.

"Liar. I was compared to you all the time," Shildina shot back, looking and sounding pretty sensitive about the subject. They spent a lot of time together now, but they still seemed to have plenty of issues boiling between them.

"It's all just passed down by word of mouth. I don't like that kind of thing," Sadeena said. For all her complaining, however, I could see Sadeena dancing with ease. At the coliseum in Zeltoble, she had basically danced through our attacks.

"Is that all we're going to find?" I asked.

"Hold on . . ." Shildina muttered, placing a hand on her fan—which was currently still a sword. "There are some residual feelings here. I sense the same thing in the other weapons."

"Meaning you can oracle them up for us?" I asked.

"No . . . I can't bring that kind of power to bear right now . . . but this type of residual energy feels like you, Glass," Shildina reported.

"Me?" Glass replied, puzzled. So now we had residual energy that was like Glass.

"You mean like how the Past Heavenly Emperor looked like Raphtalia?" I asked. Shildina looked at me and shook her head.

"I don't mean they have similar faces. There's a lot I don't know about spirits. But this quality I am feeling from it . . . It's not her, not identical, but seems to have some strong connection to her," Shildina explained. I, for one, didn't really have a clue what she was talking about. "There isn't a personality stored here. It's not that strong. But there is a powerful intent to do . . . something. It's a very strange case, that's for sure."

"Can you skip to the end here? What do you want to do?" I said briskly.

"Okay. Glass, I want to use my oracle powers to possess you," Shildina responded.

"Hold it." Kizuna was the first to respond. "That's that pretty horrible thing you did to one of Miyaji's allies when you were saving me, right?" During the fight to recover Kizuna, Shildina had used her oracle powers to bind one of Miyaji's women, a spirit, taking possession of her by force and siphoning off her strength. Even I'd not been all that comfortable with it. No wonder I sometimes found myself thinking of her like a soul eater. If that was what she wanted to do to Glass, we might have to proceed with care.

"That's right. I can't get ahold on this residual energy right now. But if I'm in possession of a similar energy, I might be able to call the two together," Shildina explained.

"Isn't that dangerous?" Kizuna asked, still on her guard.

"I'm not going to suck her dry like I did that enemy. It will drain her considerably though," Shildina replied.

"Very well," Glass said after a pause. "I think we should give it a try."

"Glass?!" Kizuna exclaimed.

"What we need right now is the same hunger for strength that Naofumi and his allies already possess. Without it, we won't be able to keep anyone safe," Glass replied. Her face was filled with determination as she talked Kizuna down. "This is just an experiment. It isn't going to kill me. It isn't even her first time doing this on a person." There might have been some issues with consent in regard to that last part, but still. "If I'm not willing to risk my own life, even just a little, it feels like I'm not going to reach the information I desire. Kizuna, I completely understand your worries. But will you let us try this?"

"It sounds like you really want this, Glass . . . but just don't take things too far," Kizuna finally responded. Glass nodded in agreement, and then both she and Kizuna turned back to Shildina.

"Shildina, please go ahead," Glass said.

"Very well. I'll give it a try," Shildina replied. Having received consent, Shildina turned her oracle powers toward Glass. Shildina was muttering some kind of incantation, but I couldn't make out any of the words. Sadeena was watching the scene with a perplexed look on her face.

"Sadeena?" Raphtalia asked.

"What's up?" I said, almost at the same time.

"Oh my. Can I help you?" Sadeena replied.

"You just have a strange expression on your face," I responded.

"I saw it too. Is something the matter?" Raphtalia added.

"I mean, I wouldn't say something is the matter . . ." Sadeena trailed off, watching Shildina as she started performing the ritual. I looked at Sadeena's face again. She rarely dropped her guard and talked about her past with me, but based on what I knew . . .

"Is it something you can't say in front of Shildina?" I guessed.

"Hmmm. I could just say it, and if she overhears us, then that's that . . . but I'm worried she would take it the wrong way," Sadeena responded. She has suffered mockery in her past for being unable to use the powers of the oracle. Of course, as she exceeded most people in everything other than that, it had likely been the only thing anyone who wanted to mock her could find fault with.

On the other hand, Shildina was the daughter that Sadeena's parents had conceived in order to replace Sadeena as the water dragon's miko priestess. As she had been raised, she was constantly being compared to her absent older sister. It gave her a complex that bordered on pure hatred, but Shildina had also possessed the oracle powers that Sadeena had lacked.

Now here Shildina was, trying to further expand her abilities as an oracle, further demonstrating an incredible talent that Sadeena did not possess. Sadeena would probably win in a straight-up brawl, but Shildina was strong too. Personally speaking, I was starting to consider the two of them pretty much on the same level.

"Mr. Naofumi, it sounds like you know what's going on here. Can you tell me about it later?" Raphtalia asked.

"Oh my! Little Raphtalia, you want to know what's getting me down? No, that's not allowed! It's too embarrassing!" Sadeena quietly slipped back behind her walls, using humor to cover her true feelings.

"Raphtalia, Sadeena doesn't want to talk about it, so let's leave things at that. If you really want to know, you'll have to persuade Sadeena to tell you," I said.

"Okay . . . I guess that makes sense," Raphtalia replied, a little sullen.

"Oh no. Now little Raphtalia is going to be 'persuading' me, is she?" Sadeena joked. Based on her reaction, I'd say she would probably share the details with Raphtalia later, who probably wouldn't be all that surprised by what was revealed either.

"It's about to start . . . I've forced this on my enemy before, but I want to make it as easy as possible on you, so please come toward me," Shildina said. Glass responded positively, reaching out toward Shildina's extended hand and then taking it. A brilliant light flashed out . . . and then Glass was standing there alone. She looked to have a bit more vigor in her cheeks than she did normally. She wasn't semitransparent either.

"This is . . . quite something," Glass breathed, looking down at her hands and checking over her body.

"What do you mean?" I asked.

"It's so amazing. I feel foolish for not having done it before now. I feel . . . omniscient, almost. It's very dangerous, that's for sure. But never having tried this before was stupid, nothing else," Glass explained.

"You really think so?" I asked. "Where's Shildina?"

"Oh dear! Sweet Naofumi, can I help you with something?" Glass's mouth was moving, her body tilting its head, but Shildina's voice was coming out. The two didn't match up at all. She was making the same kind of half-asleep face that Shildina often made. It felt strange to see that on Glass.

"This is kind of weird to watch, but . . . I have no idea why you think it's so amazing, not at all," Kizuna commented.

"Kizuna, you should give it a try yourself," Glass replied.

"What's happening with permission to use weapons?" I asked. That side of things was likely to get complicated, with the fan vassal weapon thrown into the mix too.

"I'll try and make this easy for you to understand, sweet Naofumi," Shildina responded. With that, Glass shifted from being a corporeal being to a semitransparent Glass and semitransparent Shildina placed over top of each other. Shildina was holding the fan, her hands over Glass's own.

"It's like I'm myself . . . and also Glass at the same time. Glass, now I'm going to try using you like the floating shield that Naofumi always uses. You just swing the fan like you always do. I'm the physical body here, so you don't worry about anything. Just act normal," Shildina instructed. With that, Glass floated up into the air and started to look like a ghost hovering behind Shildina. Glass made some hesitant noises and then started to move the fan vassal weapon. It left her hand and started to move like a Float Shield. But it really just looked like the barely visible Glass was moving the vassal weapon around. She seemed to be able to move it pretty nimbly too.

"We can also do this," Shildina said, taking up her sword herself and dancing around with it as a counterpoint to Glass's attacks. "Sweet Naofumi, give us something to hit. Think of Glass as a ghost or like a floating fan."

"Sure, okay . . ." I replied, not entirely sure what I was getting myself into. I readied my mirror, and Glass and Shildina started to hammer on it with their dance attacks. The attacks from the fan were the biggest threat, so I took them on my body and then used a Float Mirror to repel further strikes. Glass's attacks clattered against the mirror, and then I redirected Shildina's sword before trying to grab Glass . . . but I passed right through her. Shildina proceeded to change her sword into the fan—

"Circle Dance Empty Formation: Moon Break!" Shildina shouted and used a skill that I'd seen Glass use in the past. It was a vertical slice with a rounded moon shape around it. Shildina could use Glass's skills now too?!

In my amazement, I barely caught it on my mirror.

"Let me have a go too!" Glass said excitedly. "Circle Dance Destruction Formation: Turtle Carapace Cracker!"

"Okay, okay!" I was already pinned down by Shildina's attack and Glass proceeded to unleash one too. I was able to stop it on the Floating Mirror, but one of the mirrors shattered.

"We can apply pressure like this and use skills in quick succession. What do you think?" Shildina asked.

"That's strong, for sure," I replied. It was like fighting two versions of Glass at once. They had only used skills during this casual test, but if they could use magic too, then the power of this technique could not be underestimated. Shildina already had all sorts of unique magic tricks of her own.

"You still managed to block everything, sweet Naofumi," Shildina commented.

"That's my role in battle, after all. I can use Float Mirror too, so long as I see things coming. That said, being able to unleash two skills at once is definitely a force to be reckoned with," I responded.

"Oh my! Shildina and Glass just got a big power-up," Sadeena said from the sidelines. Raphtalia was nodding too.

"This is more than just the two of you attacking at the same time, correct?" Raphtalia confirmed.

"Yes. I've checked my status, and it has combined completely with Shildina's," Glass replied. Which meant they had Shildina's level combined with Glass's status from energy. If this new pair got serious in battle, it would be quite the sight to see.

"The issue seems to be consumption of energy. It's not going to be easy to keep fighting like this for extended periods. Even pounding a few soul-healing waters won't let us use this for long," Shildina said.

"Wow . . . healing using soul-healing water won't help? Maybe we should try using some earth crystals on Shildina," I pondered out loud. Testing my suggestion, I discovered that using earth crystals while Glass was possessed turned them into energy. If we combined soul-healing water with earth crystals, we could create a new healing potion specifically for Shildina that would extend her possessed state.

"So we can't touch Glass?" Kizuna asked. I reached out to confirm it and my hand passed right through her.

"At least . . . not right now," Glass stated.

"I bet I can if I do this," I replied, focusing life force in my hand and then trying to grab her arm again. This time it worked. "I thought that would do it. I'd heard that life force and elemental attacks can still affect a spiritual body." It probably wouldn't be a significant issue, as any attacker would have to actually be able to grab her first. With Glass attacking with the floating weapon, Shildina following up, and both of them using skills at the same time and magical support, they were going to be powerful. The two of them working together should be able to pull off all sorts of stuff.

"That should cover the combat side of things. Let's take a look at what we're really here for," Shildina said. She reached out to the weapon found in the Holy Tool Grotto, placed her hand on it, and started to read the information from within it. Then Glass narrowed her eyes in concentration before suddenly grabbing her head as though she was about to collapse.

"Glass! Are you okay?!" Kizuna exclaimed.

"Yes, I'm fine . . . No problem. Shildina is just letting the residual intent from the weapon flow into me," she explained, putting up her palm to indicate she was okay. "It is just like Shildina said . . . but I do sense intent, an intellect behind this. It feels very strange." After a short while, perhaps having completely collected all of the intent from the weapon, Shildina removed her hand and turned to the ghost-like Glass.

"Well?" Shildina asked.

"I see it now . . . All sorts of knowledge and techniques have come into me," Glass replied.

"So let's show sweet Naofumi and the others," Shildina suggested.

"Good idea," Glass agreed. "Kizuna, Naofumi, please take a look at this. This is the technique found in the weapon that my master said was lost." Glass spread her fan, and her awareness merged with Shildina, ready for me to provide some magic at any time. I obliged by incanting some support magic and firing it off.

"Secret Circle Dance: Pulse Rebound! Into . . . Circle Dance Reverse Formation: Lawless Counter!" Glass proceeded to repel my support magic, then catch up with it and use Lawless Counter to further adjust its direction. "This Secret Circle Dance seems to be a technique. Adding some power and unleashing it should allow it to be performed in rapid succession . . . if I can master it."

"Okay then," I said, impressed. If she could do that without a cool down, we would really be getting somewhere. That was exactly the kind of technique we had come here looking for.

"There are lots of other techniques and knowledge in here. It's pretty incredible," Glass said excitedly, shooting off a few of her new techniques to try them out.

"What kind of knowledge?" I asked.

"Let me see . . . The location of the country called Amachiha, for a start, and what kind of place it was are filling my mind like my own memories. The endemic plant life and culture of the place . . . it definitely seems like it was the

Demon Dragon's country. We should search for that next," Glass suggested.

"Sounds like quite the haul then. All thanks to Shildina," I said.

"Yay! Sweet Naofumi, heap more praise on me! More!" Shildina laughed. I proceeded to do so, thanking her and petting her on the head. But that caused Glass to put her own hands on her head, somewhat uncomfortably, and blush red.

"Okay, okay! Can we split up now?" Glass asked, flustered. She must have been feeling what I was doing to her body as well.

"Okay," Shildina agreed and ended the oracle state just as Glass had asked her to. Glass became corporeal again and landed on the ground . . . then tilted her head.

"Hold on. The details of how to use that technique have faded from my head . . ." Glass said. Shildina raised one hand and placed what looked like a soul into an ofuda. Writing appeared on the ofuda . . . and it turned into something like what she had used to call back the Past Heavenly Emperor. I stared at it for a moment and realized I was able to appraise it.

Oracle Ofuda
Quality: divine. A collection of residual energy and soul fragments. Used in a special ritual.

That explained how she made those things.

"That's because I was using my oracle powers through you, Glass. Once we ended that state, it makes sense none of it would stay in your head," Shildina explained.

"So these are the powers of an oracle . . . a very strange experience," Glass marveled. Even among my motley crew, Shildina had perhaps the strangest powers, I'd give her that.

Then, with a moan, Glass staggered again.

"Are you okay? Glass?" Kizuna moved over to her and offered some support.

"You need to watch out for the comedown," Shildina advised.

"Indeed. This is the price I have to pay. We will need to be careful when applying this in the future," Glass responded.

"That's our issue," I said. "Right now, Glass possessed by Shildina is the only one who can repel the cancellation magic." From what I had seen so far, it wasn't going to be something we could just replicate on a whim. We needed to break the whole thing down or we wouldn't be able to copy it easily.

"If I can perform it in front of my master, that should help with an analysis. After that, I'll just have to practice as hard as I can," Glass stated.

"I wish it was easier to learn. Like a skill," Kizuna moaned.

"Kizuna. You are still so lazy at heart, aren't you?" Glass admonished. She sounded like Ren, Itsuki, and Motoyasu, back when they had complained about having to train. It was going to be important to drill this technique into everyone who could learn it in order to have it ready to respond to anyone using cancellation magic.

"You and I in particular, Kizuna, are forced into defending when fighting humans. We can really benefit from learning this kind of redirecting and evasive abilities," I said.

"I know, I know," she replied. S'yne, meanwhile, had clearly watched the technique Glass unleashed carefully and was already trying to copy it. She had her familiar firing off some magic and was intently trying to send it back.

At that moment, the Raph-chan face icon popped up in my field of view.

"Hey, perfect timing. That's the signal from Raph-chan," I said.

"Does that mean the two masters are reaching the peak of their battle?" Glass asked.

"Looks like it. If they've got that out of their system, we should report everything that's happened here and have them analyze that technique," I said.

"Right! We all need to learn it as quickly as possible!" Raphtalia agreed. Glass nodded. "It does feel like things went very smoothly for once." I had to agree with that sentiment—however, if Shildina and her super-useful skills hadn't been here, we wouldn't have acquired half as much.

"Be careful what you wish for, and all that. We still need to keep our guard up," I cautioned.

"I understand," Raphtalia replied.

"I think you're reading too much into this. Can't we just enjoy having been powered up a bit?" Kizuna asked, as easy-going as ever. I wanted to remind her that nothing was as expensive as a free meal. We needed to be ready to pay the price for this, whenever it might come.

"Crack a smile, little Naofumi. This is good luck," Sadeena said.

"Yay! Praise me, praise me more!" Shildina added.

"I'm only basing this on past experience! Come on, move it!" I said. And so we recovered the lost technique for handling cancellation magic and headed back toward where the old man and old lady were fighting.

The high level of skills that the old lady and old man unleashed was creating an exchange of one powerful move after another. There was maybe even more to see here than a fight between heroes with holy or vassal weapons. It was like watching a bout from a fighting game playing out before us—complete with all sorts of crazy shouts and cries as each move was unleashed.

The old lady landed a long combo on the old man, ending it with a throw. The old man was back on his feet at once and retorted with his own throw combo into a launcher.

"Hah! You really are obsessed with that fan, aren't you? Well, I've stolen your style already!" the old lady crowed, snatching a fan from one of the old man's students, spreading it wide and attacking. "Observe! I've already created a new attack incorporating it! Hengen Muso Fan Style: Paper Blizzard!" The old lady created a ball of life force, then hit it with her stolen fan to create a blizzard of life force that blew the old man away.

"You think that will stop me? Circle Dance: Divine Wind!" The old man proceeded to blow away the life force attack from the old lady. "Don't think you're the only one who can steal attacks either! Circle Dance: Turtle Carapace Cruncher!" Then he launched what looked like a life-force-based attack himself—and a lot like Glass's own Turtle Carapace Cracker skill. The two of them were fighting at an incredibly high level. I'd been told that Hengen Muso Style wasn't picky about weapons, and here was the truth of that. The old lady was applying one attack after another to her weapon.

"Amazing! Drawing in techniques from other styles and immediately creating new techniques! That's my master!" Glass enthused as she and all the other students from her style watched the battle intently.

"I think we'll leave it here," the old man said with a nod.

"Hah! We'll settle this next time," the old lady replied. Thus, the fight came to an end with the beaten-up and battered old lady and old man shaking hands. It seemed to have the desired effect too; hit with the passion of the old lady, the old man said all his concerns had been resolved. A pretty violent way to work out your issues, if you asked me.

"You have some potential! I would be willing to accept you as my student. Carry on and make Hengen Muso Style your own!" the old lady said.

"You learn so quickly, but I fear you might be too old already. But with some training I think you could become worthy to carry the name of my style!" the old man replied. Neither could understand the other and yet their words almost seemed to be getting through; I wasn't all that impressed myself. The old man looked really pleased with himself, which I didn't like either.

"Are you feeling better now?" I asked him.

"You bet," he replied.

"Okay then. We went ahead and checked out the place you meant to take us," I told him. Then we explained to them both the weapons and techniques that we found in the Holy Tool Grotto.

"Hmmm . . . from the sound of the technique, it could be similar to a lost Hengen Muso Style one. I would very much like to see it performed," the old lady said.

"Yes. Glass! Show us this lost technique," the old man said. Shildina used her oracle powers to possess Glass again, and Glass proceeded to perform the variety of residual techniques for the old man and old lady. There were numerous ones along the way that I really had no clue how she was pulling off, and it made me feel again that my own skills were rough and unpolished. The old lady and old man had become transfixed, childlike looks on their faces as they observed the whole performance. Glass was similar at times. Had she brought us to a den of combat fiends?!

"Quite an interesting flow of life force! Like this, maybe? No—" the old lady said.

"Hah! Dance like this, creating a flow of planna, and then apply some strength—" the old man cut in. The two of them were already starting to try and copy the movements of the possessed Glass. It looked like they wanted to learn these new techniques as quickly as possible.

"They've got the key points down already, much faster than us. It will only be a matter of time before they learn them," Raphtalia commented.

"Looks like it. Once those two old goats can perform them, they should be able to teach us," I said hopefully. The old lady was a good teacher, I'd give her that. I leaned closer to defense, so in many cases I was basically teaching myself. S'yne had taught me a few things, just casually. That was about it.

Looking at them again, the two old masters were indeed getting the hang of the techniques much faster than us. It was easy to learn a skill but much better to be able to use something like a technique. This should greatly increase our options when it came to dealing with nullification attacks—exactly what we needed in the coming days.

While waiting for the old masters to finish their analysis, we focused our own efforts on learning the techniques as quickly as possible and returned to the castle.

After returning to the castle, we concentrated on hammering the techniques into our allies. Rishia and Ethnobalt had no complaints, and even Itsuki joined in without comment. L'Arc was a fighter by nature—a natural—and he looked pretty happy to have the old lady and old man doing some hands-on training. He still pissed me off by worrying about me stealing Therese from him though. I was too busy to worry about anything like that!

With the old lady and the old man both in the castle, the training area was now starting to overflow with their combined students. The Hengen Muso Style term "invasion of culture of other words" did pass through my head a few times . . . but I decided not to pay it too much mind. Kizuna, as expected, only managed to obtain a fairly half-hearted knowledge of how to use life force and how to release it. She hadn't been as derelict in her duties as Ren, Itsuki, and Motoyasu had been, but until the waves started, she had just been a normal adventurer. Even after we left the last time, she had lived a pretty laid-back lifestyle, mainly just fishing and sometimes training with Glass.

"I can't believe I have to join in this training that Ethnobalt is always doing," Kizuna moaned.

"I kept on telling you to stop having so much fun and get some training done," Glass admonished her.

"I was . . . just in my own way!" Kizuna responded.

"We seem to have a very different definition of 'training,'" Glass said, her eyes cold. It sounded like Kizuna had really been letting loose.

"This is a serious issue for our upcoming battles. Stick with it and continue your training," I said.

"What about you, Naofumi?!" Kizuna replied.

"I trained and acquired those techniques after leaving this world the last time. It was a pretty rough time, but I made them mine," I told her. I'd mainly trained with Raphtalia and Atla back then. I felt a wave of nostalgia for a moment, thinking about how Atla's attacks had helped me gain an understanding of the concept of life force. "Although I admit, it was a bit of a blow to find an energy-boost-type power-up method after learning life force," I said.

"If you've got a power-up method, we don't need this!" Kizuna exclaimed.

"Silence! The vassal weapons and holy weapons in this world might not even have it," I retorted.

"Indeed. Once the analysis is complete, let's have my master and Raphtalia's train everyone," Glass suggested. She seemed a lot happier with the situation after seeing how strong the old lady was.

"Learning the techniques from your style will be useful, Glass, but there's no harm in having them learn Hengen Muso Style too. We need everyone in the castle to learn these abilities for the battles ahead!" I proclaimed. And so the research into these new techniques became our top priority.

Chapter Three: The Work of Men and Monsters

"The time has finally come to return to the realm of my dominion!"

"Boo!"

A few days had passed since we returned from the head temple of Glass's style and started our training. The Demon Dragon, who had been leaving in the mornings and coming back late at night every day, had finally reached the vicinity of the territory she used to rule. We were therefore all now riding on the back of the super-sized Demon Dragon, flying through the sky as we headed toward this new destination—the place we hoped to recover whatever trinkets the dragon had squirreled away and investigate Glass's roots.

The party comprised me, Raphtalia, Raph-chan, Kizuna, Glass, Chris, the Demon Dragon, Filo, the killer whale sisters, and S'yne—who was as quiet as ever. Filo had been complaining that I was giving the Demon Dragon too much attention, and so I'd brought her along as well. Itsuki, Rishia, and Ethnobalt were along too, but they were caught up in talk about training, translation of their texts, and possible hidden codes. So they were at a distance from the rest of us. L'Arc and our remaining allies were back at the castle, training with the old lady and the old man. They had wanted to come along, but we needed to leave some defenders behind. If something happened, they could quickly call us back.

Still . . . we definitely had quite the gathering. It was like some kind of crazy school trip.

"So this is the land you once ruled?" I asked. The terrain looked pretty imposing. We had been flying over barren wastes with strange spiky rocks sticking up from the ground for a while. This place had its own unique ecosystem, and once we cleared the wilds, we came to fields of cross-shaped trees standing like grave markers. I first thought they were made of stone and was surprised to learn the truth.

When you looked at it on a map, this place seemed pretty big. Big enough for the other nations to squabble over, that was for sure.

"Impressive, isn't it? This is a marsh called the Graveyard of Death," the dragon said.

"As opposed to what? The Graveyard of Life?" I quipped.

"I can use my magic to create a mist here," the dragon continued, ignoring me, "turning it into a maze with no escape."

"It wasn't easy to get through, I can tell you. The mist was thick right up into the air, so we couldn't use the ship vassal weapon like we did with Kyo's hideout," Kizuna recalled, sounding almost wistful. I didn't need to ask how she crossed it, anyway.

"Beyond this, there are the magma flows, and then we come to my castle," the dragon said.

"Wow, okay. Just the bare necessities, huh?" I said.

"It is not as bad as it looks. With my permission, all may pass with ease. With my permission, that is," the dragon repeated. So it was a barrier that required some kind of verification.

"Something like the barrier in Q'ten Lo," I mused.

"Hmmm . . . based on the route you took, Shield Hero, it could indeed be said to be similar to that. When I was making use of the residue found in this land, such a concept was indeed in my head," the dragon admitted.

"With all the fighting among the other nations over control of this place, I guess you've got bigger fish to fry now," I said.

"For a while the people were free, and this was a place they could live their own lives . . . but they soon got caught up in the conflict. L'Arc led the way in taking in the refugees, saving many of them, but some surely remained here in their ancestral lands," the dragon explained. Kizuna hadn't made the same mistakes as the Church of the Three Heroes, then. That was good to hear. Immigrants too . . . It sounded like L'Arc was getting things done. He was a king, after all. I kept on forgetting that.

"Still, my demise certainly caused issues for the towns and villages under my control," the dragon commented.

"Have you let people know you are back?" I asked.

"I decided to save that until I reach the castle. The humans appear to have failed in their own foolish attempts to rule and returned to being governed by monsters," the dragon explained.

"They have?" I asked. Glass narrowed her eyes and nodded in response to my question.

"After we lost Kizuna, I paid a visit here and someone told me that the enemy of the humans hadn't been monsters after all . . . It had been other humans," Glass told me.

"That's tough to hear," Kizuna said. "Everyone had seemed so willing to work hard and make this a better place."

"Kizuna, our journey was not a complete waste. Lots of people have come to join us. We simply respected the wishes of those who wanted to stay behind," Glass explained.

"Yeah, I get it . . ." Kizuna said.

A bunch of people had decided for themselves to become the slaves of monsters. Other nations had been too aggressive, and those originally living here had not been permitted to establish their own nation. From the perspective of those on the attack, taking what they wanted had probably seemed like a better option than letting tomorrow's enemies get a foothold today.

I could see how some would, when faced with such selfish invaders, choose the monster masters they had known all along over new rule. Those people had probably come to the conclusion that humans would hurt them and monsters would protect them.

Taking risks on new things could pay off for some people. But supply was never infinite—as one gained the upper hand, another must face some disadvantage.

"Still, I was surprised to learn of such a nation within my lands," the dragon said. The Demon Dragon had been more than puzzled to see the materials on Amachiha that Glass and the others had found.

"You don't remember it?" I asked.

"You know how the Dragon Emperor operates, don't you? If fragments are lost, whatever they contain is lost with them," the dragon said, explaining the situation to everyone. "I also didn't rule all this land all the time. Over very long time periods, borders can shift and change."

"So was the nation shaped by external factors?" I said.

"That's right. I do have some ideas of where it might be, based on what I can recall. Sometimes I would even build cities on the seabed," the dragon reminisced. I could understand the concept; the dragon was like some demon king who kept on coming back to life periodically.

"We're going to do a thorough investigation of all the ruins and endemic plant life we can find," I said.

"Excellent, Shield Hero. I will provide as much information as I can to guide you to what you desire. All I ask for as payment—"

"Stop it with the sexual harassment. Considering how

friendly you seem, are you sure Gaelion hasn't corrupted you?"
I asked. At this suggestion the Demon Dragon's entire body
twitched and she looked away from me. That seemed to suggest
she had indeed been influenced.

"Hah . . . even if he has caused some strange emotions
within me, it does not change the fact that I like you, Shield
Hero," the dragon said. "Having been touched by your anger
and rage, your desire to burn down the whole world, how could
I not fall for you?"

"Sure, sure, whatever," I replied. I didn't have feelings like
that anymore. All I had right now was rage toward Bitch—
however, I wouldn't say I'd totally got over that other stuff.
It was just that, thanks to Atla, I wasn't as concerned by that
anger—by that hatred—anymore.

"One thing, Shield Hero. When are you going to copu-
late with the holder of the katana vassal weapon?" the dragon
asked. "I have been watching through your window with bated
breath, every moment expecting action to start."

"Hey! You can cut that kind of creepy stuff out!" I raged.
Sexually harassing me was one thing, but I didn't need Raphtalia to get dragged into it.

"Don't worry, Master! I always make sure to drive her off!"
Filo reported, giving me a thumbs-up. I had been hearing some
strange scuffles outside my window recently. This seemed to
explain them. So were these two the new Atla and Raphtalia?

"You won't be around forever!" the dragon said with a laugh.

"Boo! Master belongs to me! I'm not giving him to you, demon face!" Filo retorted, as articulate as ever.

"Well done, Filo," I told her. She'd been driving off this obsessed pervert without me even knowing it. That was worthy of some praise.

"Thanks so much!" Filo said with a giggle.

"Bah! I am about to receive all the praise your precious master can muster! Just you wait and see!" the dragon snarled.

"Boo!" was the best Filo could manage. From the sidelines, I couldn't help but think the two of them really did get along.

Then I noticed Raphtalia looking over. I knew exactly what she was thinking. She didn't need to make that face.

"Hold on? Naofumi, I thought you and Raphtalia were getting it on every night!" Kizuna interjected. Why was she getting involved!

"As I said upon reuniting with Raphtalia in this world—but I guess you weren't there—I'm not going to start doing stuff like that when the worlds are all in such peril," I said. I also pondered that not acting now might lead to regrets later, but that was a separate subject.

"I understand. I don't want to create anyone else like me . . . so I need to put my duty first," Raphtalia added. Kizuna gave a long hum, while the dragon gave a chuckle.

"Sit on your hands for too long and you'll find I've taken your spot in his bed," she said.

"Shut up. You're not getting into my anything," I shot back.

"Well . . . I also decided that setting a dangerous precedent might cause more trouble for Mr. Naofumi," Raphtalia said, looking over at Sadeena and Shildina for some reason.

"Oh my," said Sadeena. Raphtalia had a point—if we crossed the line, the sisters were likely to show up and ask to get involved too. Or more likely they'd get so strong we wouldn't be able to fend them off. That would eventually lead to the Demon Dragon trying to get involved too—but I'd never allow that.

"Mr. Naofumi works so hard every day and every night, into the small hours, doing all sorts of things already . . . I must not add to those burdens," Raphtalia said. It sounded like I needed to make some room in my schedule. I had my cooking, crafting, meetings to keep morale up, and my own training; throwing romance with Raphtalia into the mix would just be insane.

Thinking all these thoughts made something twinge inside me, however. A pain in my chest. Oh, I certainly hadn't forgotten the things I thought when I *purchased* Raphtalia. Was I pretending to be a good guy now—a guy who buys slaves, pretending to be good? Was any kind of romance with Raphtalia ever going to be permitted for such a guy?

I could almost hear my own voice, talking to me, making these accusations.

"Man, Naofumi, things are rougher for you than I thought," Kizuna said.

"Kizuna, perhaps you could take a leaf from his book and work harder yourself," Glass suggested.

"Hey, I've been working hard recently! I'm learning to cook, and I'm joining in with practice too! I'm far better at collecting materials than Naofumi too!" Kizuna stated.

"Sure. I'll give you that last one," I admitted. She had really helped reduce the burden placed on me by cooking too, which had allowed me to focus more on my crafting.

"Glass, I think we need to help Mr. Naofumi and Kizuna with their work, however we can," Raphtalia said with a slightly admonishing tone.

"You're right," Glass said after a pause. "We are relying on the holy weapon heroes too much. Fighting isn't the only thing a weapon holder can do." Glass really brought the conversation together. "I'm going to keep doing my best, so, Kizuna, please stop doing nothing but fishing."

"Ah . . . I know, I know. I'm trying," Kizuna replied. Hopefully this would help keep her focused. It would be a major coup if it did.

"Now then! I see it ahead. My castle!" the Demon Dragon crowed. I looked ahead to see a broken-down castle, just a crumbled old thing beyond the fields of magma.

Chapter Four: A Visit to Demon Dragon Castle

"So this is your castle, Demon Dragon." I climbed down from her back, joined by the others, and looked over the ruins of the place. It looked like the demon king's castle from an old RPG I played when I was a kid, just more rundown. There had been a place much like that in the sequel, and I thought for a moment I was having a flashback.

"It did take some damage when we defeated the Demon Dragon, but I don't recall it being this bad," Kizuna commented. I looked over at her. I was starting to get the feeling that in the time between her summoning and defeating the Demon Dragon, Kizuna had enjoyed a pretty orthodox adventure. The me who had been filled with dreams right after my own summoning probably would have been quite jealous of her experiences.

"Much of it was maintained by the Demon Dragon's magic, but the suffering people raided it for whatever they could get their hands on, and the battles for this land were waged right here. It's not surprising it ended up like this," Glass explained. It sounded like after Kizuna and her allies defeated the Demon Dragon, people came to raid the castle almost right away. Looters, opportunists, scum . . . people with no common decency. I shook my head.

"Hah. Pathetic fools, grubbing in the mud. I pity them, that's all." The Demon Dragon didn't sound impressed either. She was probably suffering under the reality of being defeated by Kizuna and her merry band and having the castle she had built reduced down to this horrible pile.

"Well, Shield Hero. After seeing these foolish deeds of men, do you feel more welcoming to receiving my love?" the dragon asked me.

"You have a one-track mind, honestly!" I retorted. I'd thought she was mourning, but she still had time to hit on me!

"I'll never allow it!" Filo was there too, glaring the Demon Dragon down. "My master is friendly with me in our world!"

"And what is the standing of monsters like in your world, I wonder," the dragon asked. We did have Gaelion, who was in a similar position to the Demon Dragon. From what I had heard, he hadn't ruled over any monsters other than those in his own lands.

"Rishia, do you know anything about that?" I asked. She was with Itsuki and not really part of our conversation. But while not comparable to Trash, she still had a lot of knowledge on subjects like this.

First, she replied with her normal silly noise. Then she settled down. "There are lots of stories of the king of the monsters, the Dragon Emperor, trying to take over the world, but I've never heard of monsters with the kind of organization seen in this one," she replied.

"The relationships between the monster factions seems like a real pain over in our world. There's nothing bringing the different groups together," I mused. With Fitoria around, the allies of the dragons probably couldn't do much. I recalled Melty saying once that Fitoria had also fought with monsters in the past, something about a griffin. Even monsters had their own junk to deal with.

"There has also long been fighting with creatures that are a little different from monsters. They're known as 'devils,'" Rishia continued.

"What's the difference?" I asked.

"That sounds like what we call "evilmakers" in this world—a name given to a higher rank of monster," the Demon Dragon said, seemingly putting some pieces together. In most of the games I played, "devils" would just be another type of monster.

"These are monsters that cannot be registered with a monster seal and rarely show themselves in front of people," Rishia went on, taking up the explanation. "Once they do, however, they are to be considered extremely dangerous." So in Rishia's—in our—world, devils were a separate entity from monsters. I still didn't quite get it. I'd have to ask Gaelion or Fitoria after we got back.

"They definitely aren't monsters here either," the Demon Dragon said, providing more details on devils in Kizuna's world. "They don't even speak the same language."

"Hard to tell them apart?" I asked.

"Indeed. They rarely come out, but they are here somewhere, lurking in this world," the dragon said. That sounded like some prime foreshadowing to me, and I didn't like it. I could only pray we would never have to fight them. "I must say, your Dragon Emperor sounds like he doesn't have a very strong hold on the reins over there," the Demon Dragon commented.

"I mean, it is Gaelion we're talking about," I replied. Old Gaelion happily called himself "the weakest," while the younger Gaelion was just a baby. No one would listen to him claiming to be the king of the monsters.

"Now compare him to me! Shield Hero, am I not so much better suited to be your partner?" the Demon Dragon said.

"First take a step back from all the sexual harassment," I replied curtly. Lack of charisma was something both of them definitely shared.

"Bah! You leave me little choice. I shall now have to reveal the extent of my wonderful rule!" the dragon responded.

"You don't give up, do you?" I replied, shaking my head.

"That's one of my best features," the dragon answered.

"Modesty clearly isn't. Aren't you forgetting why we came all the way here, anyway?" I said.

"I remember. My trove of treasures, correct? And the articles of the pacifier of this world," the dragon promptly replied. At least she could stay on mission. With the Demon Dragon leading, we headed into the ruins of the castle.

"We will need to break my own seal, of course. But for the really important articles, we'll need to call the Four Heavenly Kings. Even if we may look upon and admire the treasures, we can't actually remove them without some additional steps," the dragon explained.

"The Four Heavenly Kings? They were already defeated, weren't they? I fought them too," Kizuna said.

"The Four Heavenly Kings is a hereditary system, so you only defeated one generation of them. I set things up so that they would rule the monsters after I was gone," the dragon explained. I hadn't expected her to have planned things quite so carefully. With powerful enemies in the form of heroes going around, planning ahead for defeat was kingly.

"So is the Four Heavenly Kings a family bound together by arrangements between sons and daughters?" I asked. Dragons were hard on the environment, so I wondered what kind of creatures they had dealings with. The Demon Dragon must have had offspring of his—her—own. Even Gaelion had adopted Wyndia and talked about having a wife and children in the past—almost all of whom were now gone. When considered in that light, Old Gaelion was quite the tragic figure.

"It takes more than that to become one of the Four Heavenly Kings. If having to be descended from me was a condition, it would cause all sorts of other issues. The system copies the Dragon Emperor in a way that knowledge and abilities can be passed down too," the dragon continued. So strength built up over generations created something far more powerful than any regular monster. I had to admit, that was a pretty clever system. Gaelion might be able to do something similar if I suggested it to him.

Then I had a better idea. I'd have Raph-chan make her version of the Four Heavenly Kings!

"Raph?" said Raph-chan. I want Raph-chan to become the demon king in our world. That would be perfect!

"Mr. Naofumi? Why are you looking so intently at Raph-chan?" Raphtalia asked.

"Boo! Master is thinking something strange again!" Filo shouted. I could only give a chuckle, still lost in my daydreams.

"The Demon King Raph-Chan Project!" I chuckled. Raph-chan immediately gave a suitably maniacal chuckle too, playing her part perfectly. Her willingness to do so was one of her greatest features.

"What are you talking about?! Stop that at once!" Raphtalia said.

"Enough nonsense. I will return to my throne and put out the call. The scattered Four Heavenly Kings should quickly return to me," the Demon Dragon said, seemingly trying to divert attention away from my incredible new idea.

"Isn't there a simpler way to get in touch?" I asked.

"I've been calling for them already, but they aren't showing up. They're happy to draw power from me when they use magic! I need to make a summons they can't refuse and find out what is going on," the dragon explained.

"So they're ignoring you!" Kizuna exclaimed.

"Do you have any charisma at all?" I asked. What was the point in having subordinates if they didn't come when called?

"I had—have—plenty, I assure you!" the dragon protested. I was starting to see a pattern among dragons—whatever world they were from, they just weren't quite all there.

"That's funny! Seeing the two of you together, Naofumi, I think the Demon Dragon may have a cuter side after all." Kizuna laughed.

"Hunting Hero! You annoying morsel! This insult shall be carved into the annals of history!" the dragon raged. The dragon also appeared to share a lot of traits with Trash. Then I noticed Raphtalia and Glass looking over at me, completely exasperated.

We reached what looked like a throne room. It was located on the first floor, making this a pretty different type of castle from what I was accustomed to. The doors weren't human-sized, of course, and if being pointlessly big meant being more important, then here we had reached the nexus of importance—but still, this castle reminded me of somewhere else. I just couldn't quite put my finger on where.

"I'm going to summon them at once!" the dragon said. She started to incant some magic in the middle of the throne room.

"My universal collaborators, those who follow me! My Four Heavenly Kings! Respond to my call and gather to me! I am the Demon Dragon, here in my castle!" A magical circle appeared, the rings getting bigger and wider . . . and then it vanished. "The Four Heavenly Kings should definitely have received the message now. They will arrive shortly." Filo made a sound that showed she was unconvinced. "Now we just need to search for my treasure hoard, the route to which has probably collapsed. With my return, I won't allow even wild monsters to lay claw or paw on the Shield Hero and his party."

Then we noticed unexpected footsteps approaching.

"Is it the Four Heavenly Kings already?" I asked.

"No . . . I don't think so. They seem like outsiders," the dragon said. With the sound of crumbling rubble, a bunch of people dressed in what looked like adventurer's garb appeared from among the ruins.

"Oh my!" Sadeena said.

"Oh dear!" added Shildina, both sisters poking me suggestively. It seemed that we were facing a Vanguard of the Waves.

Level 78

That was odd. Other status did pop up for a moment, but then it vanished. Why was I seeing level and status information?

I hadn't done a thing myself. The Demon Dragon at my side seemed to be performing some kind of magical operation. Had she done something?

"Someone beat us to it. I didn't expect to find anyone here . . ." said the guy who seemed to be the leader of the adventurers. His party seemed to be comprised of women, including one with what looked like dog ears. A type of demi-human? I'd not seen one like her before. She almost looked like a monster. She was not someone we saw elsewhere . . . Maybe it was due to this being the territory of the Demon Dragon.

I focused my attention back on the leader. He seemed to be in his late twenties and of a similar build to me. He had a look of pure confidence on his face—confidence and ambition.

"Who are you?" I asked.

"How about introducing yourself before you start asking questions of others?" came the reply. I remembered giving Glass much the same greeting when we first met her. I decided that we might as well exchange names. Otherwise, I'd just end up calling him by another silly nickname.

"We're—" Kizuna started the introductions.

"Wait." The voice of the Demon Dragon rang out inside my head—presumably inside all of our heads. "Do not let them know you are heroes. I have a plan. This is my territory. These poor fools will soon rue the day they wandered in here." Things could get complicated, then, but we were dealing with a Vanguard of the Waves. Kizuna and the others would complain if we attacked first, and that was what separated us from them—not fighting unless we had to.

"Hunting Hero," the dragon continued, still speaking in our heads. "You like to try and talk things out, don't you? You don't want to just squish these interlopers where they stand, correct? Then I will give you some leeway. But if they should trample on our good graces, I will deal with them in Shield Hero fashion! Do you understand?" Kizuna frowned a little at the Demon Dragon's words and then nodded. What the hell? "Deal with them in Shield hero fashion?" Itsuki and the others seemed to have understood what she meant by that too. Everyone seemed to think I was going to attack them right away!

We were going to have to have a discussion about this later.

"In that case," the dragon continued, speaking to us in our minds, "Fan Hero, you speak for us. Tell them we are adventurers."

"I am Glass. These are my companions," Glass said, immediately doing as the Demon Dragon asked. She must have considered it the logical course of action.

"Okay. What are you doing here?" the leader replied. That was what we wanted to know about them, of course. I wondered why he was being so arrogant . . . but of course, this was a Vanguard of the Waves. There was no point in expecting anything else from him.

"You asked for my name but fail to introduce yourself?" Glass asked. The Vanguard of the Waves looked angry for a moment at that comment but then took a deep breath and recovered his composure before replying.

"My apologies. This is hardly the place for a casual encounter, after all. But is there any real need to share my personal information with anyone encountered in such dangerous surroundings?" he responded. He was the one who asked us to introduce ourselves, and now he said there was no need to! He was starting to piss me off already. A cool moron . . . I'd have to call him Ren II. The real Ren probably would introduce himself in this situation, so it wasn't a perfect match. But he still reminded me of Ren from back when we first met. If his tone had been milder, I would have gone with Itsuki II. In any case, it didn't sound like I was ever going to find out this guy's name.

"Very well," Glass conceded. "What are you doing here?"

"What do you think? The same as you, I bet. Fighting monsters and searching for treasure in the famous castle of the famous demon king," Ren II replied. It wasn't quite the same, of course. We were looking for treasure, but it was treasure that had belonged to the Demon Dragon in the first place, so we were really just here to pick up some things. We didn't plan on fighting monsters either. But any monsters not under the Demon Dragon's rule would get a beating if they tried something.

"I'm sure you've already sensed this, but we're strong," Ren II boasted. "Understand?" I shook my head as subtly as I could. I wanted to shout, "So what?" He had balls on him too, boasting about his strength at level 78. When I glimpsed his stats, they had been half of Sadeena's when she was that same level.

"Do not engage with him," the dragon told us, again in our minds. "Say that we don't sense any monsters so we were going to split up and search for treasure."

"Yes, okay," Glass continued. "We are here in the Demon Dragon castle searching for treasure too. I can't sense any monsters nearby, so we were planning on splitting up and searching before meeting back up."

"Huh." Ren II snorted. "You do have quite a large party."

"Indeed. Would you like to join us?" Glass asked innocently.

"No. I'm not one for teaming up without good reason. What's the point in finding treasure you have to share?" Ren II replied. On that point, I could almost see where he was coming from . . . but he continued to completely underestimate us. "If we meet again in these wide ruins, so be it." With that, Ren II and his party moved on. I wondered if we should just let them go.

"Why did I see his level and status?" I wondered out loud, really only talking to myself.

"Ah. I see what's happening," the Demon Dragon replied— still inside my head. For a moment, I thought she was going to answer my question, but then she looked over at some rubble and carried on. "They are watching us from over there. After hearing that we are planning on splitting up, they are waiting for a chance to strike. They have likely realized that you are heroes. He was overconfident in his own strength and so will likely try to tackle us alone," the dragon continued.

"So it's like a horror movie. One by one, we get picked off until our entire party is wiped out," I said.

"It's not going to be that easy," Kizuna stated quickly.

"If he's one of the resurrected, I just thought it might be a possibility," I replied. They were the kind of people who loved such cowardly, cunning tricks, after all. He might think they had an opening here, but even when they didn't, these were the kinds of people to fly onto the attack.

"I have taken stock of him already. He is small and insignificant. There is no need to bother the hands of the Shield Hero with someone on his level," the dragon continued.

"It doesn't sound like he has ties with Bitch and her forces, then," I said. This guy didn't seem to have any of her agents with him. If they had been present, capturing them and making them talk would have been my top priority. For one, I really wanted to know how they were finding the resurrected in the first place. If we had that information, maybe we could start to interfere with it.

That was probably asking too much. They seemed to just be providing general guidance rather than detailed orders.

"Fan Hero, give the order for us to disperse. Everyone, split up and start exploring on your own. Once you are alone, then they should launch their attacks," the dragon said.

"I'd really rather they didn't," Kizuna said, still hoping for a peaceful resolution.

If that was the plan anyway, I should act as a decoy. I was the best equipped to handle a surprise attack, and I could call in Raph-chan if I needed her. I signaled my intent, but the Demon Dragon shook her head.

"Shield Hero, we are the only ones here who understand your value. We need someone famous in this world and who has the kind of weapon they would want to capture," the dragon explained. She was right—here in this world, I was just the Mirror Hero. Even if there were rumors of me being a hero from another world, I hadn't done a great deal in this one. On the other hand, Kizuna and her allies had turned around a dangerous situation, warned the other nations about the resurrected, and defeated the Demon Dragon herself in the past, making them much more famous than me.

The dragon continued to explain her plan. "Let us have the vassal weapon holders go off on their own, and then, everyone who doesn't pick up a tail, come and meet back up. This is my land, my home, so I can track their movements without any problem." These poor fools had set foot in the territory of the very dragon we had with us. They might have wanted to set a trap for us, but it would be easy to trap them instead. "I will make contact with those who are being pursued. If you do not hear from me, return here. Meanwhile, I will tail the tails. Shield Hero, you can use your mirror as a relay, correct?" The Relay Mirror ability I had unlocked with that last mirror now allowed me to view the intended destination for things like Transport Mirror. The Demon Dragon was carrying a mirror, so I could use mine as a relay for it.

"Everyone," Glass said, playing her part. "Start the search. Dismissed." We split up and started to explore the Demon Dragon's castle.

Chapter Five: Appraisal Camouflage

I walked slowly through the ruins of the pointlessly huge castle. The place really was massive. Perhaps due to the need to accommodate monsters, the corridors were wide and the ceilings were high. I would have been willing to bet there was an entrance to an underground labyrinth behind that throne, just like in that game. If so, this was all a waste of time . . . However, when I thought of monster castles from my rich game experience, I thought of poisonous pools or mysterious barriers or all sorts of strange traps.

Just then, a strange shadow moved across the corridor in front of me. It looked at me and seemed to give a bow before departing. From a glance, it looked like a massive monster with two big horns. I wondered if it was one of the Demon Dragon's minions. It hadn't been an animal. It was too unique for that. If I had to choose something . . . I'd say it was a very muscular sheep. That didn't sound right. From the castle around me and the monster I just saw, it was like I was walking through Siltvelt Castle again. Maybe that was it—this place looked like Siltvelt. If these monsters could understand human language, they might fall into a category similar to a therianthrope. If that was the case, this place really would be just like Siltvelt. In this world, those like therianthropes, who were very removed from a humanoid form, might be bunched in with monsters. We had seen that kappa, after all. Kizuna had said that was a monster. Now the king of these monsters had taken a liking to me, and so they were welcoming me here.

It all felt a bit uncomfortable.

I sensed something and turned around. S'yne was there, silent. This really was starting to feel like a horror movie. If she was there, she should have spoken up. Even if splitting up was only a ruse, we still needed to stay apart.

I might not be getting any alone time, not anytime soon.

Still mildly aggravated, I returned to the throne room as per the plan. Everyone else was back too . . . apart from Glass. Now this really was heading down the horror route.

"Okay. Everyone other than the Fan Hero has returned," said the Demon Dragon, still talking in our heads. "Shield Hero, the relay."

"I'm on it," I said.

"Is Glass okay?" Kizuna asked.

"No need for concern. For now, they are simply tailing the Fan Hero," the dragon reported. I popped a Float Mirror and adjusted things to see beyond the target mirror. The Demon Dragon also adjusted the mirror she was holding, and we got to see a live transmission of events.

Glass was walking through the ruins, on alert but not too

tense. From the look of her surroundings, she was pretty far from the throne room by now. She definitely wouldn't be able to hear us talking or anything like that.

With a roar, the dog-eared girl from the party suddenly burst out and leapt toward Glass. Glass gave a short exclamation and smoothly diverted the incoming attack, then smashed her assailant with a corner of her fan. The dog girl howled in pain, dropping onto her butt and holding her head in her . . . paws? Was I imagining things, or did she seem like a little kid?

"What are you doing, attacking us without provocation?" Ren II and the rest of his party appeared, shouting accusations.

"That's my line. She was clearly intending to do me harm. Explain this," Glass said coldly.

"Your line? That's my line!" Ren II articulately replied.

"Yeah! The mean girl hit me!" the dog yapped. I wanted to slap the lies right out of her mouth myself. If Filo ever did anything like this, she'd be out on her ear, no question. Unless it involved kicking Motoyasu, of course—as it had once before. I was all for more of that. Filo wasn't a liar; she just hadn't been told what was going on. Once we discovered the truth, she had answered everything honestly.

"Master, are you thinking about me? I would never do anything like that," Filo assured me.

"I know. Lies are wrong," I replied. Filo nodded, and I gave her head a stroke.

She laughed. "I got another stroke!"

"That's the way, Filo. Don't copy that. Melty would get angry with you too," Raphtalia added.

"I know, I know. But why is she acting like that?" Filo asked.

"They want to create an excuse to attack Glass. Then they'll try to explain it away by saying the place is so dangerous they didn't realize she wasn't a monster," I explained. We continued to watch the images.

"You can't lie your way out of this," Glass said, turning her fan reluctantly on Ren II and his party.

"My apologies. This place being what it is, we are on edge too. She probably couldn't tell the difference between a monster and a human for a moment there," Ren II explained. I'd not really thought too hard about what I said to Filo, but I'd been right on the money. I hated the feeling that I was starting to understand the minds of these morons. "That said," Ren II continued, "you clearly have considerable skills and yet you chose to counterattack. I think you should apologize."

"You are the ones who attacked first. I expect you to apologize to me," Glass responded.

"I did. Didn't you hear me? Now you apologize," Ren II retorted. He was like some kind of scummy gang member—he thought just a casual "my apologies" covered it.

"My apologies," Glass managed after a pause. "Does that satisfy you?" Immediately after Glass completed her own token apology, however, the dog-eared girl who got whacked started to thrash about.

"It hurts so much! I'm going to die! Die, die, die!" She was laying it on a bit thick—there was hardly a mark, from what I could see.

"Are you okay?!" Ren II quickly took the bait. "Hey! I can't forgive this level of brutality!"

"Why don't you use some healing magic? An ofuda? A potion, even? If she really is dying," Glass responded, keeping her cool but looking despondent. Ren II didn't even seem to hear her.

"You think you can get away with this just because you're a vassal weapon hero? You're not suited to that vassal weapon, not at all!" Ren II accused.

"I see no connection between your companion attacking me and my vassal weapon," Glass replied. I agreed with her. All she had done was repel an incoming attack. And she had barely hurt the one attacking her. This was like someone faking an injury to get a payout. Glass didn't need a guy like this telling her she wasn't fit to hold a vassal weapon—and before that was even an issue, Glass hadn't even revealed that she was a vassal weapon holder in the first place. Ren II and his goons all had their weapons out, looking ready to attack Glass at any moment. This was the height of stupidity, that was for sure.

"You won't get away with this!" Ren II spouted. He was

like a moth to the flame, seriously. He didn't know the burn that was waiting.

"Hey, check it out. The girl who said she was going to die is taking part in the fighting too," Itsuki pointed out.

"Just impossible," Raphtalia bemoaned. Rishia made her normal stupid noise, which I overlooked. "It's all very contrived, but I guess it makes sense within his own twisted internal rules," Raphtalia continued.

"A fight for the honor of his injured comrade, right?" I confirmed. Launching an attack first and then complaining about the resulting beatdown—maybe I should have called him Motoyasu II. But no, even Motoyasu hadn't gone this far. Glass was gripping her fan tighter in clear annoyance and rage.

"I wouldn't push your luck. Just leave before you upset me any further. You can still back out of this," Glass warned them.

"Silence! You have hurt my companion and now come back with this arrogant attitude? You have no right to order me around!" Ren II said. He proceeded to draw his sword and charge at Glass alongside his female companions. Glass flowed like water, redirecting Ren II's sword with her fan, sliding past him while smashing him with the edge of her weapon, and then thundering another blow into the dog-eared girl as she closed in. The short exchange already produced all sorts of screams and cries of pain. Another of the party launched a fireball from the rear. It was magic from an ofuda probably intended as support, but Glass took it on her fan and sent it right back.

"My magic is coming back?!" the poor fool exclaimed.

"What?! She's attacking us? She seems short-tempered for a hero!" another shouted.

"I'm going to defend myself! Of course, I am! Cease your insolent assault or prepare to pay with your life!" Glass was losing patience, that much was clear. Ren II seemed to think they could still win, however, and a smile spread across his face.

"You won't be talking like that for long! Just hand over that weapon—" he started, about to jump back into the fray. That was when the Demon Dragon put the mirror down in a position from which we would still be able to observe and flew off to land between Glass and Ren II. The moron and his party observed the scene, a little perplexed.

"Stop causing trouble in my castle," the dragon said.

"What? It talked?!" Ren II and his party looked stunned. The dog-eared girl was frozen to the spot just by a glare from the Demon Dragon.

"Holder of the fan vassal weapon, you may fall back. I will handle this, just as we planned," the dragon said. Glass fell back from the dragon's position, although she didn't look all that happy about it.

"What the hell are you?" Ren II shouted.

"Are you unable to infer anything from my words? This is my castle. Understand? I normally wouldn't even bother to converse with pond scum like you, but at the moment, I'm trying to show a softer side of myself," the dragon said. Although I knew the answer, I hoped it was not for my sake.

"You have changed, haven't you?" Glass said, completely ignoring Ren II.

"It's one of the best things about me. I wouldn't say 'changed' either. I've grown," the dragon replied. I wasn't sure "grown" was an apt term for it either.

"The demon king and the heroes are in league with each other?! This is insane! Unforgivable! We have to make this public knowledge, for the sake of the world!" Ren II shouted, his face a mix of tension and joy at this revelation. Now a robber was talking about protecting the world.

"Hah. It only means we are beyond the times when heroes and demon kings should fight. If you don't understand that, there's little more I can say—just that, in your ignorance, you are unfit to be heroes," the dragon spat at Ren II and his party, gradually changing from the baby dragon form into something just a little more intimidating. Influenced by the Demon Dragon's magic, the walls of the corridor—ruined or otherwise—expanded out to accommodate her new form. This castle was a real box of tricks. "There's nothing to worry about. The holder of the fan vassal weapon will not participate in the fighting. I shall fight you, along with my minions."

"Hah! If we kill you, then we'll be the heroes, and the heroes working with the demon king will all be criminals! Everyone!

This is our decisive battle!" Ren II shouted. His party members shouted back eagerly, seeming to think they were going to win. Their morale was high, I'd give them that . . . but I had to wonder if they could see the disparity in combat strength.

I glanced over at Kizuna, and she had an annoyed look on her face too.

"You're not going to ask if we can let them go?" I asked her.

"I thought about it . . . but these Vanguards of the Waves have caused a lot of trouble for me too . . ." Even Kizuna sounded exhausted from trying to protect them from their own stupidity. "The Demon Dragon has given them plenty of chances to run away, and they must have heard the talk about what happens if you fight her. If they had begged for their lives, I would have stepped in."

"They are taking this battle on, under their own free will, so is it even our place to stop them?" I added. Let them walk into the meat grinder, see if I care.

"They're pretty much definitely Vanguards of the Waves at this point," the killer whale sisters chimed up, identifying them immediately. There was no reason to protect them any further.

"I understand. But this isn't bravery. It's recklessness, surely. The Demon Dragon is at least as strong as when I fought her, if not stronger now," Kizuna said.

"I bet she is. Rather than recklessness, I'd say they are being controlled by their desires," I replied.

The Demon Dragon raised her claw and the monster who had bowed to me earlier appeared from the darkness.

"I, Dainbulg of the Earth, one of the Demon Dragon's Four Heavenly Kings, have now arrived at the call of my master . . ." the beast said. That did make sense. One of the Four Heavenly Kings, he was quickly joined by two further shadows.

"I, Krimred of the Flame, one of the Demon Dragon's Four Heavenly Kings, have now arrived at the call of my master . . ." said another.

"I, Akvol of the Water, one of the Demon Dragon's Four Heavenly Kings, have now arrived at the call of my master . . ." said yet another. Each of them bowed their heads toward the Demon Dragon and then turned to face Ren II.

Hold on, I thought. The name was "Four Heavenly Kings." We were missing a king!

"What about Kuflika of the Wind?" the Demon Dragon asked.

"We have heard nothing," one of the three said.

"Okay," the dragon replied. That was not the moment for just an "okay"! She was dragging down the excitement level here!

"You've left yourself open!" Ren II took the brief conversation as an opening, leaping at the Demon Dragon with a roar. He really did seem to lack self-control. The Demon Dragon raised a claw again and a magic circle appeared in the air around

Ren II, binding him in place. He screamed, his party screamed, and amid all the screaming I still couldn't make out if anyone was shouting his name. This was becoming a pattern now. *I may never learn the names of any of my enemies, ever again.*

"Papa!" the dog-eared girl shouted. So he'd raised her—no wonder she was such a bitch.

"Attacking someone during a conversation!" The dragon snorted. "As someone I respect once said, 'That is not an opening, but a chance to prove your better quality.' You failed in that chance, resurrected."

"Release him at once!" one of Ren II's party shouted as Ren II himself continued to scream. More of the women shouted in rage as they leapt into the fray, but the three of the Demon Dragon's Four Heavenly Kings stood in their way. I wondered how this ragtag bunch of fools could believe they could possibly win.

"How do you know that?!" Ren II managed to exclaim.

"Because we already know everything about you. Do you see? Did you think you were special, that no one would be able to spot the truth?" the dragon mocked.

"Bah! So what! There's no way you can hope to defeat us!" Ren II prattled, still sounding pretty confident. The Demon Dragon released her binding on Ren II and tossed him back at the women. With a grunt, he recovered, rolling across the ground to come up ready to fight some more. If he wanted to run, this was his chance . . . but we didn't have to step in to save him. He'd brought this all on himself. I could just sit back with the popcorn (I could have really used some popcorn) and watch the fireworks.

"Hmmm . . . I still can't say I really feel good about that," Kizuna said, furrowing her brow as the scene unfolded.

"These resurrected were selected exactly because there is no talking to them. That's the issue here. They can only get along with shitty women like Bitch," I said. If they were willing to listen to reason, we wouldn't be watching the current display. Maybe we could gather together some protobitches ourselves and use them to manipulate the Vanguards, but it seemed unlikely. Pigs might fly . . . but they probably wouldn't.

"Even so, if we explained everything to them, they might be able to let go of these mistaken ambitions that drive them," Kizuna persisted. That love she felt for everyone was well-suited to a hero, I had to give her that. But the ones she was feeling it for right now were resurrected, handpicked and poisoned by the puppet master behind this entire mess. Others like them had already caused so much trouble for Kizuna and her allies. Those experiences had definitely hardened L'Arc and Glass, if not Kizuna.

"If they pretend to play along, but put some other horrible plan into place, we're the ones who will end up paying the tab. We don't have the leeway to offer them any sympathy," I explained.

"But still!" Kizuna exclaimed. I understood where she was coming from. I really did. But the only way it was possible was to convince them, and that simply wasn't possible. Kyo, Takt, Miyaji, and every resurrected we had talked with at length was the same. The longer we talked, the more they sank into survival-of-the-fittest rhetoric and the less they listened to anything we had to say. Yet when we displayed our superior strength, they were quick to resort to cowardly means. If they simply took the knee after being defeated, it might at least be said they stood by their beliefs. But defeat only made them complain and struggle and cause more trouble.

To put it plainly, there was nothing more we could do. There was no survival-of-the-fittest theory that only applied selectively to those you could defeat. We'd fought them more times than I was counting now too. We were well past the time of hoping for an exception to the rule.

"Even if they did listen to what we had to say, and decided to join us from the bottom of their hearts, their heads would probably just explode," I added.

"Sounds more than likely, from what we've seen," Itsuki chimed in, nodding. That was the other issue here. If they tried to explain who they were, they were silenced by having their very soul shredded apart. The one behind them, the one who assumed the name of God, caused them to explode if anything they said risked revealing more about them. Such an explosion was definitely a possibility, and there were no guarantees that they wouldn't just betray us. Even if we used a slave seal . . . or in this world, a slave ofuda, we couldn't trust them.

As I was debating this with Kizuna, a change occurred in the battle between the Demon Dragon and Ren II.

"We're not finished yet. If you think that kind of attack will take us out, you've got an ugly surprise coming!" Ren II raged. He was completely underestimating his opponent, or perhaps just unable to give up . . . Maybe there was a reason. I didn't really care, but I had to wonder what was up with the guy. He was facing four big monsters, one of them the Demon Dragon herself, and yet he looked so confident in his victory you would think he had already won. Everyone around me seemed to be feeling the same thing. No matter how you looked at this situation, he wasn't going to win. "Everyone!" Ren II shouted. "These guys are all bluster! We can defeat them, I promise you!" I didn't know what the resurrected had been like during their lives, but I guessed they were reborn with game knowledge from when they were alive, like the other three heroes from our world. So this guy might have played a quest to defeat the Demon Dragon and thought that he knew the stats of the enemies he was facing . . . That might explain it. With his stats, though, he couldn't ever hope to take down the Demon Dragon on her own.

The Demon Dragon had made some adjustments to the sealing ofuda system that Kizuna had employed and delighted in showing me how much she had grown. She was also receiving the growth-adjustment blessing from me, as unlocked by Gaelion, and had worked hard on leveling up. She'd even had a class-up already. I remembered her boasting about how her stats increased when she transformed. And here she was, now in her grown dragon form, far more suited to battle. She was bipedal, unlike Gaelion, which meant she could incant magic at any time.

"Hmmm. You don't seem to think much of me . . . but maybe that's only reasonable," the Demon Dragon admitted to Ren II. "Resurrected! As this place will be your graveyard, allow me to share a little mercy with you. The holy weapon and vassal weapon holders, commonly known as 'heroes,' have a resistance to being analyzed. Even if you try to force a peek at their secrets, the best you will get is maybe their level. It's impossible to see any details."

"Huh?" I wasn't sure where this was coming from, but it was true—that was what happened when I got a glimpse of Ren II's status earlier.

"That's why it took so long for me to get a look at you. That's why I've been stalling for time," the dragon said. Then she clicked her claws, and it was like something was repelled away. Ren II's face visibly paled, and then he suddenly turned his back and ran without giving his allies a second look. The woman and dog-eared girl all shouted and called after him in surprise.

"This is all part of the plan!" Ren II called back. "Everyone! Buy me some time!" The women followed his orders, including the dog-eared girl, grabbing their weapons and leaping into battle.

"Hold on! I'm coming with you!" shouted one of the women. She had a bitchy-looking face, exactly the kind of woman I simply couldn't stand.

"Can you crawl any lower, scum? Casting aside your allies and running for the hills? I have nothing more to say." The Demon Dragon raised one hand, stopping the incoming magic from the women. The walls in the direction Ren II was running then closed up tight, and the three Four Heavenly Kings also moved to block his progress.

"The resurrected party attempts to flee. They fail to escape," I said.

"Huh? Mr. Naofumi, you aren't wrong, but why are you saying it like that?" Raphtalia said.

"Raph?" said Raph-chan. I guess RPG jokes didn't work out here. It was always hard to run from boss encounters anyway—traditionally speaking.

"Naofumi, can you please stop making your unfunny jokes at a time like this?" Raphtalia asked.

"I mean . . . trying to run away? Isn't that the joke here?" I countered.

"Why do you think he suddenly decided to run?" Kizuna asked.

"I think I know. I'm guessing he can appraise enemy stats," I said. Various people made surprised noises. That would explain why I had seen his status, due to the reflective properties of my mirror.

"Bah! Out of my way! I know! Scroll of Return!" Ren II took out an escape item. Here in this world, transportation items were sold in stores.

"That doesn't work on the Demon Dragon's continent," Kizuna said blithely. There had to be a dragon hourglass somewhere, restricting the use of other such items.

"Impossible! I paid good money for this special-order Scroll of Return, and it won't work?!" Ren II fumed. It sounded like he had a pretty special item there.

"You are hopeless, truly. I am the embodiment of evil. You think your trinkets can work in my presence?" the Demon Dragon said. It sounded like Scrolls of Return were sealed off when she was around.

"We should get the Demon Dragon to give us that later and analyze it," Itsuki suggested.

"A Scroll of Return that leads to a dragon hourglass in another nation could be dangerous indeed," Ethnobalt muttered in reply. He was right. If they had something that dangerous, we would need to know and be prepared for it.

"Do you think you might want to tell your friends here the

truth? That you can't hope to defeat us, no matter how hard you try?" the dragon said. There was a look in her eye, like she was observing a piece of trash.

"That's not what this is!" Ren II protested.

"If you really don't want to spill the beans, you force me to do so," the dragon continued. "This insect has the ability to view the status of others, without them even noticing it, and he decides from that information whether or not he can win. He's only ever chosen the battles he could win . . . thus far." That was pretty much what I was expecting. I looked over at Itsuki.

"I've heard of abilities that allow one to determine the strength of others. They are called 'analysis' or 'appraisal,' or all sorts of things," Itsuki informed me. He had freaking super-heroes in his home world, so I guessed it made sense someone would have that kind of quirk.

"Like being able to see status in a game?" I asked.

"There might be people who see it like that. There's some personal differences in that side of things," he replied. He had told me that there were lots of different abilities. "There's also magic like that." One of his allies during the Church of the Three Heroes incident had been into that stuff, I recalled.

"That is why," the dragon continued, with a pause for effect, "I used a little trickery to trick his tricky little eyes and make us look much weaker than we actually are." Turning to Ren II, she asked, "And how did that turn out for you?"

He had foolishly attacked Glass under false pretenses and thought he could defeat the Demon Dragon even after learning who she was, because what he was seeing was telling him it was all a bluff. That had actually been a trap laid by the Demon Dragon. But upon the removal of her magic and the reveal of the actual numbers, Ren II had quickly realized that his team didn't stand a chance and made a run for it, leaving his allies behind to buy him some time, presumably with their deaths. I hadn't thought I could think any worse of him, but he proved me wrong again. He didn't care what happened, so long as he survived.

"That can't be!" one of his women said. "The beast is lying, correct?"

"It has to be! We can win, if we combine our strength!" another said.

"T-that's . . . that's right! Fight hard and we can win! But I need some time to unleash my new technique. I need you to b-buy me . . . buy us that time!" Ren II exclaimed. His stuttered delivery didn't help things, however. The women seemed to have worked out what was going on, and each of them started to pale too.

"You would continue this farce? Pathetic. And you think you can fight a hero like that? Hardly worth wasting the breath to laugh about," the dragon said.

"I was just being tricked!" This came from the Bitch-like

bitch at the back, who had provided support magic. "I haven't done anything wrong! I will give you these others as a sacrifice, if you will just let me go!" She had both hands clasped together, almost like she was praying to the Demon Dragon.

"You would betray me?!" Ren II raged.

"Betray? That's hardly the word for it. I learned of the revival of our ruler, the great Demon Dragon, so I accompanied you all here in order to serve you up to her," the woman declared. I'd seen this kind of transformation before. We were all shaking our heads as we watched.

"There seems to be a lot of women like her around. L'Arc and Glass filled me in with the details," Kizuna said.

"Tell me about it. Maybe these other worlds are just full of Bitch-type women," I mused. I'd seen so many now who did the cruelest things for the most selfish reasons. If this was an average day as an adventurer, I never wanted to become one.

"Stay back, peasant. The one I care for hates scum like you the most," the dragon said.

"That can't be! This is a misunderstanding! Please, I beg you—" she started. The Demon Dragon whipped her tail, smacking the shitty woman in the face and sending her flying away with a scream and then a crunch. Rolling across the ground, she ended up at Ren II's feet.

"Silence! Speak such filth again and I will squish you on the spot. If you wish to survive, stay silent," the dragon ordered, ignoring the woman she had battered (she had probably been knocked out) and looking at Ren II instead. If he was the mouse, she was the cat—or maybe a lion was a better analogy. "I'm not about to let you escape, so come on. Attack me." The dragon unfurled her wings, letting them get the whole "king of monsters" experience. This was all intended for me, obviously. She wanted to show off exactly how strong she was.

Ren II looked sick. From his perspective, he had just walked into the bad end of the game called life. I didn't know how long they had been adventuring for, but they must have known there was something called a "demon king" at the end of it. They must have made some really bad choices to end up here. They were now faced with a battle that wasn't going to just turn out to be one of those annoying "unwinnable events."

The dragon gave a chuckle. "You aren't wrong. If you can defeat me here, without any holy or even vassal weapons, you will indeed become known as a hero. Bring every fiber of your being to bear. This is someone who I have taken a liking to. She stood firm against me. And even with the gap of power between us, she ultimately contributed to taking me down."

"That's because . . . she was a hero, surely!" Ren II protested. He probably thought the Demon Dragon was talking about when Kizuna had defeated her and that Kizuna was the one that the Demon Dragon had taken a liking to.

"No, not at all. She was no hero. When an actual hero was

in trouble, she put her own life on the line to contribute to the fighting. I know none more worthy of respect than her for her bravery," the dragon replied. I knew who the Demon Dragon was talking about. Anyone who had fought the Demon Dragon in our world would likely be able to tell. It was Atla. In that moment, at my instruction, she had leapt into the fray without a second thought. I'd had a plan to win, of course, but it had still been a very brave act. She had cornered the Demon Dragon that had all of my abilities. There was no denying that achievement.

The dragon continued, "Now comes the big test. If you wish others to think of you as a hero, prove yourself. Turning your back and fleeing from a powerful foe isn't something a holy or vassal weapon holder will smile upon. Understand?" Rishia could speak from experience on this point. Itsuki, who definitely did understand this, was looking at her. "No miracle is going to come for one like you, however. One who thinks only of himself."

"I'll show you! I'm not going to meet my end here! Come on, everyone!" Ren II shouted, his body shaking while he tried to encourage his retinue of women to follow him into death. Unfortunately for him, they didn't seem interested in his proposition anymore. If they fought here, then they could surely only die. Most of them now looked pretty half-hearted in their fighting stances.

What followed was difficult to watch. Another one of the women was sent flying away, also knocked unconscious. Ren II started to beg for his life in exchange for those of his allies, a real Bitch move. Then he started to say he would bring regular sacrifices if the dragon let him go. Not so long ago he had been trying to kill Glass, and now the guy was begging her for his life. Glass did try to stop the Demon Dragon. Since she had fought this kind of enemy so many times up until now, it was too little too late.

These guys weren't worthy of life. It was that simple, ugly though it was. And so the "fight" between the Demon Dragon and Ren II's party came to a swift conclusion.

Chapter Six: A New Heavenly King

"This reminds me of something. I've heard that bears don't kill their prey before eating it. They eat it alive, toy with it, which is what makes an attack so horrible," I said. Glass, who was just returning, placed her hand over her mouth at these words.

"What's with the general knowledge?!" Kizuna interjected. Raphtalia nodded in agreement—she had just been a beat too slow.

"Just seeing that fight, it made me think of that," I said. Their bodies were scattered across the floor, looking pretty much intact. That was their bodies though. The Demon Dragon had dragged out their souls and eaten them alive. She had done it before. I had only ordered her to remove a soul in order to check something. Eating it had just been a little bonus for her. Normally, a shikigami like Raph-chan was required to see souls, but for some reason we had been able to see them when observing them through the mirror.

Glass, a spirit herself, had therefore been forced to watch the Demon Dragon feasting on one, live and uncut.

"Well, Shield Hero! Are you not impressed?" the dragon asked.

"You certainly are a beast," I replied.

"One of my best features!" she enthused.

"You've been saying that a lot recently. Are you trying to force a catchphrase? I'm not going to allow that," I warned her. I didn't see that as an appealing feature either!

"They were nothing but scum, in any case. Having creatures like that crawling in this world makes me sick," the dragon said.

"I can't disagree with that," I replied. I understood not wanting to die—who didn't?—but I would never understand trying to survive by sacrificing one's allies. Immediately after I was framed, if no one had believed in me at all, I might have done the same thing . . . but I'd like to think otherwise. I would certainly never turn my back on all my friends now, people with whom I'd come through so much.

There was something I needed to ask. "One thing you said back there, Demon Dragon . . ."

"Ah. You mean when I praised those who helped in my defeat? From among them, I give the highest regard to the blind tigress," the dragon replied. As I suspected, she had been talking about Atla. For all her bluster, she seemed to acknowledge the strength of Kizuna and her allies too.

"I don't think Atla would be especially moved by praise from you," I reported.

"I wouldn't be so sure. As two who have been inside your shield, I think we share the same feelings. In fact, my feelings for you may have originated with her," the dragon mused.

"You're saying it's Atla's fault you turned out like this? Just be quiet, please!" I was getting sick of talking to the creature.

"Anyway." The Demon Dragon finished talking with me and then incanted some magic in the direction of the corpses. Moments later all of them stood back up, vacant expressions on their faces. Rishia gave a high-pitched scream, and for once I agreed with her.

Fresh Zombie

They even had monster names. As we marveled at this gross spectacle, Kizuna frowned.

"Any adventurers unlucky enough to be defeated by the Demon Dragon become zombies and go on the attack," she explained. One might call that "recycling," but it seemed a little much.

"Fear not. I have not instructed them to attack intruders. Rather, they will begin repairing my castle," the dragon informed us. So they would be working on construction until their zombie bodies failed them. *Lovely.* I was really starting to wonder if we had made the right decision by adding the Demon Dragon to our forces. "Fear not," she said, but that only had the opposite effect.

"Naofumi, this is the Demon Dragon," Glass said. "Do you understand that?" I pondered for a moment. She was definitely more dangerous than Gaelion, in all sorts of ways. Even if she was in love with me, she was still a demon king.

"This is simply a form of the 'survival of the fittest' that they themselves subscribed to. Why worry about what happens to reckless fools who don't know their place?" the dragon asked. That made sense to me. Defeat would always mean losing everything. Whether monsters and humans were different or not, we were humans and so would generally side with our own kind. But with the world in crisis, it was impossible to sympathize with the Vanguards of the Waves, who believed they were justice and kept trying to kill the heroes.

"Humans can use that kind of magic too, right?" I asked. I'd seen Necromancer as a job in various games.

"You know your stuff, Shield Hero," the dragon replied.

"Kyo did something similar too," I recalled. The previous holder of the mirror vassal weapon had manipulated bodies in a similar way—and now it was getting harder to justify us doing it too.

"You can leave corpses lying around here, and if they fall in a place with especially powerful magic, they will turn into zombies of their own accord," the dragon revealed. "Even if you bury them, the same thing will happen. All will follow my orders, the one true ruler of this land." So zombies could just spring up from the ground. It was just another bizarre natural phenomenon from another world.

"That doesn't make it okay to play around with bodies," Kizuna retorted.

"Hah. I never expected you to understand anyway," the dragon shot back. The two of them started to glare at each other.

"We can deal with such problems once the waves are resolved. Okay?" I said.

"Well said, Shield Hero. I love how much you can just overlook," the dragon purred.

"Sure, whatever. You were sad to see the castle like this too, Kizuna. So, both of you, just give up for now please," I told them. After the Demon Dragon had been defeated, humans had been in here, fighting and pillaging. Neither side was in the clear. Humans were more than capable of fighting amongst themselves too. Everyone just made up their own rules, and anyone who disagreed with them got a show of strength. It was up to those living in such times to decide whether they wanted to abide by such rules or fight back. Like how Melromarc, who had hated the Shield Hero, came to accept me as a hero.

"I really just have to let this go?" Kizuna moaned.

"We can simply seek to make the world a better place, a little at a time," Glass told her consolingly. Itsuki often used a similar approach . . . but it didn't get much of a response from Glass. I looked over at Itsuki, and he had a weird expression on his face.

"Where does true justice lie? A difficult topic, eh, Rishia?" he said quietly. I already knew the noise Rishia would make and just blocked it out—she wasn't ready to engage in any meaningful discussion, still shocked by the zombies.

"Well then. An interesting interlude, but shall we get back to what we originally came here for?" the Demon Dragon asked, looking over at the three Four Heavenly Kings. Of course, we needed to find the Demon Dragon's treasure trove and investigate similarities with Q'ten Lo. The three of the Four Heavenly Kings who had shown up all saluted the Demon Dragon. "These visitors might be human, but do you recognize them as my guests?" the Demon Dragon asked them. All responded in the affirmative. "You may not like it, but the world faces destruction if we do not join forces with the heroes. You must accept the severity of this situation."

"As you command!" all three replied. From where I was standing, it looked like all three of the heavenly kings were practically shaking in their (figurative) boots.

"Well then. Perhaps you can explain yourselves. Why did you not answer my call the moment I returned to this land?" the Demon Dragon asked. The grotesque faces of each of the heavenly kings twisted into expressions of fear.

"That was because . . . we sensed your presence from multiple places, and were unable to determine which was actually you," one of them said. Multiple Demon Dragons might be explained by her being the Dragon Emperor, her broken core passing to Kizuna, then using that core to waken the Dragon Emperor. Kizuna had kept a number of them around too.

"I see. You do make some good points, but—" The Demon Dragon raised a claw and lightning arched out to hit the three heavenly kings, making them scream and roar in pain. With disgust in her eyes, the Demon Dragon started to incant magic toward the twisting three heavenly kings. "I think this generation of Four Heavenly Kings underestimates me. Feel for yourselves just where your power comes from!" There were veins popping in her forehead. She looked so angry. I wasn't scared of her anger so much as the sparks it caused in the air all around us. "Kuflika of the Wind didn't even bother to show up! Do you actively seek to disappoint me?" the dragon asked.

"Mistress Demon Dragon! Please, mercy!" one of them begged. The others joined in, pleading for their lives. They weren't hostile toward us, however, and the Earth one had greeted me civilly when we first met, so I decided to try and offer them a lifeline.

"Multiple Demon Dragons, they said. Maybe the harpoon vassal weapon holder has some Demon Dragon fragments and is running experiments on them? If that's the case, it would be a big problem," I mused from the sidelines. My worst-case-scenario theory made the Demon Dragon stop torturing the heavenly kings and look at me.

"I see. They did create that twisted creature, didn't they? Maybe they are doing something similar with my fragments. That does sound possible," the Demon Dragon mused.

"It's just one possibility," I said.

"Always best to be prepared for the worst. Very well. I will overlook any transgressions this time," the Demon Dragon concluded.

"Mistress Demon Dragon, we are indebted to your mercy." The heavenly kings stood straight and saluted again.

"Kuflika of the Wind, however, is an entirely different story. Any who fail to even show their face will be punished. Even in death it should still be possible to at least respond. Intentionally failing to appear can only mean I have been forsaken. I am stripping the current Kuflika of the Wind of her title as one of the Four Heavenly Kings," the Demon Dragon proclaimed. She incanted some magic in the throne room and one of the four sparkling magic circles shattered, causing a large crystal to appear in the claw of the Demon Dragon.

"As you command!" The three heavenly kings all bowed their heads.

"I felt some resistance, but I am the one who assembled this power. Any attempt to resist me will be quickly put down. I am the Dragon Emperor, master of all magic! You cannot hope to escape from me," the Demon Dragon stated. I wondered exactly what she meant and what had happened to the Kuflika creature.

The Demon Dragon looked happy with the proceedings, anyway, and turned to the crystal in her claw.

"Hmmm . . . what to do with this . . . I know." She drummed her claws on her chin for a few moments and then turned to look . . . at Filo!

"Filolial of the Shield Her—ah, you are a humming fairy now—by the name of Filo," the dragon said. Filo made a surprised exclamation, sensing what was happening and going on guard . . . or, rather, hiding behind me. "After you were taken by the Demon Dragon in your world, you fought him, didn't you?" the Demon Dragon said.

"Sure. So what?" Filo asked. I wasn't liking the direction this was taking either.

"This is the perfect opportunity for me to repay that debt, with interest," the Demon Dragon replied and proceeded to throw the crystal at Filo. "Now you shall command the mighty power of one of the Demon Dragon's Four Heavenly Kings! Filo of the Wind, rise to glory!"

"No! Master, save me!" Filo squawked.

"Stop, stop, stop! You can't just—" I started, then stopped talking and acted in order to use a mirror and prevent the speeding crystal from hitting Filo. The crystal shattered into mist and hit me . . . and then something passed inside me. In the next moment, Filo—who had been behind me—arched over backward!

"There you go! I have delivered it to you through the blessings of the Shield Hero! Is there nothing I cannot do, truly?" the Demon Dragon exclaimed. Filo let out a shout, crouching down with a glimmer around her . . . and then she stood back up.

"Boo!" Filo shouted.

"Filo! Are you okay?" I asked.

"Boo! It doesn't hurt, but it feels like it's swelling up inside me!" she replied.

"You see, my dear Shield Hero, there is nothing to worry about. This is an expression of my true feelings for you. Take a closer look," the Demon Dragon suggested. I did as I was told, checking Filo's status. First, I noticed that her race had changed from humming cockatrice to heavenly king of the wind. So "heavenly king" was a race? All her stats had more than doubled too. Filo wasn't receiving the filolial adjustment or cowlick blessing here in this world, so I had been a little worried about her stats; now she looked like I could really rely on her.

"It's like your cowlick has been powered up," I said.

"Boo! I don't like it," Filo replied, as disgruntled with her hairstyle as ever. I thought the cute cowlick she had received from Fitoria was quite charming.

"I wouldn't turn into a monster yet," the Demon Dragon cautioned. "Let things settle a little first."

"Boo!" Filo retorted.

"Shield Hero. Fear not. I may have appointed her as one of the Four Heavenly Kings, but she cannot be punished like you have already seen me punish the others. That is another mark of my feelings for you. My mercy, and a fine gift," the Demon Dragon said.

"Boo!" Filo continued.

"If you can make that power your own, you will be able to fly like me with everyone on your back. They have been too heavy for you until now, haven't they?" the Demon Dragon said.

"Really?" Filo smiled for a moment. "Boo!" Then she was angry again. I wished she would just pick one!

"Hey . . . are we sure this is okay?" Raphtalia asked. I was right there with her, of course. Sadeena and Shildina were watching the proceedings with caution on their faces, while Itsuki and Rishia were frozen in place in surprise. Ethnobalt's eyes were narrow, and he was clearly ready to fight at any moment.

"Demon Dragon, if you keep pulling stuff like this, then you're really going to make us mad!" Kizuna threatened.

"What do you mean by 'pulling stuff'? I am simply making myself useful to you, that is all," the Demon Dragon replied innocently.

"If you could be a little more objective about it . . . Well, no matter," I said, giving up.

"Boo! Yes matter!" Filo retorted. All that booing from her, this was getting us nowhere.

"Why did you do that?" I asked the dragon.

"It's something you will need to face the challenges ahead, surely. When we have the time, I also intend to teach the heroes some of the magic I have developed," the Demon Dragon explained.

"Is that the 'disposition awakened' thing on the enhanced Demon Dragon weapons?" I asked.

"Correct," the Demon Dragon explained. The True Demon Dragon Mirror had an unlock bonus called "dragon magic disposition awakened." It sounded like the Demon Dragon was planning on teaching us some magic. "You will awaken to my own magical formula. To put it in terms you will understand, Shield Hero, it is like the Way of the Dragon Vein. But you will be able to draw power from it no matter how far away you are. Forming a contract with a powerful monster will allow more powerful magic to be used," the Demon Dragon explained.

"There are mentions of this in ancient texts," Glass said. "Talk of a form of magic originating with the Demon Dragon that only certain monsters are allowed to use."

"Correct. It's a type of magic that one of the past Dragon Emperors sealed away in order to prevent foolish humans from using it. I have simply broken that seal," the Demon Dragon said. It sounded like some kind of ancient magic. Ethnobalt had quite a jealous look on his face. There was no need to worry—we'd get the dragon to teach it to everyone.

"It sounds something like black magic," Kizuna commented. "Like making a deal with the devil."

"Indeed," I replied, not sure I liked that much either.

"You must learn it too, Hunting Hero. I will permit you to use the Four Heavenly Kings. Form powerful contracts with them all." It was like the Demon Dragon was giving Kizuna and her allies their own unique magic.

"What about us?" I asked. It might be a different magic system, but I should still be able to learn it.

"Think of it as an extension of the Way of the Dragon Vein. It feels very similar. Ask for the minions you share your blessings with to lend you their strength, and you should be able to do it," the Demon Dragon said. That sounded pretty promising. Once I got back to our world, I'd have to sit down and give it a try. "I will aid you, of course. I can support your incanting, Shield Hero."

"I'm sure you can," I said dismissively. No need to pay any mind to her continued attempts to allure me.

"It sounds like we just got some very important information in a very offhand manner," Kizuna pondered, looking a little perplexed.

"I bet Therese will be able to use it right away," I said.

"Indeed. She should have no trouble. I hope everyone will be able to keep up too," the Demon Dragon replied.

"Uwah . . . this sounds like a good thing, but also pretty

hard," Kizuna said. She sounded like a schoolkid who didn't want to study. All sorts of homework piling up—but this was homework that could get you killed if you didn't finish it.

"Now then . . . as we originally planned, we must search everywhere to find if anything remains of my treasure trove," the Demon Dragon said. We began the search right away, following her lead into the castle. The Four Heavenly Kings seemed to have got the message and were obeying the Demon Dragon completely. The fact they didn't rise up against her was proof of the dragon's charisma. But I still wasn't sure she had any of that, to say how she treated me. Maybe they just couldn't refuse her at all.

As I was pondering all of this, I decided to try talking to one of them—Dainbulg of the Earth, if I recalled correctly—as we headed toward the treasure trove.

"Hey, why do you follow her orders? You must have seen some pretty nasty stuff," I said.

"No, not at all . . ." Although Dainbulg of the Earth didn't seem very keen on doing so, they had been ordered to answer all of my questions, apparently. "You do not seem to fully understand, so allow me to explain. Mistress Demon Dragon has been revived with powers far in excess of her past form. So much more power, I tremble to consider where it might have come from." Okay. Maybe it was the result of my power-up methods. I looked over at the Demon Dragon for some kind of confirmation, but she looked away and struck a silly pose. She really didn't look like a demon king to me. "That is why we kings have no intention of disobeying anything Mistress Demon Dragon asks of us. This is just another move toward the inevitable, conclusive war that must come with the humans. In order to achieve that, we must first overcome the waves." He seemed like a pretty loyal goat-like thing, I'd give him that. "Still, hero from another world who has won the heart of Mistress Demon Dragon . . . I sense something in common with you. You are worthy of being among us," the king concluded. I had no idea what he was sensing. It must have just been a casual compliment.

That did remind me of something people had told me in Siltvelt though—that I had a strange presence about me. I remembered some of them noticing it as soon as they looked at me. Was this some other facet of the power of the shield as a holy weapon—something that helped make monsters and animals like me? Even Ethnobalt was a bit like that around me. Maybe there was something there.

"Okay. Here we are," the Demon Dragon said. We had reached the end of a very twisty corridor, and there the Demon Dragon used magic to blow away collapsed rubble to reveal secret stairs leading downward. She headed down them and then opened a large door at the bottom.

Chapter Seven: The Demon Dragon's Treasure

"Wow! This is the treasure trove? It's an underground cavern, but it looks really nice!" Kizuna exclaimed. I had to agree. It was a massive underground limestone cave. Sunlight seemed to be filtering in from somewhere. The light was captured on exposed gemstones lining the walls and illuminating the entire interior. In the middle of the cave there was another structure made pretty tastelessly out of gold.

"That's—" Kizuna said.

"Yes. It's the dragon hourglass for this castle," the Demon Dragon confirmed. There in the garden of the building stood the dragon hourglass. Vines wrapped around it. It looked a bit like the one from Q'ten Lo.

"Now, I shall combine my strength with that of the Four Heavenly Kings and break the seal," the dragon said. The Demon Dragon started to incant some magic.

"Boo! Stop making me do things I don't want to!" Filo protested, upset at the proceedings. It was like she was being forced to take part. Having confirmed that the barrier surrounding the building had vanished, we gingerly approached the structure. I took a look at the plants covering the dragon hourglass. They looked like camellia. They had a bit of an unsettling color about them—evil-looking, you might have called it.

"They look pretty evil," Raphtalia said. "Like the bad twin brother of sakura lumina."

"Yeah. I guess these are this world's version of sakura lumina . . . If they are camellia, then maybe we should call them camellia lumina. But there's something about them . . ." I mused, trailing off.

"This place is filled with magic, after all. Some strange mutations can surely be expected," the Demon Dragon said. She almost sounded proud of it, which was definitely odd.

"Think we might find something like the sakura stone of destiny?" I asked.

"I'll have to take a look around to be sure . . . Those stones are created over a long period of time by the sakura lumina, or so I'm told," Raphtalia told me.

"I thought they just came out of the ground," I said. Mutated camellia lumina probably weren't going to give us much luck then—no sakura stone of destiny in this world.

"Glass, please come over here. We won't be able to get the exact same effect, but let's try the Heavenly Ritual," Raphtalia said.

"It can work even with these plants around the dragon hourglass?" Glass asked. Raphtalia led her over to stand in front of the dragon hourglass. It did seem like Glass was in the position of being the Heavenly Emperor for this destroyed nation.

Sadeena and Shildina also knew the ritual from Q'ten Lo, and they were able to put on a pretty convincing performance.

However, neither the dragon hourglass nor the camellia lumina seemed to be responding as desired. I might have seen a little movement, nothing more.

"Did it work?" I asked.

"The response is a little weak," Raphtalia confirmed. "It did seem to be aware of us though." She tilted her head while touching the camellia lumina. It seemed there was some cross-compatibility with heavenly powers.

"Hmmm . . . there's something interesting about this tree." The Demon Dragon had taken an interest in what Raphtalia was doing and muttered to herself as she analyzed the situation. "That reminds me, Shield Hero. Your minion with the fan vassal weapon can combine with one of your other minions now, correct? Why not give that a try?"

"Yeah, good idea. Shildina, try combining your strength with Glass," I said. Shildina nodded, coming forward from where she had been lurking in the back and reached out for Glass. Glass took Shildina's hand, the oracle powers kicked in, and the two of them combined. The camellia lumina immediately started to glow more brightly. Flower petals gathered around Glass and Shildina, forming a magic circle. It looked a lot like Raphtalia's Sakura Sphere of Influence.

"Power is flowing into me," Glass said with a gasp.

"I feel it too. It feels like my residual memories have been refreshed," Shildina said. The two of them stood ready and then spoke in unison. "Camellia Sphere of Influence, deploy!" At the call of their voices, the magic circle became fixed in the air.

"The details of the ceremony may not be exactly compatible . . ." Raphtalia said. They proceeded to recreate the ceremony as close as they could to the one performed in Q'ten Lo, and the camellia lumina continued to glow . . . before finally going out. It didn't seem to have worked.

"I think—in Q'ten Lo terms, that is—that would have appointed her as Heavenly Emperor," Raphtalia said. Shildina shut off her oracle powers and Glass checked herself over.

"I don't have access to the same power I just felt," she reported.

"So it's only when you are combined with Shildina," I mused.

"It seems that way," Glass said. It was something else that was probably too hard to practically use, then.

"That said, having camellia lumina around is great. Plant them carefully in your territory and they should boost your experience," I told her.

"They have that effect too?!" Kizuna exclaimed.

"Yeah, that's how they work back home," I replied. It made quite a difference, having them around. Our breeding plans had worked well and you could see them all across Melromarc now.

"Why do you think the camellia lumina didn't respond when it was just Glass, then?" I pondered.

"Think about how she differs from Raphtalia, maybe," Kizuna suggested.

"Okay, well we worked out that Raphtalia was the daughter of some royals who fled from a nation called Q'ten Lo," I said.

"Glass is from the line of a country that was wiped out long ago," Kizuna added.

"Maybe that means she's too distant a relation. But the oracle power brought up some residual ancestor stuff and made it work," the Demon Dragon said. That made us all fall silent for a moment. It sounded possible—and like there were just too many differences between the pair of them. Glass raised her hand and Raphtalia twitched. This was starting to get uncomfortable. It was like we had considered them to be the same for so long, but actually that wasn't the case.

"Ah . . . I'm not bothered by this, don't worry," Glass said.

"Well, okay," Raphtalia replied.

"You've registered now anyway, so even if your bloodline isn't that strong, maybe you can compensate in other ways. With some training, you might be able to use it alone, like Raphtalia can," I suggested.

"Indeed. I'm not giving up now. It seems there are still some secrets to find in this world," Glass said.

"Anyway!" Kizuna said, cutting through the awkward moment. "If we have the materials for these pacifier weapons, we're going to have an easier time of it going forward, right? So let's have a look around for them," she suggested.

"Good idea. Take a branch of camellia lumina and we'll see if we can transplant it later," Glass suggested. We finished the survey of the dragon hourglass and moved on to fishing for some of the Demon Dragon's treasure. What we found were a whole bunch of rare gems and all sorts of magic-related tools.

"Hey! This looks promising! Take a look!" The Demon Dragon lifted up what looked like a gun from among all the junk and showed it to me. "You make ofuda bullets and then fire them with this. A pretty interesting idea, don't you think?"

"It looks kind of useful," I said noncommittally.

"You agree, right? But you need to imbue it with magic in order to fire it. If you can't imbue it with magic, you may as well just throw the ofuda at the enemy," the Demon Dragon admitted. Okay, so it was just trash.

"The guns from our world have wider applications than that," Itsuki said—and he was the Bow Hero. "The bullets can be made to contain fire, and the weapons have good range too."

"If you want range, you'd be better off just attaching the ofuda to an arrow. If you apply enough energy to make this shoot long range, the whole thing will just explode," the Demon Dragon revealed.

"So it's just a toy shaped like a gun," I said. I understood the feeling of wanting to make something like that, though, rather than just using magic. I was an otaku myself, prior to becoming a hero.

"I guess so. Just an odd, toy-like weapon," the Demon Dragon said. The search continued, and more and more junk of a similar nature was revealed. A lot of it would probably reach a good price if sold, but in terms of gear, there wasn't much to beat what we were already using. We didn't need old works of art.

"Booze!"

"Drink time!" The killer whale sisters found a stash of something alcoholic and looked ready to call it a day.

"No slacking off!" I shouted.

"I have collected the best beverages from across the world. Shield Hero, will you join me?" the Demon Dragon asked.

"I'll drink you all under the table," I threatened. I knew where my strengths lay.

"Very well. Let us see which of us can better hold our drink!" the Demon Dragon replied.

"Mr. Naofumi! Don't give in to her games! She'll pretend to be drunk and then attack!" Raphtalia shouted.

"Raph!" added Raph-chan.

"Boo!" said Filo.

"I'm sure she has something like that planned . . . but this stuff does look like it would be good for cooking-enhancement experiments. Let's take some of it back," I decided. We might find some potent brew that allowed for full magic recovery with a single mouthful—we couldn't afford to miss out on that.

"Booze it up! Little Naofumi! This stuff is delicious!" Sadeena howled.

"Oh my! It was worth coming all this way after all!" Shildina added. The killer whale sisters wouldn't be any good to us now. Shildina looked ready to get off-her-face drunk.

"Look, Shield Hero! A statue of me!" the Demon Dragon proclaimed, ignoring the killer whale sisters and continuing to boast about her stash. It was a Demon Dragon made of gold though. Pure trash. It had been polished to an intensely annoying gleam too.

"Melt it down and turn it into coins!" I shouted.

"Huh, I guess you don't like that one. Maybe I will have a Shield Hero statue made instead, then. That's all I need, and then . . . Oh yes, delightful," the Demon Dragon mused.

"Make anything of the sort and I'll kill you. Just what are you planning to do with a statue of me?!" I asked.

The search continued. Then we happened across what looked like stone tablets set into the old walls of the horrible-looking building. There were a number of them there. It was something the Demon Dragon liked to collect, perhaps.

Then I realized I had seen tablets like this before somewhere.

"These are hero text tablets, aren't they?" I asked. They looked really similar to the ones in Q'ten Lo. Tracing the carvings on them, I could tell they were faintly responding to the light. "It would be super convenient if they had holy weapon power-up methods written on them or something," I said. We had been planning to explore the rest of the Demon Dragon's nation for stone tablets later, so finding them here would be a stroke of luck. Then I took a closer look. "There's lots of text on them . . . and I can't even read it." That was strange. In our world these tablets appeared to be written in Japanese, and I could read them easily. Different worlds meant different systems—I should have learned that by now.

"Oh, those old things. There was this religion that had a problem with me, and my forces 'collected' those from the head temple. They are like a prophecy, if I recall. It's about the heroes who will be summoned here to face the waves at the end of times," the Demon Dragon said.

"What?! In our world I heard they were being kept by the Church of the Four Heroes!" Rishia exclaimed. I wasn't sure where she came into this.

"We have these too?" I asked. If that huge church had information like this, they should have hurried up and brought it to me. It always seemed to be the case that by the time such information arrived, I didn't really need it anymore.

"We do. The Church of the Four Heroes in Faubrey has a

secret room, or so I have heard, that only the heroes and the bishop may enter," Rishia continued. I shook my head, wondering why I was only hearing this now, in a place like this.

"I'll have to put checking that out onto my list of things to do," I said.

"That's the thing . . . When Takt rebelled, the church denounced him for breaking with tradition. In order to put the pious ones back in their place, Takt's forces destroyed all the tablets," Rishia relayed. My eyebrow twitched in anger. So I couldn't read them after all. I almost wished Takt was still around so I could kill him again.

Those guys, the Vanguards, loved to trash tradition. They had surely targeted the tablets on purpose, seeking to destroy anything that might give us an advantage.

"Kizuna," I said.

"Okay . . ." Kizuna stepped up in front of the stone tablets and placed her hand on one of them. It looked pretty worn down . . . Then text from the stone tablet illuminated and floated upward, with a mark that looked like a fishing rod.

"Let's see what it says . . . single hero for whom this message will glow. One who knows the joy of hunting. One who continues to struggle even against such harsh restrictions. You cannot consider the one who lurks beyond the waves to be a person. Open your awareness to the meaning of hunting. Aim for the moon . . . and you will be able to hunt even a god." Kizuna paused. "That's what it says."

"I don't know what half of it means, but it definitely seems to be on the money," I said. Our enemy, the one causing the waves, was known as the "one who assumes the name of god."

"The meaning of hunting? Do you think I've been doing something wrong?" Kizuna asked.

"No idea. It says aim for the moon! Are we meant to go into space?" I replied. That would be quite something—from fantasy to sci-fi. Kizuna made a noise like she was thinking. Was it wrong to want the tips we received to be a little easier to understand?

"The moon . . . You know what, in the memories of a past Dragon Emperor, I seem to recall an ancient vessel designed to travel to the moon," the Demon Dragon said, suddenly getting involved in the discussion again. The lines of "fantasy" were definitely starting to blur.

"Can't you fly to the moon?" I asked. I'd seen summoned dragons breathing fire in the void of space in certain RPGs I'd played.

"Even I can't reach the moon. Library rabbit, isn't it said that your ancestors originated on the moon?" the Demon Dragon asked Ethnobalt. Right, rabbits in Japanese culture— living on the moon, making mochi, all that jazz. Indeed, I might have thought the ship vassal weapon he originally had could have taken us to the moon.

"I don't think I've ever heard anything of the sort. Maybe

those records have been lost in our long history," Ethnobalt said. It sounded like he had no idea.

"Hmmm . . . very well. We'll just have to keep on searching," the Demon Dragon concluded.

"Indeed. It sounds like a lead, so we just need to keep chasing it," I affirmed. That seemed like the only tablet that was responding . . . As I looked around, I saw another one of them glowing softly. The tablets showed four weapons, and it was the ones with the hunting tool and what looked like an ofuda on them that were illuminated.

"Based on the one you read, Kizuna, it looks like only the Ofuda Hero can read this one," I guessed. "Does this mean someone holding the ofuda holy weapon is close by?" Everyone was immediately on alert. The only ones with any chance of launching a raid on this party were S'yne's sister and her forces. I looked around, tense for a moment longer, but there was no sign of anything happening.

In fact, it was completely quiet.

"I can categorically state that it would be impossible for anyone to reach this point undetected while I am in the castle," the Demon Dragon said.

"I know some folks who just might pull it off," I replied.

"Hmmm . . . yet none seem to be appearing. We should investigate that stone tablet," the Demon Dragon said.

"I guess so. Kizuna, give it a try," I told her.

"Sure thing, but . . . hold on. This looks different from the one I read," Kizuna realized.

"What?" I took a look myself. The text on the one with the hunting tool and ofuda definitely wasn't Japanese. Ethnobalt moved over and ran his paw over the stone.

"It is an ancient language, but one from this world. However . . . the changes in design make it hard to read. Rishia, can you make anything out?" Ethnobalt asked.

"Actually, I can," Rishia replied. Our head researcher, coming through again! Having someone around who knew about this stuff was super convenient. "I think I can read it, even. Has the design of the letters really changed that much?" she asked.

"Maybe it is selective about who gets to read it," Ethnobalt mused.

"I can't read it either," the Demon Dragon confirmed.

"Maybe it's set up so that monsters can't read it," I said. "Rishia, go ahead."

"Yes, of course." Rishia started to read the floating letters. "This tablet appears to be a list of the candidates who can be summoned as heroes. That's what the part I can read says," Rishia reported.

"The candidates who can be summoned due to the waves, huh?" That reminded me, the holy weapon spirits had talked about this topic. I wondered if that meant the heroes who could be called had been determined far in the distant past or if there was some kind of prophet who was giving out this information. "When I was inside the shield, I heard about this. There's a list of candidates to be summoned. Why don't we find out what number you were, Kizuna?" I said tauntingly.

"Why me? No thanks," she replied.

It would certainly suck if you found out you were low down on the list. I had apparently been the shield spirit's first pick . . . and my name wouldn't be here anyway.

"About that . . ." Rishia pointed at the tablet so I could see what she meant—the part about the hunting tool had been completely scraped off. It didn't look like something that had occurred when the tablet was stolen. More like wear with age.

"Bah!" I said with some gusto.

"Naofumi, please don't be so mean to me," Kizuna said.

"That's right. What is your problem with Kizuna?" Glass said, both of them frowning intently.

"Mr. Naofumi, please don't take things too far . . ." Now Raphtalia was on my case too. Even Raph-chan climbed up on my head and beat at me with her paws. Okay, I'd definitely gone too far. I was aware myself that I'd been complaining a bit too much recently.

"Okay, okay. I'm sorry," I said.

"I'll read what I can from the ofuda section . . . The text here is like writing from Siltvelt," she said. She started to follow the text with her eyes and read it aloud.

". . . born from . . . and given life to replace one with duties to perform; who can recreate any technique. You who have run from that role, swimming beyond the worlds in pursuit of freedom. The ofuda holy weapon will surely come to you. That's what it says," Rishia finished. The text for the first part has been erased, and it was quite long. Rishia had read out the part that could be read, but . . .

"Is that stuff all true? About the Ofuda Hero?" I asked.

"I don't know. The Ofuda Hero I met was a student who looked like he loved games," Kizuna replied. Everyone had their own stuff to deal with, in the end—stuff they didn't always want to share with other people.

"Hey, Shildina," I said.

"Oh dear!" she replied. I was having her check all the junk for any residual memories.

"Can you extract any residual information from this stone tablet?" I asked. "If there is a strong lingering intent, you can hear things, right?"

"Hmmm, there's nothing left, so I can't read anything. I can tell the magic behind this is incredible though," Shildina said. Having the text floating like that was quite something.

"There must be some other reason for this response. Maybe it was just a mistake," I said.

"You think so?" Kizuna replied.

"We can't worry about it too much right now. At best it's

just talking about a hero who can be summoned," I said. If they were needed, they would be summoned when the time came. We couldn't sit around hoping for aid from someone who wasn't here. I needed better information than this unreliable poetry. Something about the holy weapon power-up methods would have been nice, but it was no good if Kizuna couldn't read it. "Back to the treasure hunt!" I shouted. Everyone shouted their agreement, and we searched the Demon Dragon's treasure trove from top to bottom. When all was said and done, we found some stuff that might prove useful as weapons, some strange-looking tools, magic items, and other materials. Filo had gotten a big power-up too, so the trip had definitely been worthwhile. We'd also managed to form an alliance with the Demon Dragon's minions under her orders. Everything was coming together in preparation for the final battle. We were also able to have the Four Heavenly Kings perform something in this world called a "job change." It was a post-limit-break class-up, making us even stronger.

Chapter Eight: An Alluring Pudding

It was the day after we searched the Demon Dragon's castle.

"This is incredibly delicious!" A shout rang out from the kitchen in L'Arc's castle.

"Who's snacking down here?" I said, looking over. "Hold on! You're that rotund noble!"

It was just before the start of our strategy meeting about how to handle the harpoon vassal weapon holder. I was working on some food to provide during the discussion, and for some reason the greedy noble who had caused such a fuss during the whole Seya Restaurant incident had found his way down to the kitchen and was stuffing his face.

"This is incredible! Such a rich flavor, but it doesn't persist for too long, leaving a sublime aftertaste. It's so addictive that every cell of my body wants more of it, hands, mouth, tongue. And yet it feels like all the impurities in my body are also being washed away! I can feel it! Just eating this will be enough to fend off all sickness, making me hardened and strong!" His rantings descended into a wild roar. He suddenly pumped what muscles he had. His clothing started shredding off, and then he started to strike body-building poses. This guy was a real freak.

"Where did you come from? Get out of here!" I'd been so

absorbed in the cooking I hadn't even seen him come in. This wasn't a kid's movie—I didn't need rats in the kitchen.

"My apologies! As soon as we arrived at the castle, he just ran away from me," Tsugumi said as she appeared, bowing her head low.

"I wondered what all the noise was . . . You always stir things up when you stand in the kitchen," Yomogi said, also coming in. She was looking at the noble with a frown on her face—before she saw the samples I had laid out.

"This looks like the studio where Kyo used to do his research. That takes me back," Yomogi said.

"Are you aware that I'm not keen on being compared to him?" I said. I certainly didn't need anyone saying I was similar to that guy. Yomogi was still lost in her recollections, however. I guess it hadn't been all bad for her. I was researching compounding and cooking, so I guess it would look pretty similar.

"Mirror guy! Hello!" It was the kid who had called me Tray Hero during the Seya Restaurant incident. His younger sister also offered a greeting from behind Tsugumi.

"Hey, Tray Kid. What are you doing here?" I had been planning on calling him Keel II, but after his tray reference, I had decided to just call him Tray Kid as punishment.

"When I told them we were taking part in King L'Arc's strategy meeting, they said they wanted to see you, so we brought them here," Tsugumi explained.

"Okay, whatever . . . just keep that noble under control. He's running off with all my food," I replied, pointing at the rotund figure who was still posing like crazy.

"Are you researching Seya's food?" Tsugumi asked.

"I might look like it, but don't lump me in with that creep. I guess this noble just reacts like that to everything," I said. He was like some kind of comedian, always overreacting. He had grown horns too, thanks to my cooking. I hoped that was just a condition unique to him. It would be an even bigger pain if people started to expect magical results like that.

"It looks like your cooking is to blame," Tsugumi said, not letting the topic drop. Did she think this noble and I were similar, then?

"If you want to find out . . . how about you try some and see?" I said.

"You dog!" Tsugumi narrowed her eyes ferociously, looking ready to strike. I didn't care. Sensing tension in the air, Tray Kid and his sister both looked at Tsugumi with worry on their faces.

"No need to make those faces. It's fine," Tsugumi told them.

"Really?" Tray Kid asked.

"Really. We aren't here to fight. Go ahead and ask what you want," Tsugumi said. It sounded like the kid had something to ask me. Tsugumi gave him a push to stand in front of me.

"I wanted to watch you cook . . ." Tray Kid said. He had the same expression on his face as the villagers often did back in my village.

"Okay . . . whatever. I'll show you later, but you have to keep that noble under control. If he complains, tell him I ordered you to do it," I said.

"Okay!" Tray Kid replied happily. What an innocent little kid.

S'yne was there too, on standby, and stuffing herself alongside the noble. She might have been a bigger threat to my cooking than he was, honestly speaking. She quietly filled her face with all my samples.

"What's going on in here?" L'Arc and the others arrived, probably attracted by all the noise. Along with Raphtalia and Kizuna, he should have been getting ready for the meeting. "I heard talking . . . What's the deal?"

"Tsugumi has brought some guests to see us. The noble is among them. He is now pretending he's a bodybuilder," I said.

"Then he leaves me no choice," L'Arc said, shaking his head. "Therese!"

"Very well. I shall punish him for eating the food samples of the Master Craftsman," Therese said.

"No, that's not what I want!" L'Arc responded. "Therese, are you trying to form a comedy duo with kiddo or something?" The two of them still had a lot to work out, clearly.

"What is all this? What's going on?" Kizuna said as she arrived.

"I take my eyes off you for a moment . . ." And Raphtalia came in and chimed in too.

"Good timing, everyone. Let's get the strategy meeting started," L'Arc said. He convinced Therese to lift the noble into the air using magic and take him, Tray Kid, and the sister away into a different room. This allowed the strategy meeting to get underway pretty quickly. We all sat down, discussed events, and planned what to do next. Everything was pretty much ready for us to go on the offensive.

As there were a lot of people involved, representatives from each group would speak. For example, Kizuna and Glass would represent her faction, while L'Arc and Therese would speak for the rulers of each nation. Rishia and Ethnobalt would provide information on ancient texts and other such articles. I was hoping this approach would make things go more smoothly. Raphtalia and I would speak for the heroes from the other world. Itsuki was more like an aide to Rishia at this point and didn't seem to have much to say.

Finally, there was the Demon Dragon representing monsters. I had put Filo with her to try and keep her in check—which sounded crazy, when I thought about it. The Four Heavenly Kings were part of the group now too, anyway.

"Let's start the meeting," L'Arc said. "What's the first issue on the table?"

"The harpoon guy. What's going on there?" I asked. There didn't seem to be any point in wasting time, so I cut to the chase.

"The scouts sent to each nation have reported some suspicious activity," Glass reported.

"Suspicious how?" I asked.

"He seems very active . . . although we don't know if it means he is coming for us or not," she stated.

"That's pretty vague information," I said.

"This is—nominally—a vassal weapon hero we're talking about, so he is quite difficult to track. If our agents get too close, they risk being silenced before they can report anything to us at all. And he is erratic in his movements, making it hard to predict where he will appear next," Glass continued. He was clearly on his guard, which would explain how slippery he was being. We were also talking about an enemy who might just pop out from this nation's dragon hourglass at any moment and I wouldn't be surprised. He was in league with S'yne's sister's forces and Bitch too. We could expect some kind of cunning strategy to play out.

"Tighten security. Prepare for all-out war too," I said. These resurrected all thought like Takt, believing they had the strategy that could easily win any conflict. Kyo had been a little more reserved in his approach, perhaps. There was also the possibility that S'yne's sister and Bitch had already laid a trap for the harpoon guy and, before we knew it, had taken the weapon from him. They continued to get up in our business, but we still hadn't seen anything from the boss of S'yne's sister's forces. When S'yne's sister showed up to poke the bear last time, she just seemed to have brought with her a random bunch of folks who had been around at the time.

"They are probably holed up somewhere, gradually gathering their forces," I said. "Like Kyo did. We might face more frenzied attackers ready to die for the cause." Yomogi made a face at that. I'd mixed a little sarcasm in too.

"They might attack in force if they determine they can defeat us," Glass said. This whole thing was a race against time. Which side could become stronger faster and then launch a strike to defeat the other? That was the issue. It felt a bit like one of those simulation games set in feudal times.

This was also the field in which the Staff Hero, Trash, excelled the most. I wondered again if we should risk bringing him over.

"Based on our past actions, I think sending a small elite force into their nation is the best move again," I said. We could send the Demon Dragon and Filo with a mirror into enemy territory and get in from there. Then we could rush their base and quickly get into the final attack with harpoon guy or Bitch or S'yne's sister—or anyone who wants a piece of us.

"Right on! Sounds like a plan I can get behind!" L'Arc

punched one fist into the palm of his other hand, already looking for a fight.

"We'll have to locate their base first, of course," Glass said.

"Right. That's the way to get a quick solution," I said. It
sounded like they had at least one spy close to Bitch. I wondered if they might have any information for us. I just wanted
to charge into wherever they were hiding and wipe the whole
bunch of them out.

"Master Craftsman, can I say something?" Therese put up
her hand to speak.

"What is it?" I asked.

"Are there any jewels among the Harpoon Hero's forces?
If so, I have a good idea about how to deal with them," she
said. Therese always came up with plans based firmly in logic,
such as reviving the Demon Dragon. So it was definitely worth
listening to what she had to say. I looked over at Kizuna and
Glass.

"Based on what we've seen so far, it seems unlikely that
they won't include at least one spirit or jewel," Glass said.

"Even if the hero doesn't have one in their direct retinue,
there is bound to be one among key national figures, which
should still work," Therese said. "If I can get close to them,
I'm confident I can acquire information from them." L'Arc was
looking at her with a hurt look on his face. I didn't like the
way this was going. "By the way, Master Craftsman . . . I know

you've been making an accessory for me, but has there been any development on that front?"

"Right. It's finished, pretty much. If I give you that, can I have the Two Spirit Charm back?" I asked her. I took out the accessory that I'd prepared for her, having really tailored it specifically to her needs. Just seeing it made Therese cover her eyes as though dazzled. That wasn't one of its effects, I was pretty sure.

Four Holy Beasts Guardian Seal: Starfire (four holy beasts blessing, all status increased (large), magic power increased (massive), sparkling power, spirit's inquisition, soul reflect)
Quality: highest quality

It was packed with all sorts of materials I had ordered from L'Arc's castle. I had created what looked like an amulet of some kind. Therese had given me her broken Orichal Starfire Bracelet, and in the central gem section I had inserted the Chikaheshi no Tama that we had found in the old man's Holy Tool Grotto. I reworked it a little and surrounded it with smaller gemstones. Once it was completed, a fire had glimmered in the center of the crystal, and stars had started to float there. For the design itself, I'd tried to make it look as cool as possible, but it still felt a little bit childish to me.

"It's blinding! Master Craftsman, please put it back in the bag," Therese said. To her, the accessory seemed to be giving off an incredible light, almost making her suffer by emitting some kind of pressure.

"I can tell it is pretty incredible too," Glass said, furrowing her brow at how dazzling it was to her.

"I guess it works on spirits too," I said. That seemed possible from the materials I had used. The Chikaheshi no Tama probably had effects on spirits.

"Yes. I think that will be a powerful weapon even for a non-hero," Glass said.

"I will meet your every expectation, Master Craftsman!" Therese added eagerly.

"Sure thing, whatever. I also put this little item together. Itsuki, you can use bells as a weapon, right?" I asked. I returned the Four Holy Beasts Guardian Seal: Starfire and brought out something else that I had cobbled together from junk obtained from the Demon Dragon's hoard.

"That's right," Itsuki confirmed.

"It can be an accessory too. It's only a prototype, but after you've copied it, Itsuki, let Therese use it," I told them.

Demon Dragon's Four Heavenly King's Bell (Demon Dragon's Four Heavenly Kings blessing, four elemental magic power-up (large), power of darkness and soul)
Quality: highest quality

The Demon Dragon had ordered the Four Heavenly Kings to give up all sorts of materials. These had included the horn of a former heavenly king and a crystallized cluster of magic. I'd turned them into a bell that looked like it would suit Itsuki and then decorated them in a manner I thought he would like. I didn't make it all myself, of course; the craftsmen from the castle had helped me too. The actual bell part had been a real pain. I had been the one who performed the final assembly.

With a cry, Therese suddenly fell from her chair.

"Therese!? Are you okay?" L'Arc scrambled up to help her at once, but she was back on her feet in seconds, eyes wide and pupils seemingly dilated as she stared transfixed at the bell. It was pretty weird—scary, honestly.

"I'm fine, L'Arc," Therese finally said. "This is incredible. It looks so evil and yet so divine . . . I fear it might lure me onto some dark path." I wasn't sure she was on the straight and narrow at the moment. It all sounded a little dangerous too. If we let her keep this, she really might turn to the dark side.

"You bet it would," the Demon Dragon said, almost proudly—I certainly didn't care for that attitude. "This is the Shield Hero's work from materials that we provided him." I could see how it might look that way to others, but personally, I felt I hadn't quite achieved what I wanted with it. The accessory dealer would surely point out all sorts of problems with this if he saw it. The materials were good, which made it *look* good. That was all.

"The one who taught me accessory-crafting would find all sorts of problems with this piece, I assure you," I told them all. This looked good just because I'd made it from materials from the Demon Dragon and her heavenly minions. Good materials, that was all. I'd been saved by those. Anyone with basic knowledge would be able to turn out something comparable. Imiya would have been able to get a few more imbued effects on there for sure.

"You say that, but it looks to be a pretty powerful weapon," Itsuki said, having finished copying it. "There's a limit to the compositions it can play, but simply as a weapon, it looks like it would perform better than the True Demon Dragon weapon."

"I see. Sounds like it was worth making after all," I said.

"It also has something called 'successive magic' as one of its unlocked abilities. I will have to verify it, but it might allow me to perform various types of magic at the same time, like the Demon Dragon does," Itsuki continued. Maybe I'd done a pretty good job after all.

He later on performed those tests, and as he had suspected, it allowed for the use of magic in quick succession. It devoured magic, SP, and EP, however, and left the user standing there as they incanted. So it wasn't easy to make use of. It also didn't play well with cooperative magic or ritual magic.

"Master Craftsman . . . or should I just call you God?" Therese said.

"I'm definitely not a god," I retorted. The one pulling the strings behind our enemies was the one who assumed the name of God. I certainly didn't want to be treated like a god myself.

"I have a plan. Please lend me that accessory," Therese continued.

"Of course, Therese. I made it for you originally," I told her. Her eyes seemed to have adjusted a little at last, and she was able to accept the Four Holy Beasts Guardian Seal: Starfire and the Demon Dragon's Four Heavenly King's Bell while returning the Two Spirit Charm.

"Thank you so much," she said. Therese put the two accessories on, and balls of floating magic started to appear in the air around her—like her magic was even more boosted beyond the Two Spirit Charm.

"Quite a display of power," the Demon Dragon said. "You are still below me, perhaps, but you could easily reach the level of a hero." Therese gave a confident giggle in reply.

"Watch out, Demon Dragon. It might only be a matter of time before I steal the throne of the one who commands magic," she warned.

"Hah, dream on!" the Demon Dragon scoffed.

"This is all thanks to you, Master Craftsman. I will respond to your expectations, I promise," Therese told me. She suddenly had a totally different personality, almost. I hadn't expected her to change so much, and it almost prompted a name change . . .

"Motoyasu III," I said.

"Mr. Naofumi? Seeing this new side of Therese made you think of the Spear Hero, didn't it?" Raphtalia said. It was getting to be like she could read my mind.

"Hey. Kiddo! What does that mean? What are you thinking about Therese?" L'Arc demanded.

"Can't you see it? Your girlfriend is undergoing a complete change in personality. If you don't have her return to her old self quickly, we'll end up with Motoyasu III on our hands," I warned him.

"I don't even know who this 'Motoyasu' is. The Spear Hero?" Kizuna asked, butting in.

"Boo!" Filo shouted. She knew who we were talking about.

"When I first met her, she seemed like such a normal, gentle girl . . . and look at her now," Raphtalia said. I could only agree with her. Kizuna and the others seemed to have noticed the changes in Therese too. It was no exaggeration to call this a change on a Motoyasu level.

"If she starts to end everything with 'I say!' then take those accessories off her at once, or it will be too late," I warned.

"Do they carry the risk of such a curse?" L'Arc asked.

"No . . . don't worry about it," I said. "Therese, tell us your plan."

"You haven't guessed it already?" she asked.

"Not without some more hints I haven't!" I replied. She looked puzzled that any further explanation was required.

"Very well. If I walk through the capital of the enemy nation, in this current state, I should be able to easily obtain information from jewels. That is how appealing these accessories are," she said.

"Oh, okay," I said, maybe expecting more. She was going to use those accessories as jewel bait—a plan exploiting the specific tastes of a race.

"If the enemy does have any jewels among his forces . . . I'll be able to turn them to our ends," Therese said with absolute confidence. I hoped that would last.

"You can go do your own thing, Therese. We'll run our own operation at the same time," I said. "As you order, Master Craftsman," Therese replied.

"Kiddo! You're going to leave Therese like this? That's too dangerous!" L'Arc exclaimed.

"If you have an issue with it, use the power of your love to return her to normal," I told her.

"You twist the situation with clever words, but you're the one who turned her into this!" L'Arc retorted. I didn't care about any of that, and this was not my fault. If anything, L'Arc was just lacking in love.

"We just have to believe that L'Arc's love can turn Therese back and continue with this fight in our own way," I said.

"You sound like a bad voiceover added to the cliffhanger for a cancelled series!" Kizuna blurted out. She was clearly quite the otaku herself. "You're the one at fault here, Naofumi!"

"Kizuna. We can't spend all our time on this one issue. We'll just have to support her and stop things from taking a wrong turn," Glass said. Glass had her head on straight. "Can we please proceed to the next issue?" I wasn't to blame for Therese. I reaffirmed that to myself. It was the lack of skill among the craftsmen of this world, and L'Arc himself, that was to blame.

"Moving on," I said, following up with Glass. "We'll have the Demon Dragon and Filo infiltrate them first. After they've gathered some local information, then we fight. That's about it."

"Boo!" Filo said, unhappy with her role—she'd been in a mood since becoming the heavenly king of the wind.

"Very well," the Demon Dragon said more amicably. "If you so desire it, Shield Hero, so be it." This was all new for Filo, after all. Still looking upset, she proceeded to produce her upgraded morning star—now a bolas—out from under her wing and swing it around. When she was in her monster form, she could use the bolas with her foot, charging in and hitting enemies as she went past, really making use of her natural mobility. I also wanted to equip her with some claws, if possible.

"We have no idea what kind of attacks they might try, so we need enhance ourselves as much as possible while we can," I told everyone. To be quite honest about it, our only plan of action was to try and discover the power-up methods we didn't know yet, hoping that they could help us win. Being able to provide magical enhancement would be a big boon too . . . However, we were making progress on the issues that S'yne's sister had warned us about. Now we could reflect nullification away. With the skill version, in particular, all it took was the right timing. The old lady and old man had researched the technique version and then taught it to us. That one worked about a third of the time, at the moment. All we could do was keep on practicing.

"Moving on. With my recent research, I have finally completed a dish that meets all of your demands—easy to obtain, easy to eat, and efficiently providing experience. I'm not talking about the ultimate in cuisine. I'm talking about efficiency here," I revealed.

"I'm not sure I understand, but it sounds quite incredible," Kizuna said. "Something also sounds a little . . . out of place about it though," she added. I ignored her. The entire concept was that they didn't have to eat too much.

I indicated for the food to be carried in from the kitchen. The noble had been snacking and posing after eating the richer prototype samples. The food coming in now was the finished dish, with a less aggressive flavor. At a glance, it looked like a chocolate cake. This came from my world—my original world, Earth—where it was called "blood pudding." In the north of

Europe, many people were puzzled by the taste even when they knew what it was made from. If I told these guys what it was, they wouldn't eat it. If I even said the name, the holy weapon translator would do its work and they would run for the hills. So I had decided not to tell them. Let them eat it first and decide based on that.

It had been hard to get the pancake-like texture, that was for sure.

"Is it a chocolate cake? It looks very rich," Kizuna said.

"Don't ask questions. Just eat," I told them. "If you want to put something on it, there's some syrup there." I placed down the blood pudding and sliced it up into pieces for everyone.

"You made this yourself, kiddo? Then it must taste great. Let's just try it," L'Arc said. He led the way and everyone started eating. Filo gave it a sniff and left it on her plate, looking at it with a furrow in her brow.

"Master . . ." she started. She was normally such a glutton; I was a little surprised at her hesitation . . . but it was definitely a love-it-or-leave-it kind of dish.

"Raph," said Raph-chan.

"Pen," said Chris. The two of them sniffed at the blood pudding on their own plates, then looked at me . . . Yeah, they had worked it out too. I'd expect no less from Raph-chan. They reacted the same as Filo . . . but were still eating it. That was the big difference.

"I see. This does look most efficient. Extremely logical, in fact. And you have made it quite flavorful too . . . well done." Ethnobalt also seemed to have worked out what it was but accepted it and started eating anyway. Raphtalia watched everyone else and then timidly started to eat it herself.

"Mr. Naofumi, it's safe to trust you, right?" she asked.

"Of course. Eat this and you'll be ready for anything our enemies want to throw at us," I said. It would be difficult to find anything better suited to bringing out the blessings of the cooking enhancement than this. S'yne was already on her second helping, I noticed.

"Little Naofumi. Could you make us something that goes a little better with a drink?" Sadeena asked.

"Yeah. How about some sausage?" Shildina asked. From their requests, it sounded like the killer whale sisters knew what was in it too! The pair of them had a good sense of taste.

"I made this myself from the same materials. What do you think?" Shildina showed me an ofuda. It seemed we had found good material.

"Hey, this is pretty good . . . Wow, hold on! I'm seeing an incredible increase in experience and abilities! And even an imbued effect?!" Kizuna exclaimed. A single slice of this was equal to an entire stacked plate of my other cooking in terms of abilities increases and bonuses. It wouldn't give all that much experience, but it was surely better than feeling bloated from eating too much. "It tastes good, but not so good you want to stuff yourself with it. It really finds a common ground."

"Indeed," Glass agreed. "If we could manage to eat some of this with every meal, we should be able to cover any gaps in the other power-up methods," Raphtalia said.

"This is amazing!" L'Arc said. "It's a bit salty, but really great otherwise!"

"I can't believe you made this," Yomogi said. "Impressive."

"I know. It's like strength is welling up from inside me!" Tsugumi agreed, also surprised. "I think I could fight all night." I was pleased that everyone seemed to be liking it, anyway.

"You really can do anything, can't you, Naofumi?" Kizuna said.

"Kizuna, we need you to learn to do things like this and to make new things of your own too. Once your issues here are resolved, I'll be going back to our world," I told her. A holy weapon hero who left everything to me, and was unable to do anything herself, was just a fool. Take Itsuki—whenever we ate now, he always played an experience-boosting song that he had gone out of his way to find and learn. It was a different piece from the Glutton God Tango that promoted digestion.

"I know, I know," she said lamely.

With that, my blood pudding was eaten up in the blink of an eye.

"If we can make this a regular dish, I think you'll all be

strong enough to face whatever we have coming," I said. "Agreed?"

"Yeah. Why not? I think it gives better stat increases than some level-ups might," Kizuna said.

"That said, I'm pretty sure we'll hit some kind of limit somewhere," I replied. After reaching a certain bonus multiplier, the incoming numbers dropped off. That was often a thing. I was pretty sure a wall like that was waiting for us somewhere up ahead.

"Now can you tell us . . . just what is this? It looks like a pancake, at a glance. Is it easy to make?" Kizuna asked. The Demon Dragon, unable to hold it in any longer, folded her arms and spread her wings to hover in triumph in the air. I didn't need her rubbing it in and waved her down. Kizuna looked at the dragon's smiling face, then looked back at me. "Did you make it from materials we found at the Demon Dragon's castle? That would make them kind of rare, right?" Kizuna continued.

"They are rare, but we have easy access. Otherwise, it wouldn't fit the requirements. We need enough to stuff every single person here, after all," I said.

". . . Hey, Naofumi. Can you just tell us what it's made from?" Kizuna said.

"It looks like nothing more than a chocolate-colored pancake with a salty flavor," Itsuki said, providing his own impressions.

"Indeed," Rishia agreed, also sounding a little puzzled.

"But the flavor wasn't chocolate," Kizuna said. "Just where is this color coming from?" Everyone was starting to look worried, like I'd fed them something terrifying. It wasn't as bad as all that.

"It's just a highly efficient dish, that's all. The detoxification process is a little annoying, but it's clearly worth the trouble," I said.

"Huh? Did you just say 'detoxification?'" Raphtalia asked. They seemed to have realized that I wasn't going to give a proper answer, and so almost everyone there looked over at Filo. The killer whale sisters were eating it while knowing what it was, so they had likely decided to keep their mouths closed. Filo was the outlier here because she hadn't eaten anything yet.

I'd removed all the poison from it. But they were all looking at me as though something horrific was inside. I felt a bit conflicted about that. They had all said they liked it while they were eating it.

"Hold on, Naofumi . . ." Kizuna pointed down to the blood pudding, her face turning pale.

"Tell me, Kizuna . . . if there was a game in which you gathered ingredients to make food and enhance your allies, what kind of ingredients do you think would make the food with the best effects?" I asked her.

"uhHuh? I guess something you'd find in a hidden dungeon

or maybe on the final stage . . ." Kizuna pondered. She suddenly looked again at the Demon Dragon, who still had a superior look on her face.

"Correct," I said. "This is blood pudding. As you might guess from the name, I mixed in blood from the Demon Dragon with the ingredients."

"Fehhhhhh!" said Rishia at once. I decided to give her that one. As soon as I revealed the truth, everyone who lacked general composure—everyone other than Raphtalia, Raph-chan, the killer whale sisters, Itsuki, and Ethnobalt—put their hands to their mouths and ran for the door.

"What's your problem?" I shouted. "This is super-efficient food. Eat it all!"

"Kiddo, seriously?! There are some lines you shouldn't cross!" L'Arc shouted back. I didn't care. We had bigger fish to fry than eating a bit of blood pudding. I found out later that L'Arc tried to throw up but couldn't—his body knew what was good for him.

"I am literally giving my body here," the Demon Dragon said, very upset. "It must not go to waste! Unforgivable!" They had eaten it, after all. Going to try and throw it up was the problem.

"I don't need forgiveness from you!" L'Arc shot back.

"After I went to all that trouble to make an easy-to-eat blood pudding! Maybe I'll try a Bloody Mary next time. At least the killer whale sisters will drink it!" I said. A more direct delivery system might increase the effect too.

"That's not the problem!" L'Arc shouted.

"Is this really the only way through the battles that lie ahead?" Raphtalia questioned.

"You aren't convincing anyway, covering yourselves in weapons and armor I made!" the Demon Dragon raged.

"We did make some stuff after we defeated you, sure . . . but that feels a little different to me," Kizuna said.

"It's the same thing, surely. We draw blood from the Demon Dragon, who then recovers it by eating and using healing magic and medicine. Meanwhile, we use that blood, which is basically power extracted from the dragon, by mixing it in with our food and eating it. It boosts our own experience-gathering. That allows us to provide the Demon Dragon with even better food," I explained. The ideal relationship, a real circle-of-life thing going on. If they didn't want to rely on the Demon Dragon, we could raise a monster better suited to the task. It was just that the Demon Dragon's blood had seemed the best suited to conversion into a foodstuff. I honestly couldn't believe any other monster would be able to provide the same volume of material as the Demon Dragon either. Maybe they would accept Filo? She was the heavenly king of the wind now. I looked over at her . . . to see her shaking her head furiously.

"Boo! What are you going to cook me into?!" she asked.

"I bet Motoyasu would eat it, no matter what I make," I said.

"What?!" Filo exclaimed. I could think of a few jokes to spin off from there, but I wasn't normally one for crude humor.

"I think Kizuna and the others would accept some chicken broth. However, it will mean you need to take a long, hot bath, Filo," I told her.

"Never!" she replied.

"Filo's leftover bathwater? That's pretty hardcore!" Kizuna said. Motoyasu would probably drink it until he drowned. Love could be a harsh mistress . . .

"That reminds me, in Siltvelt there was that dish made with milk from female therianthropes. Wasn't there . . ." Raphtalia muttered, her eyes off in the distance. I'd heard about that one.

"This dish is top-shelf stuff," I said. "If you're not going to eat it, go ahead and get killed in battle and hold us all back!"

"That's dirty, kiddo!" L'Arc retorted. I mean, some of them might not like the flavor, but this was by far the most efficient food I could make at the moment.

"Think of it as a nutritional supplement," I said. Yomogi and Tsugumi had said something like that. They should think of it as something used by those cubicle warriors who needed a kick to make it through another hour of overtime.

"Dammit," L'Arc cursed.

"We might even drain the dragon dry and get rid of her!" I said.

"Give it a try if you can!" the Demon Dragon crowed. At least she was playing along.

"It feels like we've reached our inevitable destination . . . How like you, Mr. Naofumi," Raphtalia said, seemingly giving up.

"Beggars can't be choosers . . . We need to do whatever we can to overcome the trials ahead," Glass said, reluctantly agreeing. The only ones who still had a problem were Kizuna and L'Arc.

Still, even though this involved a little force-feeding, the enhancement using the mirror vassal weapon was going well. The book enhancement was proceeding too. My worry was how much of a difference the holy weapon power-up methods that we still didn't know about were going to make for our enemies. In terms of levels, we would just keep raising them—without knowing how far we should be taking it.

"Hmmm." The Demon Dragon was frowning a little. Her ears pricked up.

"What is it?" I asked.

"I sense a strange presence closing in within my territory," she replied. I wondered what that could mean—another visitor like Ren II, perhaps. In the same moment, a messenger appeared in the meeting room.

"Emergency report, King L'Arc! We've received word that hostile forces are marching toward our borders," the man reported.

"Looks like they've seized the initiative," I said.

"Bah! Very well! Let all our allies know! Prepare to march!" L'Arc shouted.

Chapter Nine: Just to Make Sure

"The enemy is advancing at incredible speed. Fighting has already started in the port! A powerful enemy wielding an axe is going on a rampage!" the man reported. The port was where Kizuna's house was located. They were making good time.

An enemy with an axe too . . . That immediately made me think of Armor.

"I know what I need to do," Itsuki said quietly, ceasing to play.

"Okay, Itsuki. If Mald is there, we should go and stop him," Rishia said, clearly planning to join him. They had a connection to the guy, after all. Armor was kind of like Itsuki's version of Bitch.

"Enhance security around the dragon hourglass. We're going into battle too!" L'Arc said. Under the king's orders, we also prepared to march with Kizuna's forces. Having the holy and vassal weapon heroes taking part in a war was not really a good look, but the enemy was already using such weapons themselves; we had no choice but to respond. If the enemy was just starting out in this direction, we might have had some leeway, but what we needed now was mobility. It was still a shame that the ship vassal weapon had yet to be recovered.

We had the mirror vassal weapon, however. It allowed us to move quickly to anywhere it looked like fighting was going to start, so that was something. We weren't completely stuck. But I still needed a registered mirror to move to. If the enemy worked that out, they could start smashing mirrors though. There was also a limit on the number of mirrors I could register, so the skill was not without its drawbacks.

"What about in your territory, Demon Dragon?" I asked.

"I can't tell. They are moving quickly. I sense a presence much like a holy or vassal weapon. I sense the same . . . wavelength, you might say," the Demon Dragon explained.

"The timing is too perfect. This must be some kind of joint operation," I said.

"It seems likely. They are idiots, which makes them hard to read. An idiot will always do the unexpected," the Demon Dragon replied.

"Any issues with your land being invaded, Demon Dragon?" I asked. The Demon Dragon's lands had been without leadership until recently. They were also the site of a raging struggle for power, leaving little there worthy of capture. This might be the moment to take the land, but I could see little value in doing so—at least from our recent visit.

"Not really. I am wondering why they're interested in my territory though," the Demon Dragon mused. I wouldn't be pleased if we had cast it aside, just for it to actually be important. It was trash for us, but treasure for them.

"Can you tell which hero it is? It's not the harpoon guy, is it?" I asked.

"Kiddo, do you think the harpoon guy isn't here? Did you hear the report?" L'Arc said.

"But they also have all sorts of strange techniques and unknown vassal weapons. They might even just use a double. Not to mention the ship vassal weapon is still missing," I reminded everyone. That fox woman during the Takt trouble was a good example of what I was talking about. Of course, if Raphtalia could use magic, then we could have done the same thing . . . and Raph-chan too.

"That's true," Ethnobalt chipped in with confidence. "Nothing can match the ship for getting around." Whether you were advancing or needed to fall back fast, that ship had the mobility to make it happen. When I thought about it from the other side, if our enemies had the ship, maybe we should have just assumed we would always start on our back foot.

"We don't know what the enemy wants, so we need to start by confirming that. I can join you instantly using a mirror. So, L'Arc, you take the others and go on ahead. If anything happens, I'll get S'yne . . ." I was about to tell her to report to L'Arc, but she grabbed my sleeve and tugged on it hard, a stern look of disapproval on her face. She was right—if they had laid a trap, or were interfering with our communications, we might not be able to move around instantly. She herself had been prevented from getting to us on multiple occasions, so I could understand the look on her face.

"I guess we don't have a choice," I said. I'd wanted to entrust this to S'yne, as she was the least tied down of all of us, but I also couldn't ignore the look on her face. Due to the location, we also couldn't use Rishia's Portal Skill to keep watch. The magical fields in the Demon Dragon's castle cut out the use of pretty much all teleportation skills anyway. I could use a mirror, but other than that, our only other option was the dragon hourglass or more specialized means.

"Raph-chan," I said.

"Raph?" she asked.

"You can sense what is happening to us, at least a little bit, can't you?" I asked.

"Raph!" she confirmed excitedly, raising one paw as though giving a salute.

"Then we'll entrust this task to you. If L'Arc and his party get into trouble, let us know," I told her.

"Raph!" she responded, climbing quickly onto L'Arc's shoulder and waving at me.

"Naofumi, are you going to the Demon Dragon's castle?" Kizuna asked.

"Just to make sure everything is fine. I'll need to take the Demon Dragon, Raphtalia, Filo, and S'yne with me. Anyone else want to come?" I asked.

"We'll tag along!" Sadeena said.

"Yep, count us in," Shildina confirmed.

"I wish to protect this place where I have so many memories with everyone, so I will accompany L'Arc," Ethnobalt declared, standing next to them with his book in hand. Kizuna's house was in the port. None of them would want that to be destroyed. It had already taken some damage during the attack from the guy who stole L'Arc's scythe.

"You're just going to make sure everything is alright, right? Then the battle here is more important," Tsugumi said, Yomogi nodding. So they were staying here too—meaning that most of our forces would be heading directly to the port. The old Hengen Muso lady would be sortieing with the old man.

"That leaves just you pair, Kizuna and Glass," I said. They both remained silent. Kizuna didn't seem sure which she should choose. She looked at Glass and then at me.

"I'm more concerned about the Demon Dragon's side, seeing as we don't know what's happening there," she finally said.

"Just to make sure, like I said," I told her. It didn't look like I had a registered mirror right where any of the fighting was happening, but we could still get back here pretty quickly.

"If you are just going to quickly check things out, we'll go with you. All I can do in open warfare is support the rear anyway," Kizuna concluded.

"I concur," Glass said. "We don't know what's happening in

the Demon Dragon's territory, but it won't take too long if we are just going to stop by." It sounded like they had chosen the mysterious movements of our enemies over protecting their cherished memories—maybe thanks to nothing more than a hero's hunch.

"Time to move out," I said. I activated my movement skill toward the mirror, opening a direct passage to the port.

"Okay! Time to settle this!" L'Arc shouted.

"I'll use this accessory to make them change sides!" Therese said, and then their entire party set off for the port town. After they had gone, I used the mirror again to connect to a mirror in the Demon Dragon's territory.

"Time for us to move too!" I said.

"Okay! Let's get this over with and catch up with the others," Kizuna replied. We headed into the mirror.

We emerged from a mirror hanging in the throne room of the Demon Dragon's castle and started looking around.

"So? We should be close. Anything?" I asked the Demon Dragon.

"Yes. They are near. They've made it right up to the gates. If we run, we can encounter them in the courtyard. However, I'm still not sure exactly what I'm feeling . . ." the Demon Dragon trailed off.

"Then we just have to go and take a look," I replied. The

Demon Dragon did just that, starting to incant some magic as she flew off ahead of us. We hurried after her and quickly made it out into the garden. The castle was basically a ruin, after all. There was little impeding the view.

That was where we finally discovered the one who had invaded the Demon Dragon's territory. The one we had come here to find was there.

"Well, well, well."

That voice already gave the game away.

"—!" S'yne gripped her scissors tight, waves of murderous rage rolling off her. I understood why. I was feeling pretty vicious myself as I raised my mirror and prepared for battle. S'yne's sister was bad enough, but—

"You really are such a pain in my ass!" That was the moment that Bitch gradually descended down on a flying ship toward the ground. She had a sharp-eyed guy holding a harpoon and a bunch of other goons with her.

"Well, well, well. It seems we didn't divide them up as well as you hoped. Just like I said. These are the lands that the dragon and Iwatani rule. You'll never get the jump on them here, and it was foolish to try," S'yne's sister said.

"Shut up! This is hardly the time for such comments!" Bitch turned to the guy with the harpoon and purred like a cat. "Right? I am your ally, now and always!" As I suspected, she had him under her thumb.

"That's right, that's right! Well said, Lady Malty! There's no reason for you to pay attention to that cold old trout!" This came from another random girl—a new cheerleader for Bitch, seemingly. I had to wonder where she found these women. It was like she had an infinite supply somewhere. Woman B II.

Bitch gave a giggle, anyway. She seemed to be in a good mood. I guessed the previous Woman B had been sent into a battle that killed her after failing to win favor with Bitch.

That didn't matter now anyway. What I really couldn't tell was why the harpoon guy seemed to be angry with us.

"Whatever. We just have to wipe these guys out, no matter what, don't we? As quickly as we can!" the harpoon guy said.

"You're going to have a nasty surprise if you think this will be that easy," I retorted. There was something off about the guy, like he was a feral animal in a corner. He had a face like Takt when his main girl was killed—or Motoyasu when he first found out Raphtalia was a slave. He certainly looked ready to fight.

I almost didn't want to ask. It wasn't going to be a thrilling backstory, not from what we had experienced so far. The best course of action was to trigger another exposition dump from S'yne's loudmouthed sister. I stared at her intently, silently giving her the signal, and she eventually sighed and started to talk.

"The reason why I rushed over here is because one of the allies of the Harpoon Hero is about to expire, even as we speak, thanks to the Demon Dragon," S'yne's sister explained.

"You claim this is my fault?" the Demon Dragon responded, puzzled at her name coming up. I wondered if the dragon really knew what was going on. A few moments later, an evil smile spread across her face (so she did know what was going on) and she started to talk.

"I see. Long ago, I scattered a selection of carefully crafted cursed items across the world. Now you want to wipe us out in order to stop one of those curses," the Demon Dragon said. I presumed these would be like the cursed items or traps you found in dungeons in a video game. It made sense that in a real setting some kind of "demon king" creature would be needed to make stuff like that.

"You really do have some awful hobbies," I told her.

"Curiosity killed . . . well, pretty much everybody. I don't care about any human dumb enough to die by one of my trinkets," the Demon Dragon replied. She really did have a philosophy for life that was never going to see eye to eye with mine. It was almost refreshing how little chance we had to get along. I could definitely understand why Kizuna and the others still held a grudge. "You can't even break a curse of that level though? I thought you had some real power behind you," the Demon Dragon bemoaned.

"That's not what this is!" the harpoon vassal weapon holder shouted. It seemed that wasn't the issue after all. But thankfully he continued without any more guessing games. "Kuflika is

about to die, all thanks to you! All thanks to you!" The harpoon vassal weapon holder pointed at the Demon Dragon and then threw his harpoon with all his might, seizing the initiative with a preemptive attack.

"Formation One: Glass Shield!" I shouted, placing a glass shield to stop the harpoon. The glass shattered on impact. The harpoon quickly returned to the user's hand, while S'yne's sister knocked down the attacking fragments of flying glass.

"Kuflika?" I asked. Who the hell was that? Even though I was terrible with names, I was pretty sure I had heard this one recently.

"I've found Kuflika's magic! It's in her! Over there!" one of the women in the harpoon guy's retinue shouted.

"What?!" The harpoon guy turned his deadly intent toward Filo.

"Huh? Filo?" I said. She didn't seem to have any idea why she was being targeted either.

"Kuflika is the name of the monster who was kicked out of the Four Heavenly Kings by the Demon Dragon yesterday," Raphtalia reminded me, seeing the puzzled look on my own face.

"Oh, of course," I said. "Kuflika of the Wind." The one that was removed as a heavenly king for not answering the Demon Dragon's call.

"Well, I can't say I expected this," the Demon Dragon said,

finally putting it together. "You've come all this way for the sake of the former heavenly king of the wind, Kuflika? Good for you," she mocked, flapping her wings and floating idly in the air.

"So now you know," S'yne's sister said. "Kuflika just collapsed yesterday. As we searched for the cause, it turns out the very magic required for her continued existence has been cut off. The only possible explanation is a loss of her power as one of the Four Heavenly Kings." We understood why they were here now, but it didn't change the fact this Kuflika was just a dumb idiot. She had to have some idea of what the Demon Dragon would do if she ignored the summons. So why did she ignore it?

"I've come to take back everything for Kuflika!" the harpoon guy shouted. Now fully in possession of the facts, the Demon Dragon gave a deep sigh . . . almost sounding mournful.

"You poor fools. That power is my magic. It's been passed down across the generations to each of the Four Heavenly Kings and accumulated along the way!" the Demon Dragon raged.

"So what! That power belongs to Kuflika! It isn't yours!" came the reply.

"Becoming one of my Four Heavenly Kings means being completely loyal to me. I have the right to bestow my own property upon anyone I please, which makes that power mine, not Kuflika's. You need to get your facts straight," the Demon Dragon replied to the harpoon guy, sounding thoroughly annoyed that any of this was necessary. It seemed to me this was like punishing a traitor, just to be attacked by the friends of that traitor for having rightfully punished them. "Is it not justice that the two-faced are punished? Are there none among you who command monsters? And if those monsters disobey your orders, do you not punish them? That's all this is."

"Silence, fiend! Kuflika is about to die all because of an awful creature like you! I'll never accept this!" the harpoon guy fired back. He sounded like the protagonist of a very different story from the one I was living in. I'd lost count of the number of times I'd faced opponents shouting this kind of rhetoric. We always ended up being treated like the bad guys by them. It made me sick.

"That's right! I'm not accepting this either!" Bitch said, finding—as always—the most annoying thing possible to say. Her eyes were laughing. She had no real sympathy for this guy or the plight of his friend. The Demon Dragon just laughed.

"I don't need you to accept anything. What were you trying to do here, anyway, in my absence?" The Demon Dragon looked over at S'yne's sister, likely presuming she would provide a better answer.

"Let me break it down for you," S'yne's sister started but then threw out an orb much like the one she had used the last time we fought.

"Ooh . . . I've been called for . . . gyah-gyah!" From the orb appeared a creature that looked like a big, purple Demon Dragon. It had the same kind of device around its chest as the artificial behemoth we had faced during our last encounter. Its wings also had a bit of a mechanical look to them. The design was like something from a monster-raising game set in a virtual world that I'd played once. If I had to give the thing a name, "metal magic dragon" sounded good.

"I am the true Demon Dragon. Gyah-gyah," the metal magic dragon said. Another abomination, and this time it could talk. They were further advancing their technology, clearly. We were always getting stronger, so it made sense that our enemies would too, but I kind of wished they would stop it.

"Just another boon from our proprietary artificial monster plan. This one is very different from the prototype you fought last time, of course," S'yne's sister said. This was a further development, then—or maybe the final form—of the artificial behemoth that we fought previously. It was a man-made monster with a holy weapon inside it. That would suggest that this one probably had a holy weapon somewhere inside it too. I hated to give our enemies any credit, but they had stumbled onto something potent here. It might even be worth telling Rat about, the woman who researched monsters in my own territory. Although she was unlikely to care about simply replicating the work of others, it would be smart to get her to try and copy it.

"If our ally, this new Demon Dragon, inherits this land, it can return Kuflika's powers! That's why you have to die! This will be the final battle!" the harpoon guy shouted. He was clearly all messed up in the head. It also wasn't the first time I'd heard this "final battle" crap. I wished this would be the final battle.

"The Dragon Emperor fragment that the Harpoon Hero's friend had . . . is that what you call them? We combined that with the fragments we had collected from other regions and made this," S'yne's sister told us.

"I will do whatever it takes to become strong—even take advantage of human technology to obtain spirit power, like this. The coming of a new age is foretold! Gyah-gyah!" The metal magic dragon started to talk again in a tone sounding very much like the Demon Dragon. Then it cast some magic on itself, turning into a mechanical-looking girl with steel wings. She moved over to the harpoon guy and started to purr, taunting the Demon Dragon. I'd seen this same kind of act with Takt's Dragon Emperor.

"Pathetic. I am ashamed I ever thought your presence feels anything like mine. Using the fragments that I gave Kuflika and her underlings for this kind of travesty? I am about to lose my mind with anger," the Demon Dragon retorted. It sounded like she had put various ploys in place to revive herself. We probably should have been all over that. It would make sense for the

Four Heavenly Kings to have Demon Dragon fragments. We'd even thought that the harpoon vassal weapon holder was doing something with Demon Dragon fragments too!

The Demon Dragon was emitting a black aura, incensed at the attitude of the metal magic dragon. At the same time, the metal magic dragon was glaring down the dragon-form Demon Dragon.

"Siding with these infidels who would profane the holy weapons. There are no depths to your foolishness," the Demon Dragon spat.

"Can you afford to pick and choose how you get stronger?" the metal magic dragon fired back. "Maybe you can—it would explain why you got yourself killed. The time has come to accept this new age, gyah-gyah."

"Silence your foul mouth," the Demon Dragon replied. "For you to speak of me in this way . . . even that other petty Dragon Emperor would see how foolish you are being." It sounded like she was talking about Gaelion. This whole thing was actually similar to Gaelion's previous battle, I realized. He had fought Takt's Dragon Emperor with a significant lack of cores when compared to his opponent. Kizuna and her allies still held most of the Demon Dragon's cores at the moment. And now this dragon was facing an opponent created from the Demon Dragon fragments obtained from Kuflika.

"You all love to talk so much, don't you?" Bitch opined. "Can we please see some action already?"

"You are the ones who love to lie so much!" I retorted.

"What was that?! How dare you speak to Lady Malty like that!" Woman B II jumped immediately to Bitch's defense. I just wanted to slap her and tell her to stay out of this. This was all such a pain. I decided to try and just ignore them.

"We'll crush your cowardly invasion!" I shouted. I certainly hadn't expected enemies to show up like this. Expect the unexpected, so they say. But this also didn't appear to be a planned move on their part. They had just used whatever means they had at hand to rush over here.

"Boo! If we lose, I'm not sure I'll like what happens to me!" Filo said.

"Tell me about it. You'll get the short end of the stick for sure," I confirmed. Filo was taking the power from one of their allies, after all. I wasn't planning on losing—we weren't going to lose—but if we did, Filo would end up like Kuflika was now.

This world continued to cause trouble for Filo.

"Oh my. I have no idea what is going to happen next, Shildina," Sadeena said.

"Me neither." The killer whale sisters probably weren't keeping up with what was going on, but they both stood ready to fight. I needed to give Kizuna and Glass a little more of a kick though—really make sure negotiations completely fell apart.

I knew what this guy would be thinking, and there was something I'd wanted to try for a while now.

"Let's negotiate. If you truly care for this Kuflika, release the harpoon vassal weapon and end your alliance with these other forces. Then we will guarantee the life of Kuflika," I told him.

"Like I would believe the word of scum like you!" he retorted, sounding very much like Motoyasu once had—and giving exactly the answer I was expecting.

"Scum, you say? And are you having fun playing at hero, Mr. Resurrected?" I jibed. That got a rise from the harpoon guy, confusion and hesitation rushing into his eyes. These guys had no poker face. Hit them with their most vital secrets and they showed you everything. "Looks like I'm right about you. Sorry, but you don't get to turn this world into your toy box," I told him.

"Shut up! This will be all settled once we win! If you're strong, you can do whatever you like!" he raged back. There it was. The classic one-sided survival-of-the-fittest thing. Once we kicked his ass he was still going to complain, you could be sure of that.

I had no more time to give them, anyway. Trying to talk things through with them had never worked before, and it would just be so much easier to kill them here. I knew that was a dangerous thought to have, but that didn't stop me from having it. There were some conflicts in the world that couldn't be solved by talking.

"Oh, Kuflika, you poor creature." The Demon Dragon laughed mockingly. "It seems the one you have sworn your new loyalty to isn't willing to give up anything to save you at all."

"Silence! Demon Dragon of evil!" the harpoon guy retorted. But from the look on his face, I guessed that one might have hit a nerve.

"Sweet Naofumi, there's someone over there holding a strange-looking ofuda," Shildina reported. We had the harpoon vassal weapon holder, Bitch, and S'yne's sister . . . and now someone holding what looked like a jet-black ofuda stood in front of the ship vassal weapon. "An ofuda," I almost exclaimed! Not another holy weapon? They had committed a lot to this battle.

The one holding the ofuda was a handsome-looking young man. Not the kind of person you really saw around me. Maybe like L'Arc, but younger—or Motoyasu when he was in high school.

"This is where I stake my claim! For the sake of the debt I owe!" the ofuda guy shouted.

"Yes, that's right," S'yne's sister told him. "You do your best, please."

"I will! I shall repay my debt to the great one by defeating these foes in battle!" the youth responded. He seemed like a pretty innocent kid . . . Maybe we could get through to him, at least. "We shall take the women alive, of course. They are all high quality . . . What perfect offerings they will make." Okay, so I spoke too soon. He was looking at Kizuna with an evil leer on his face. Forget this guy too, then. He was clearly lost in blind devotion to someone on the other side. There was nothing more difficult than convincing someone to change their ways when they already knew they were doing evil stuff.

"What about L'Arc and the others?" I asked.

"Well, well, well, I did want to focus on them, but here we are. We sent plenty for them to play with, anyway. After that debacle last time, I ordered those who can't play well with others to go cause chaos elsewhere," S'yne's sister explained. It sounded like she was talking about Armor. Bitch was still here though, which seemed like an oversight to me. "We've deployed a monster carrying a holy weapon over there too, along with vassal weapon holders from other worlds," S'yne's sister continued. I swore under my breath. They weren't holding anything back this time. They might have rushed into this, but they were bringing out all their big guns.

"Can Raph-chan make it over?" I wondered out loud. I thought about C'mon Raph, and a cross appeared over the Raph-chan icon. It was like she could come but couldn't right then. L'Arc and Itsuki were likely facing a tough battle too.

"You seem to be getting quite full of yourselves for beating some street performer last time," Bitch said. "I've got something that will stop you dead today!" She displayed what looked like a whip. She looked like a stuck-up little child showing off her favorite toy. I'd seen that whip before! It was the one Takt had used. They even had the whip seven star weapon! And they'd given it to Bitch? Pearls before swine!

This was likely the reason she had been laughing so much, anyway. I couldn't escape the feeling that we were about to get steamrolled.

"Seeing as we are fighting enemies who can nullify or even reflect magic, we thought she could use a little more oomph," S'yne's sister explained helpfully. But she didn't look happy about the decision. A seven star weapon was wasted on Bitch, surely. All she did was hang back and snipe from behind the real action, just like before, but now with a whip.

"They aren't holding anything back this time. We need to finish this quickly, then," the Demon Dragon said, floating in front of us with her arms crossed, then looking at me.

"Hah. Poor fool. I have a holy weapon in my body, which has been enhanced by almost all of the power-up methods known to this world. Do you really think you can defeat that? Gyah-gyah!" the metal magic dragon ranted, sounding like some insane ruler. That was some nasty new information to be receiving at this juncture too. They had all the power-up methods of the holy weapons and likely enhancements from six vassal weapons too. We didn't know if Miyaji had told them about the musical instrument's power-up method, but it was safe to presume they had that one too.

Meanwhile, we had one holy weapon and seven vassal weapons. If we factored in the enhancement rate of the holy weapons as a multiplier of three, they had eighteen and we had ten. The issue would be how to cover that gap of eight points.

It felt like too big of a gap, honestly speaking. I wasn't really basing my enhancement multiplier on anything other than a hunch there, so the vassal weapons might do better than that . . . but I was also thinking that retreat might be one option. If we considered that all the weapons that S'yne's sister held had their power-up methods implemented, that only opened the gap further. Unless we could fill that gap with powerful support magic, there seemed to be no way to win this battle.

"Hah. Poor fool! That's my line. Thinking you can win like this . . . I will show you what a true hunger for power looks like!" Maybe the Demon Dragon had some kind of a plan, because she wasn't backing down a step. "Listen to the voices of the holy weapon and know the suffering of the vassal weapons. You cannot hear the pain of the spirits? You are unfit to call yourself a dragon. Return to me and become part of a true dragon again."

"That's my line, gyah-gyah!" the metal magic dragon retorted.

"For Kuflika! We will defeat you!" the harpoon vassal weapon holder shouted at the Demon Dragon and Filo, with his allies all joining in. Those two were their primary targets here.

Chapter Ten: The Importance of Anger

"Here we are then, Shield Hero. Have you ever considered that there must be a reason why I have developed such feelings for you and why my minions swore fealty to you so easily?" the Demon Dragon asked, ignoring the riled-up metal magic dragon completely. I had really thought that had been the moment the fighting would start. It sounded like she had something to say though, so I answered the question.

"Not really. It's because of the hero power-ups I've given you, right? Now you are much stronger than the past Demon Dragon, right?" I said.

"Do you think that alone would allow me to forcibly take the power from Kuflika, one carrying one of my fragments, someone I practically created?" the Demon Dragon asked, pressing the point. At the time she had muttered about some kind of resistance, but she had also clearly become strong enough to ignore it completely. I didn't really care about that. "I would have become stronger than my past self, even without you nearby. But that's not all. I have obtained even greater power now." Multiple magic circles started to overlap over the Demon Dragon's body. I shook my head. My status floated up uncalled for, and the weapon book icon was displayed.

"Hey! You're not hacking my stats again!" I shouted. It felt like a violation on the same level as having my account hacked. The Demon Dragon got a little power back and look what she did with it! Pretending to be on our side, just waiting for an opening to strike!

"Demon Dragon! Just what are you planning?!" Glass and Kizuna both shouted at the dragon.

"Shield Hero, listen carefully to what I am telling you," the Demon Dragon said, a serious expression on her face, completely ignoring the questions and protests from our side.

"What do you mean?" I said.

"You heroes are trying to turn your back on the power of darkness and treat it as though it never existed at all. That is again why I ask this of you," the Demon Dragon continued. The skill icon for Formation One: Float Mirror flashed, and at the same time a skill called Change Mirror, a conversion of Change Shield, also appeared. "The hatred, the disgust you felt for the world in the moment was justifiable anger. Do you think that denying that anger, pretending it never existed, and withstanding so many terrible things without ever getting angry . . . do you think that is the correct approach? Truly? You cannot truly believe that is mercy?" the Demon Dragon asked. I hesitated, unsure how to answer. My Shield of Compassion was a temporary power, bestowed upon me by Atla. When I walked between life and death and was reunited with Atla and

Ost again, they had led me to a desire to save the world and save everyone in it—a desire that was real and true.

That said, the Demon Dragon was making a point I could not deny. Those feelings, and the anger I held within me, were kept in very different places.

"I don't care what you say! I've made my decision. I will not rely on anger . . . will not use the power of rage again," I said. With the power of compassion that I had been blessed with, I had already lost access to the Shield of Rage and the Shield of Wrath.

"Mr. Naofumi . . ." Raphtalia took my hand and squeezed it.

"Does the girl who gave you your compassion also deny your anger? Does she tell you to never get angry again?" the Demon Dragon said, pressing her point. I stammered for a moment, glancing over at Raphtalia. Atla . . . would surely have affirmed my rage in this instance.

"Demon Dragon . . . just what do you want to make Mr. Naofumi do? If you are trying to lure him off the righteous path, I will stop you!" Raphtalia declared.

"Holder of the katana vassal weapon, the Shield Hero's rage and his kindness are both elements that comprise the Shield Hero. See now that losing any of those parts will have a negative effect. Understand my words. A time will come when something important will emerge. It must be obtained no matter the cost," the Demon Dragon said cryptically. Change Mirror was automatically selected for me, and the mirror to change it to was then also selected. The shield selected was Mirror of Wrath. This was an item that the Demon Dragon had enhanced in the past by interfering with my shield. In principle it looked like a +11 AF. The Rage rank was now IV.

"Having rage is why you also have compassion. You have forgotten a vital component of your heart. Allow me to show you how to really use that power," the Demon Dragon said. I could feel something flowing up from deep inside me and moving into the Demon Dragon. At the same time, Formation Two: Float Mirror and the Shield of Compassion were forcibly activated, trying to suppress the power of my rage.

In response, the Demon Dragon just started to demand more power from me. Beast transformation support appeared, which I had used on Fohl and Sadeena in the past. I grunted with the effort.

"Mr. Naofumi?!" Raphtalia stammered. My armor was starting to transform, like when I had used the Shield of Rage. This time, though, I could feel both anger and warmth mixing in the armor.

With a terrible roar, the Demon Dragon drew in more power from me and started to transform. She quickly became bigger and more powerful than when we had fought her in the past. I grunted again, alternatingly assailed by the rage that

swirled in my heart and the images of everyone I wanted to protect—Raphtalia and Atla, Filo, Melty, Sadeena, Shildina, S'yne,
Keel, Ruft, and everyone else in the village. I didn't dislike it
either—it made me feel strong and capable of protecting them.
Having something absolute, something you had to protect at all
costs, created hatred for those who would try to destroy it. That
was what I was feeling.

In the weapon book, the name of the weapon somewhere
between rage and compassion floated into view . . . but I was
unable to read it.

"Don't worry," I finally managed to reply. "I'm not going
to get swallowed by rage." A time limit then appeared in my
field of view, like the one I had seen when I was controlling the
Shield of Wrath. It was set to thirty minutes.

"I'm still not sure about this . . ." Raphtalia said.

"She's being so aggressive about it. The anger might win
out!" I said pointedly, but the Demon Dragon just replied as
mockingly as ever.

"That is one of my best features. You need to show the
Shield Hero who is boss sometimes, holder of the katana vassal
weapon," the Demon Dragon said, looking over at Raphtalia.
What was she trying to get Raphtalia to do, exactly?

"That's not the issue here!" Raphtalia shouted back.

"Oh, but it is," the Demon Dragon replied. "You must
not deny the rage of the Shield Hero. Share that anger, share

your tears, share the quiet moments, and share the struggle to overcome; that is true compassion." The Demon Dragon was warning us that I was yet to overcome my anger. I needed to stay calm, stay calm without getting angry . . . but that just wasn't possible right then!

"We're going to discuss this again later!" I raged. The Demon Dragon just laughed.

"You don't have to understand it now. Just make sure you don't pretend your rage does not exist," the Demon Dragon said. She really was a masochist, loving it even when I got mad with her. "Now then, heroes, take a good look at your weapons created from my materials," the Demon Dragon suggested. Kizuna, Glass, Raphtalia, and S'yne all did so.

"The True Demon Dragon weapons have a rage effect applied to them now. They look much stronger," Kizuna reported.

"Look at this power!" Raphtalia exclaimed. "They aren't even cursed weapons. This is good. I feel such power flowing up from inside me, too." I shook my head. Was this another dragon effect? Everyone, including Raphtalia, had something like a black aura surrounding them, indicating they had been powered up.

"I feel power rising from inside," Kizuna said. The blood pudding was having an effect too, I was sure. I didn't like the direction this was taking though. At this rate, my rage would be required for the Demon Dragon to reach her Wrath Dragon form every single time something happened.

"I think this . . . might be just what we need," Raphtalia whispered, looking at the black and yet burning katana in her hand.

"Naofumi, what should we do? Who is going to fight who?" Kizuna asked.

"The Demon Dragon and Filo have been called out already," I replied. The terrifyingly transformed Demon Dragon was facing off with the metal magic dragon.

"Boo! This isn't my fault!" Filo was having a bad day, for sure. So it was the Demon Dragon and Filo versus the harpoon guy, his goons, and the metal magic dragon. The numbers seemed a little unbalanced.

"Aren't you going to call in the other heavenly kings?" I asked.

"I sent them to the port. They would just get in the way here anyway. More isn't always better," the Demon Dragon replied. *Okay . . . whatever.*

"Hey! Don't forget about me," said a voice.

"Kizuna! Watch out!" Glass shouted as the guy with the ofuda holy weapon threw a card-like ofuda at her. Glass managed to knock the attack out of the air just in time, but her expression was harsh.

"That was powerful for just a probing attack," she said, her hand looking numb. The simple act of repelling the incoming attack had hurt Glass considerably, meaning we were indeed facing very powerful foes.

"Glass! Are you okay?" Kizuna asked.

"It does hurt a little," Glass managed after a pause.

"I have all sorts of ways we can fight you, so be careful. I can use magic too. If you think you can stop me, go ahead and try," the ofuda guy said, a handsome smile on his face.

Then Shildina moved over to stand next to Glass.

"I think you could use some help," Shildina said.

"Yes, I think so. I'm not going to be able to handle this alone. Shildina, please aid me," Glass said.

"I'm going to fight for sweet Naofumi too," Shildina replied. They combined their strength, overlapping again as the oracle powers were activated.

"Well, well, well, you do have some fancy tricks," S'yne's sister said.

"Indeed, I do. You would do well not to underestimate me in this form," Glass warned. "Kizuna, please provide support from the rear. If you see an opening, you know what to do," Glass said.

"Okay! We'll annoy them as much as we can, right, Chris?" Kizuna said.

"Pen!" the familiar replied. Kizuna had summoned Chris and was ready to fight. It looked like Kizuna, Chris, Glass, and Shildina were going to fight the one with the ofuda while offering support to anyone else who needed it if an opening presented itself.

My only other concern was the ship floating in the sky behind the harpoon vassal weapon holder and his goons with its cannon trained upon us. I expected them to start firing at any moment. As it had formerly been Ethnobalt's weapon, we knew what kind of attacks it could perform. But since it was stolen, we had no idea what kind of modifications might have been made. Withstanding whatever barrage it unleashed was where I came in, of course.

There was no sign of Bitch coming down from the ship.

"Dear little S'yne, I don't need you making any trouble, so let's play together again," S'yne's sister said.

"—!" S'yne replied, although I couldn't hear any of it.

"S'yne has—since the last defeat and is—expect a result—last time!" her familiar said, maybe filling in some of the blanks.

"You'd better pull your weight this time!" Bitch complained down at S'yne's sister. She had proven herself to be very strong, so I could see why her allies would complain about her only fighting S'yne.

"Well, well, well. Should I fight Iwatani? I don't mind if I do, but what do you think S'yne will do then?" S'yne's sister mused. S'yne decided to make her sister's mind up for her, turning her sewing vassal weapon into a ball of yarn and launching a preemptive strike. Threads launched from the ball and flew out in all directions, striking at all of the enemies. That looked useful for keeping them all pinned down. Even the metal magic dragon was getting caught up in them.

Looking at the threads, S'yne's sister slammed her own chain weapon down onto the ground.

"Binding: Multi-Headed Orochi!" she shouted. Chains appeared from four directions and blocked the passage of the threads.

"Hah! We can shred such attacks with ease!" Bitch said.

"But can you keep doing it?" S'yne's sister asked. "The instant you let your guard down, those threads will get you. With Iwatani here, they have even more applications." She just loved explaining things, regardless of the side she was on.

"I wasn't sure you would notice," I said. Using my mirrors made instant transmission of the threads a possibility. They could pass through my mirrors and spread freely across any desired space. What I really wanted to do was put a mirror behind Bitch and bind her up all at once.

"You must understand," S'yne's sister continued, giving a dose of reality to Bitch. "Having that dragon nearby will place restrictions on your own magic—magic that doesn't work on Iwatani anyway. The point therefore becomes how well we can fight without their interference. And you want to just ignore S'yne? Please. You'd better start helping."

"Whatever are you talking about?! You need to keep her off our backs and take all of the others out too! You can use magic, right?" Bitch said, issuing orders as haughtily as ever. I hoped they would keep fighting like this until it created an opening to strike.

"Well, well, well. You should be the one to do that. The one who suggests something is normally the one to carry it out, correct? You've been awarded all sorts of blessings, and yet you still want more! And you think I'm getting full of myself. If I just start shooting off magic, that dragon is going to take steps to stop me. I don't want to have to deal with that," S'yne's sister said, a taunting smile on her lips. Her entire attitude seemed to subtly suggest that this was Bitch's last chance. Bitch clearly was on uneasy footing with her new friends.

I just wanted them to fight more. Fight each other! The rage surged to overtake me, and I struggled to force it down again.

"Which means I will pin down Iwatani and S'yne," S'yne's sister said.

"I'm not going to forget this slight!" Bitch shouted.

"Lady Malty! This is the time to show your worth!" one of her goons shouted. They were behind the others. Bitch had the whip in one hand, seemingly preparing to use a skill. She had learned her lesson about firing off magic at me—I would just send it right back. Maybe they would try for some cooperative or ritual magic, something a little harder to interfere with. It must be nice, I pondered for a moment, to be able to access forbidden magic using an accessory. These guys all sucked!

"Raphtalia, do you know what to do?" I asked.

"Yes. This time we have to fight her," Raphtalia replied. That meant Raphtalia, S'yne, and I would be fighting Bitch and her goons—primarily Woman B II and the ship vassal weapon.

"Little Naofumi, can I fight the harpoon hero?" Sadeena asked.

"Think you can take him?" I asked.

"I'll need support from you and the others, little Naofumi. I just want to see how good he really is with that harpoon," Sadeena said. Of course, she used a harpoon herself. If this worked out, stealing the weapon away from him—like Itsuki had done against Miyaji—was not out of the question. Proving a clear difference in personal quality and claiming the weapon would definitely be a good outcome.

"Shall we begin? Allow us to demonstrate how foolish you are for turning your weapons on us!" At this shout from the Demon Dragon, both sides all started to attack at once.

"Now! Play our trump card!" Bitch shouted. It seemed a bit early for that, but the metal magic dragon and ofuda holy weapon holder both shouted in agreement. The two corrupted holy weapons started to release a kind of vibration that gave the air a purple tint. It scattered into the surrounding area.

Bitch gave an unnerving giggle as my mirrors started to shake. It wasn't just the mirrors either—Raphtalia and Glass's weapons were affected too.

"What's this? What's going on?!" Kizuna didn't seem to be affected. I glared at Bitch, wondering what she was planning. I was sure I had felt this before, somewhere . . .

"Vassal weapons! Respond to my call and obey my orders!" Bitch intoned. The mirror was shaking even harder, as though trying to resist.

"Mr. Naofumi!" Raphtalia looked over at me with a worried expression. More cowardly tricks—I should have expected no less from Bitch. This was also the same trick they had used when they stopped my shield and Itsuki's bow from working.

"You are the true holders of those weapons, are you? So what! Is that enough to resist this power?" Bitch crowed. "I strip from you your right to hold those weapons!" Another vibration shook the air. The mirror, katana, and fan all seemed about to comply with Bitch—then the mirror fired off a beam to protect the katana, and the hunting tool holy weapon protected the fan. Her ploy didn't seem to have worked.

"Bad luck! Looks like corrupted holy weapons can't make the grade when it comes to stripping the right to use vassal weapons," Kizuna said, sounding very pleased with herself.

"Hah. Your very first move is to try and steal our weapons? How very boring," the Demon Dragon added, almost sounding disappointed.

"You are joking! It didn't work? What a waste of time!" Bitch clicked her tongue, which just annoyed me more. I wanted to kill her so badly. I wanted to kill her right there!

"They have a holy weapon too, so it can't be helped. Even if it comes from another world, working together with the vassal weapons allowed their holy weapon to stop you," S'yne's sister said, providing her normal, impartial analysis. In this case, she seemed to want to mock Bitch. These guys always tried to weaken us like this! I was just pleased it didn't work, or we would have been right back to having to fight without weapons again.

"I'm not leaving this opening unexploited!" The Demon Dragon twisted a paw and countless balls of black magic appeared in the air, flying toward the metal magic dragon.

"My universal collaborators! Respond to my call and materialize your magic power!" Even as she launched the first attack, she was incanting the second.

"Fool! Have you forgotten who I am? Gyah-gyah!" the metal magic dragon spouted.

"We'll see who is the fool here . . . I am the Demon Dragon! Now you will learn that your comprehension of me is fatally flawed!" the Demon Dragon replied.

"And so what if it is? Eat this! Lightning Strike Dragon: Ten!" The harpoon vassal weapon holder lifted his harpoon and then charged right at the Demon Dragon, his body wreathed in lightning. It was a power-up skill! But without knowing which holy weapon it was coming from, there was no way to copy it. Life just kept getting harder.

"Little Demon Dragon, he's going to appear to come at your head but then aim for your body," Sadeena said—at some point, she had climbed onto the Demon Dragon's back and was now giving advice.

"Then I know how to respond," the Demon Dragon said, lowering her head and avoiding the attack. The harpoon vassal weapon holder circled around, still a crackling ball of lightning, and tried to strike at her body, but she knew what to expect and shut him down. She followed up with a grunt as she swung her tail, striking the harpoon guy hard. He grunted in turn.

"What was that?!" he exclaimed.

"That was a pretty powerful attack, from the look of it, but easy to avoid once you know where you are targeting," Sadeena told the harpoon guy from her perch on the powered-up Demon Dragon's back.

"I'm surprised you could see that," the Demon Dragon said.

"I'm pretty good with a harpoon myself," Sadeena responded.

"Very well. Stick close to me now!" the Demon Dragon shouted.

"Of course! Let's both win some praise from little Nao-fumi!" Sadeena replied. The dragon made a sound of agreement, and I shook my head. I didn't need that pair, of all people, starting to get along.

"Now! This is the moment to form some magic! Have a taste of my power with my complete command of magic!" the Demon Dragon roared.

"Fool! I'll show you that I'm superior with magic in every possible way! You shall learn the terror of a holy weapon! Gyah-gyah!" the metal magic dragon sniped back. Then they both started to intone the exact same magic!

"This power, a precursor to victory, is the ultimate magic that can eradicate all and give mercy to my companions . . . The Dragon Emperor, ruler of this world, commands it! Provide almighty power!" The Demon Dragon finished first and turned to look at us, while the metal magic dragon was frowning for some reason.

"I'm not going to help my master's enemies," Filo said. The Demon Dragon's magic could be made more powerful by borrowing power from those who had contracted or collaborated with her. And Filo—who had been appointed as one of the Four Heavenly Kings—had denied that request from the metal magic dragon. Then Filo took her bolas out from her wing, spun it around, and threw it at the harpoon guy.

"Uwah! No way!" The harpoon guy toppled over, his legs tangled in the bolas. He was back up almost at once, but it bought us some time. Filo's throwing attacks were pretty useful too; I had to give her credit for that.

"Gah! Curse you, Heavenly King, and your failure to see which of us is your true ruler! But I can manage even without your aid, you will soon find! Gyah-gyah!" said the metal magic dragon.

"Too slow. No matter how fast you can incant, magic from a king without any subordinates will never match mine!" the Demon Dragon exclaimed.

"She has someone collaborating with her! Me!" the harpoon guy roared. It looked like maybe he was helping out.

"Let us see how you fare under our assault. It will be interesting to see how big a gap we can create. Blessing of the Demon Dragon's Four Heavenly Kings!" The magic that the Demon Dragon composed flew right for me. It was coming in really fast. But seeing as we hadn't been plunged into the chaos of open battle yet, I could still respond. "I will determine when it goes off. Shield Hero, multiply it!" the Demon Dragon said.

"Yes, I've got it. Formation One, Formation Two, Formation Three: Glass Shield! Into . . . Mirror Cage!" I adjusted the angle of the two floating mirrors to catch the incoming magic. In the moment it touched the Mirror of Wrath floating mirror, it turned a sickly color. It reminded me of Sacrifice Aura. Immediately after that, it touched the Shield of Compassion mirror and turned back to a normal color—the compassion had purified it. My gut told me that we would have paid some nasty price, just like with Sacrifice Aura, if it had been activated after hitting the Mirror of Wrath. Getting the order in which it hit the mirrors mixed up could definitely be dangerous.

That risk was also worth it, however, because I could tell it had been increased by more than just a normal reflection. Then it hit the third glass mirror . . . and that was when I trapped it in the Mirror Cage.

"Here it comes. Everyone! Get ready!" The Demon Dragon roared. In that same moment, the cage was ripped apart. Then the Demon Dragon support magic that I had multiplied rained down on us.

My stats saw an immediate jump upward. It was hard to calculate exactly what the modifier was, but it was at least equal to if not above Liberation Aura VIII.

"Demon Dragon! Harpoon and Dragon Protection: Ten!" The metal magic dragon did not miss a beat, casting some support magic on her own allies.

"Well, well, well," S'yne's sister said. "You shouldn't be relying too heavily on support magic." Both her and the metal magic dragon started to incant more magic.

"They are leaving an opening for us, so let's take it," the Demon Dragon said.

"Come on, little Filo! Let's pull our weight!" Sadeena called.

"Okay!" Filo agreed. The Demon Dragon flew straight for the metal magic dragon, while Sadeena grabbed Filo's legs (Filo had turned into a monster that looked like a big eagle) and they flew straight for the harpoon guy.

"What?! They don't even have vassal weapons, but look at that speed!" their target shouted.

"That's because little Naofumi has piled so many enhancements onto us! We're not giving any ground to you!" Sadeena shouted back.

"That's right! Master's meals give me lots of energy!" Filo added. The wind wreathing her also enveloped Sadeena's harpoon, and Sadeena also used some gemstones to access the Way of the Dragon Vein as she charged right for the harpoon guy.

"This is a copy of that technique you just used," Sadeena said. "If you don't avoid this, I'm not going to have any fun today at all." Transformed into a bullet of speeding wind, Filo shifted her trajectory slightly from the harpoon guy, zooming high up into the sky while Sadeena continued flying directly toward her target.

"You think such a direct attack could hope to—" But his bravado was cut off with a grunt as he avoided Sadeena's charge but then got hammered by that same bullet of wind, which turned almost 180 degrees in the blink of an eye and smashed into him. The two of them had known exactly where the harpoon guy would dodge.

"Oh my, you didn't avoid that? I even showed you which hand I was holding it in to make it easier for you," Sadeena jibed, still completely in her comfort zone. She might be lacking in output compared to him, but she was completely winning when it came to technique.

Not one to be left behind, the Demon Dragon grabbed onto the metal magic dragon in that same moment, opening her mouth wide and taking a breath. A blast of black fire was unleashed from deep inside the Demon Dragon's throat, glimmering with light as it burned.

"Have a taste of this! New Star Blacksun Fire!" the Demon Dragon roared. The metal magic dragon gave a complementary roar of pain. I'd seen flames like those before. They were the same as Dark Curse Burning.

The Demon Dragon breathed fire on the metal magic dragon for a while and then backed off again. Her target groaned.

"Cursed fire . . . the recourse of a coward," the metal magic dragon finally managed to say.

"You will have a difficult time purging the fire of my rage! So hot it burns even the darkness. Do you think you can treat it? Well, just in case . . ." She snapped her claws together and I felt something change in the air around us. "I've created a magic pocket that delays healing. Any who stand against me . . . had better not need medical attention for a while." The Demon Dragon seemed to have every base covered, including creating a field that impaired the effects of healing magic.

Chapter Eleven: Opposing Nullification

I turned my attention away from Filo and Sadeena—I had my own battle to fight, after all. The slow staring contest with S'yne's sister continued, but she was incanting magic all the while.

"You're wide open!" Bitch taunted. "Air Strike Backwhip V!" She unleashed a whip skill that ignored range and attacked from behind. She really did love surprise attacks. I had been expecting just such a cowardly attack, however, and it was easy to stop it.

"Formation One: Glass Shield!" My life-force-imbued glass shield caught the whip as it tried to strike me from behind. The glass shattered and flew toward Bitch.

"Lady Malty! Save me!" one of her retinue screamed, grabbing onto her.

"Hey! Get off me! Oww!" Bitch complained. Some of the fragments actually hit her.

"Whatever are you playing at?" S'yne's sister said, narrowing her eyes as she watched the scene unfold. She seemed to have used up all her patience with Bitch now.

Raphtalia rushed in toward S'yne's sister, keeping her body low, drawing her sword in a Draw Slice.

"Instant Blade! Mist!" she shouted. The effects from her scabbard allowed her to attack in haikuikku, but S'yne's sister still managed to avoid the attack.

"Well, well, well. Very scary stuff," she taunted. She had seen it coming a mile off. Just how fast was she, I wondered again after seeing her avoid an attack at that speed.

"Spider Wire!" S'yne grabbed the opportunity to try and limit her sister's movements, but her sister swung her chain around and swept away all of the incoming threads.

The best plan looked to be for Raphtalia, S'yne, and me to keep S'yne's sister's attention focused on us—she was the real threat here—then seizing an opening to take down Bitch and the others. In order to achieve that, though, I needed to get aboard the ship.

As we tussled back and forth, Glass and Shildina—buffed by the Demon Dragon's magic—launched into battle against the guy with the ofuda holy weapon.

"I order you here and now," the ofuda guy intoned. "My ofuda . . . respond to my call! Lightning! Pierce my foes! Chain Lightning: Five!"

"Hah! Circle Dance Reverse Formation: Lawless Counter!" Glass reflected the magic unleashed by the ofuda holy weapon holder, and then Shildina threw her own ofuda in response.

"I'm skilled at handling lightning. I order you here and now. My ofuda . . . respond to my call! Water . . . disperse this lightning! Lightning Drain!" Water extended from Shildina's thrown ofuda, adjusting the trajectory of the lightning. "Did you really think such a simple attack would hit us?"

"How about this then?" the ofuda guy replied.

"You'll have to deal with our attack first. Shildina, together!" Glass said.

"Let's go!" Shildina agreed. Glass splashed some soul-healing water over her body while Shildina gripped an earth crystal, and both of them turned their fans into swords. They had the Wave Sealing Sword, a unique weapon that was a fan but could turn into a sword. Glass closed in with the guy with the ofuda holy weapon, with Shildina swinging her sword right behind her. Even more impressive, she had found a second sword from somewhere and was fighting with two.

"Wave Sealing Sword: Zero Formation! And then special skill . . . Sword Dance: Mizuchi!" Glass shouted, cutting vertically, then adding a spin.

"Twin Water Dragons Sword Wave!" Shildina was right behind her, providing a magical sword technique using her two swords with ofuda added. The guy with the ofuda found himself under a series of dragon-themed attacks. He gave a grunt.

"You're good, I'll give you that," the guy with the ofuda said.

"I'm not finished yet. Have a taste of this! Reverse Return Strike!" Shildina turned into her killer whale form for a moment and unleashed a tail swipe. Then she immediately chopped at his body with both swords.

"Uwah! You are both full of surprises," the ofuda guy said, leaping backward.

"Formation One: Pit Trap!" Kizuna immediately created a hole at the ofuda guy's feet, toppling him to the ground with a grunt.

"Another cowardly attack . . . you won't defeat me like that!" The ofuda guy gave a roar, placing ofuda floating in the air around him like Ethnobalt and Kyo had done with the pages of the book vassal weapon. Using them as stepping-stones to climb up into the air, the guy with the ofuda holy weapon launched a follow-up attack.

"I can handle enemies who move like a rabbit," Shildina said—perhaps talking about Ethnobalt. The way this guy was using his holy weapon to make new footholds for himself was similar.

"You can't handle your weapon yet, can you? Just like all the resurrected, you lack experience. Take this! Direct from my master! A combination attack with a style from another world!" Glass shouted. Joined by Shildina, they turned their fans back into swords and each unleashed their own attack.

"Circle Dance: Turtle Carapace Cruncher!"

"Hengen Muso Fan Style: Paper Blizzard! Circle Dance Zero Formation: Reverse Snow Moon Flower!" It sounded like

Shildina shouted the wrong attack name. She had learned some Hengen Muso Style techniques but didn't have a complete understanding of them yet, so her degree of recreation was low. Because she was combining her power with Glass, however, she still managed to activate it. A skill much like Glass's own huge attack, Reverse Snow Moon Flower, was triggered. Wind blew up around Shildina, and flower-petal pieces of ice attacked her enemy.

Glass followed up at once, launching the defense-rating attack the old man developed right at the ofuda guy. He tried to dodge it and defend against it, but Shildina's skill still hit him. Even I felt that one—a real nasty combination attack. Their target groaned.

"Quite a nasty attack, even though you are so weak," the ofuda guy replied, a hint of panic creeping into his face as he responded. He had the kind of face that suggested he loved to call other people cowards.

"I think there's a nicer way of saying that. At least call us creative," Glass replied.

"Your weapon feels like it is mainly intended for using magic anyway. Shouldn't you be working with your allies to launch some big magic spell? You're not suited to close combat," Shildina analyzed calmly. The ofuda guy didn't seem happy with that suggestion either.

"Thank you for the advice, but I don't need it from the

likes of you. There is only one who is allowed to caution me so openly," he replied.

"Like we know about your silly personal rules," Shildina shot back.

"Don't get full of yourself just because you've got a pretty face," he retorted.

"Full of what? Even having a pretty face won't get sweet Naofumi to look my way," Shildina replied.

"Clearly Naofumi doesn't care about looks. Look how he acts with the Demon Dragon. I think her analysis of him was correct," Glass chipped in. I would have loved to step in and put them straight, but I had my own battle going on.

"I think I'll give you a lesson on how to actually use ofuda," Shildina said. "With some instructions on surprise attacks too. You'll see how the miko priestess of carnage fights!" She closed her fan and took out an ofuda, then started to incant some magic. Glass pressed her own attack against the ofuda guy, protecting Shildina.

"You can't expect these attacks to get you very far for long! Hah! Intense Cascade: Five!" At the shout from the ofuda guy, a vast volume of ofuda flew out to cover the vicinity closing in around Glass. But she danced and whipped up a wind around herself to divert the attacks and create an opening to escape.

"Circle Dance Evade Formation: Wind Dance Melody! A powerful attack, to be sure, but that hardly matters if I can dodge it. We can also use this to pin you down. Kizuna!" Glass shouted.

"I'm here! Double Lure!" Kizuna cast in her lure, and in the same moment it hit, Glass slammed the ofuda guy in the shoulder with her fan.

"Circle Dance Destruction Formation: Turtle Carapace Cracker!" Glass made every word linger as she hammered the attack home. The ofuda guy screamed as something exploded inside him, blood rupturing out. I had to admit, the sight of a handsome guy getting his comeuppance felt good.

"Your high stats worked against you in the end," Glass commented.

"I'm not finished yet! Things are just getting fun!" he retorted with a laugh.

"Then you'll just have to enjoy it alone," Shildina said. "My magic is ready."

"You aren't the only ones who can attack!" the ofuda guy shouted. "Take this! Art of Fire! Blazing Ball: Ten!" He bypassed the ofuda completely and unleashed some magic from this world. It was definitely different from the ofuda magic.

"Another direct attack. Are you even trying to hit us?" Shildina asked. Accompanied by Glass, the two of them slipped easily beneath the impressively sized incoming fireball and continued to close in.

"I order you here and now. My ofuda . . . respond to my

call! Water and wind! Attack the foe who stands before me!" Shildina's magic caused a shoal of watery fish to appear, wrapped around in wind. "Wind Fish Rush Down!"

"You aren't trying either!" the ofuda guy shouted. "You can't expect to hit me with that!" He seemed to be focused on defense now, with his ofuda out to dodge or block any incoming attacks. However, he had failed to look closely enough at his surroundings. He had failed to identify which attacks Shildina was most skilled with.

"I lead the power of the ofuda here and ask that it be realized. Vein of the earth! Ofuda! Lend me power!" Shildina continued. "Sweeping Ofuda Tempest!" That looked like hybrid magic based on the Way of the Dragon Vein, which meant she could probably imbue it with additional strength. Her ofuda proceeded to float up into the air and fly toward her target.

"That is the mark. See if you can avoid it," Shildina taunted.

"Your attack can't hit me if that ofuda doesn't. You seem to favor attacks that take a long time to launch, do you not? Maybe you should have incanted after you marked me," the ofuda guy replied.

"I have to incant the first hit or it doesn't work," Shildina explained.

"I see. That only raises the bar higher. If I smash that ofuda out of the air, all your efforts will have been for nothing," he said, keeping an eye on Kizuna and her support while fending off Glass's attacks. Shildina glanced at the flying ofuda . . . and then it happened. From behind the ofuda guy, Glass stuck an ofuda onto those she had already deployed.

"What?!" he shouted. Now that they had a designated target, the watery wind fish started to fly toward it. They were like homing missiles. Shildina continued to summon more water wind fish, sending out countless fish toward her enemy.

"Shildina currently possesses me, you see. That means we have to share everything required for activating magic. Oh, and look! Chris wants to take part too!" Glass said.

"Pen!" Chris replied. Glass drew in her fan and prepared to launch a skill, and then Chris appeared and turned into an ofuda. Glass attached it to her fan and started to dance.

"Circle Dance Zero Formation: Reverse Water Wind Fish! Penguin Peck!" She elevated it to the level of a hybrid skill, Glass's Reverse Snow Moon Flower mixed with the water fish Shildina created, and then Chris added too. The whole pile of attacks plowed toward the ofuda guy.

Perhaps because of mixing attacks, there were now clones of Chris too! Each time one of them hit, it fragmented apart and vanished. They weren't dying. They were just attacking while mixed in with the skill. I looked on in admiration, wondering if Raph-chan could perform a similar combination skill of some kind.

The ofuda guy gave a moan, losing ground in his attempts

to defend against the attack. The power that the combination of Glass and Shildina brought to the table really was a big help.

"If you can't deal with rating attacks, you better not try and defend so much," Glass suggested.

"Where . . . where is such an attack coming from . . ." the ofuda guy gurgled. Then I noticed that Glass and Shildina had—quite creatively—worked in some Hengen Muso Style life force as well. The poor punching bag didn't know how to deflect it and was spitting up more blood as a result. He was still holding out, but that was about all I could say for the guy.

With an impotent roar, the ofuda guy launched another large fireball at Shildina and Kizuna.

"I've told you this thing is too easy to see coming," Shildina told him. It was pretty big and pretty fast, but both Shildina and Kizuna easily avoided it.

"Hitting you wasn't what I had planned," the ofuda guy managed, even scraping out a laugh. "Art of Fire! Fireworks Ball: Ten!" From where the ball landed, it turned into a massive pillar of flame and then exploded further. That was some serious area-effect magic.

"The final work of a fool . . . Secret Circle Dance: Cursed Return!" Shildina took out her fan and swung it toward the incoming magic, focusing a part of the exploding flames . . . and then returned it toward the ofuda guy.

"What? This can't be?!" It was hardly inspiring final words.

Then he screamed as the fire hit him. Shildina was already using the new secret techniques in combat! I was impressed. This was a magic-conduction technique similar to the Gather technique that S'yne had taught Atla and me. I was struck again by how many varied attacks everyone in my party had—I could barely keep them straight myself.

"Your cooking is something else, Naofumi," Glass commented. "My attack power has never been so high, and the cost of the possession has been reduced to a trickle too. But I still can't contain my gag reflex at thinking about food made from the Demon Dragon!"

"Try to make a snack to go with alcohol next time, okay!" Shildina requested again. The effects of the "food doping" were pretty easy to see, anyway. Along with additional experience and the permanent ability boosts, it also offered temporary stat boosts. It even offered a boost experience rate, making it easier to level up. But that information didn't matter to us right then. I was still struck by the difference in Glass's reaction—almost dejected—and Shildina's—simply offering an unbiased impression.

"It's working! One more big push!" Kizuna shouted support from the sidelines while focusing on attacking the holy weapon using the hunting tool.

"I'm ready! He's very tough, though. If this is the difference in enhancement between us, we are going to have an uphill struggle," Glass commented.

"We can do it!" Kizuna shouted back.

"I'm not finished yet!" the ofuda guy said. So those hadn't been his final words after all. He was looking intently at his own ofuda, which seemed to pulse somehow. "This is the sealed power of my weapon. The power of the cursed ofuda! Feel it across your pathetic bodies!"

"I'm not scared of curses. I've been through enough of them," Shildina said offhandedly. It was a classic Shildina line. She had handled all sorts of dangerous stuff back in Q'ten Lo.

"—!" S'yne trying to speak got my attention back to our battle. Glass and Shildina looked to have things under control.

"Take—!" S'yne's familiar doll was heading into battle alongside its mistress. They were both sticking close to S'yne's sister. S'yne was using her scissors as two swords and attacking over and over again. Although each time it almost looked like she would get hit, S'yne's sister was dodging with an almost annoyed look on her face.

"Well, well, well, you have improved even since we last fought. You always were a hard worker, S'yne," her sister said, even as she weaved through S'yne's enraged attacks. She was preparing to cast the nullification magic, so she was focusing more on just avoiding attacks for the time being.

"Not—lose—time," S'yne said.

"No one likes a stubborn girl, little sister," S'yne's sister said. I had hardly been able to hear a word S'yne said, with all the sound skipping. But S'yne's sister frowned. All her advice seemed to do was rub S'yne the wrong way. Her eyes hardened and the frequency of her attacks increased. She was playing into her opponent's hands, though, it felt like to me. Any opening she got, S'yne sent out threads to interfere with the other enemies around us, but S'yne's sister blocked them with her chain each time.

"Here we go! My magic is ready. Disarming Shot! Earth Explosion: Ten!" S'yne's sister shouted.

"Have some of this too!" the metal magic dragon added, both of them launching their magic at the same time. That suited us perfectly. Although it was from two separate sources, the area of effect for the two was linked together. The unlocked effects of my weapon visualized magic for me at the moment, so that made this all the easier.

Up on the ship, Bitch was gripping her whip and gathering her power. She was clearly planning to attack in the moment that we were weakened. I wasn't going to allow that.

The magic that S'yne's sister unleashed closed in first. I used a mirror to knock the flying enhancement magic toward the nullification magic, then used my new skill to rebound it away.

"Release Rebound!" Matching my own timing, Raphtalia and Glass both also unleashed their own skills for nullifying enhancements. With an immensely satisfying sound, the nullification magic S'yne's sister cast was sent flying away and turned into mist.

"Well, well, well. You learned that quicker than I expected. But what about this?" she asked slyly. The metal magic dragon unleashed more magic, even as the Demon Dragon viciously attacked.

"Universal power of my mighty core! Respond to my desires and materialize your magic power! I am the Dragon Emperor, ruler of this world. My power is the strength to conquer all, the ultimate magic that can eradicate all! My foes fall before me! The Dragon Emperor, ruler of this world, commands it! Nullify all magic! Demon Dragon Freezing Pulsation: Ten!" A second wave of enhancement-nullification magic was unleashed, and the dragon even had the next one all lined up too. Would it be debuff magic next, I wondered. That's what I would have used.

"We have a plan in place for that too! Secret Circle Dance: Pulse Rebound!" Glass shouted. She and Shildina opened their fans and started dancing again, applying power along the incoming magic and then repelling it away even as it came flying in.

"Me too, of course!" Everyone else pulled it off about a third of the time, but I had a slightly better success rate than that. All I could do was defend, after all. With all of this power being drawn out of me so unnaturally at the moment, I felt as though I could send any incoming magic back the way it had come. With rage and compassion at war within me, I simply couldn't be stopped! "Hold on a moment. What name did the old lady give this? Ah, right. Hengen Muso Style Lost Technique: Magic Eradication!" It involved filling my mirrors with life force, collecting the enemy's magic using the Gather technique, and then sending it flying away. As a side effect, it could also scatter magic within a two-meter area around the users. But pulling that off required a level I hadn't reached yet. Being able to apply Gather like this made it easier to use than I had expected.

I was using floating mirrors to do it. When the magic hit the mirror made from the Mirror of Wrath, fire exploded out from it, causing a minor tornado. That had been a clean hit, so maybe it had an attack hitbox. It must have triggered a counterattack.

Raphtalia was also using draw slices to chop down the incoming magic.

"What? What is all this?!" S'yne's sister exclaimed in surprise.

"Did you think there was only one way to counter you?" I responded. "You have to realize that you aren't the only ones who can pull off all this unpredictable stuff." I was pleased! We had more than proved we could do it, knocking away nullification magic and getting rid of it for good. That would keep us much safer in battle.

"Phew! Yep! I've got a handle on it now!" Kizuna was putting what she had learned into practice too, protecting Sadeena and Filo before the magic hit them.

"We're going to be playing catchup forever," Raphtalia said.

"Well, well, well. You've certainly been putting some time in," S'yne's sister said, giving us an annoyed round of applause. She still seemed pretty at ease.

"What magic are you going to use next? I'll send it right back at you," I said, mirrors ready.

"Bah! Stop getting carried away!" the metal magic dragon said, glaring at us.

"If you want us to stop, stop us," I replied. I was loving the look in her eyes. I always wanted my enemies to look at me like that.

The battle was growing more chaotic.

"Well said, Shield Hero," said our dragon. "Your taunts provide a thrill for me too." She was starting to piss me off more than our enemies, to be honest. There was no defeating the sexual harassment dragon.

"Hold on!" Bitch squawked. "How are you letting them get away with this? Hurry up and weaken them! This isn't what we agreed on in the meeting!"

"Well, well, well. Did you expect Iwatani and his allies to just sit on their hands? It's arrogant to think that we would be the only ones making any forward progress. You need to be ready for just these kinds of things!" S'yne's sister replied.

"What are you talking about?! You guys are strong enough to trample any efforts they might make! So start trampling!" Bitch demanded. S'yne's sister looked displeased at this, shrugging even as she fended off S'yne's barrage of attacks.

"The problem with fighting someone is you never know what they are going to do. You're sitting up there, removed from everything, watching the big picture. Maybe you should pull something out from your bag of conniving tricks to help us," S'yne's sister pointed out.

"Hold on. You're going to blame this on me again?" Bitch raged. I was just enjoying the show. There was nothing quite like watching two enemies you hated tearing into each other. I wanted to keep watching for the rest of the night, but we didn't have that kind of leeway here.

The cannons on the ship vassal weapon had already started to fire down on us.

"Stardust Blade!" Raphtalia was using what was also a long-range skill, her Stardust Blade, to fire stars up at the ship vassal weapon in the sky, but her efforts didn't seem to be having much of an effect. I wondered if I could get up there using a Movement Mirror from a glass shield.

Then I had a better idea.

"Formation Three: Glass Shield!" I shouted. I used Glass Shield and Mirror Cage to intercept the incoming shells and prevent them from interfering with any of my allies. I was able to make it through using Stardust Mirror, but it was still a pretty tense situation. I certainly didn't have the leeway to try and get up there myself. I needed to deploy Raphtalia as support for someone. That was becoming clear. The battle had only just started . . . In mere minutes we were also being pushed onto the ropes . . . The future did not look bright, not in that moment.

"I've got plenty more for you yet! Eat this!" The metal magic dragon unleashed a stream of magic.

"My power is the strength to conquer all, the ultimate magic that can eradicate all! My foes fall before me! The Dragon Emperor, ruler of this world, commands it! Lower everything! Demon Dragon Lowering Pressure: Ten!" The metal magic dragon was trying to send out more balls of magic. I looked over at the Demon Dragon and gave a nod, not liking the synchronized feeling with her.

"What a coincidence, my little fragment. I was just incanting that magic myself. Allow me to make use of yours," the Demon Dragon said, taking advantage of the flow of magic created by the incanting of the metal magic dragon to immediately complete the incanting of her own magic.

"Demon Dragon: Raging Reduction!" A cluster of black magic balls was formed, interfering with the magic the metal magic dragon had been trying to trigger.

"No! Never! I have the power of a holy weapon at my command! You can't stop me like this!" The metal magic dragon raised a hand and tried to force out the balls of magic . . . but I could see it all, which meant I could also reply.

Using Gather again, an application of life force, I moved my mirrors into position, placing them in front of the magic before they flew, knocking them into a Float Mirror, and then sending them back. Of course, the final thing they hit was the rage-infused Mirror of Wrath. After this impressive combination, the Demon Dragon also clicked her claws.

"What?!" The metal magic dragon's shout was then drowned out by screaming—joined by the harpoon guy and his entire party as the magical lights unleashed by the Demon Dragon crashed into them all.

"Well, well, well. Look out!" S'yne's sister knocked the magic away from herself.

"Hah!" The guy with the ofuda holy weapon did the same thing. I wasn't sure how the ship was doing it, but it was knocking the magic away too.

"My strength! My power! My entire body feels like its burning . . . Is this a curse?! But I'm not finished yet! I've just fallen to plus/minus zero, that's all!" The harpoon guy checked his own status, then turned hate-filled eyes on us. With the enhanced magic and debuff magic at the same time, his stats had hit no positive, no negative adjustment . . . but that couldn't be right. He had the Rage Curse on him, so he had to have some negative on there.

"I'm not done yet. You were created from me, nothing more. Take another level of nullification magic." The Demon Dragon unleashed more magic toward the metal magic dragon. "Universal power of my mighty core! Power of the Four Heavenly Kings! Respond to my desires and materialize your magic power! I am the Dragon Emperor, ruler of this world. My raging power is the strength to conquer all, the ultimate magic that can eradicate all! My foes fall before me! The Dragon Emperor, ruler of this world, commands it! Nullify all magic that I desire! Demon Dragon: Selective Freezing Pulsation!" The magic was complete, and powerful light flared out from the Demon Dragon's claws.

"Again? What a nuisance." S'yne's sister sighed. Once again the magic failed to hit her, the guy with the ofuda holy weapon . . . or anyone from S'yne's sister's forces, Bitch, or the others on the ship vassal weapon.

"You only nullified enhancement magic? That's another dirty trick!" the harpoon guy fumed, looking at us as though we had killed his parents or something.

"If the shoe was on the other foot, you'd be calling this a skillful piece of strategy, right?" I jibed in reply. Anything done to them was cowardly. Anything they did was exceptional. I'd read of enemy generals who praised the tactics that defeated them, but in real life no one was celebrating having junk like this done to them. That was real warfare for you.

"I couldn't resist it all!" the metal magic dragon said with a grunt. She had thrust her hands in front of her, trying to weaken the incoming attack, but it had clearly just been too powerful for her. The Demon Dragon was still one step ahead of her. They might have the edge in terms of raw power, but the Demon Dragon was far more experienced. The metal magic dragon and the harpoon guy could barely handle their respective weapons, to be honest.

"I've still got a move or two!" the metal magic dragon said with a roar, choosing to ignore the Demon Dragon and fly directly at Filo. Filo crossed her wings and prepared to engage, unleashing haikuikku.

"How is she so fast?" the metal magic dragon gasped. "Why?! I might be debuffed, but I still have a holy weapon! Why can't I keep up? Gyah-gyah!"

"The Four Heavenly Kings receive their blessings from me . . . Now I have been powered up. It makes sense that they would be powered up too . . . does it not?" the Demon Dragon said.

"Boo!" Filo still didn't sound especially pleased about any of this. "I'm feeling all angry, so now I'll sing that fun song that I went to listen to with the bow guy!" Filo said. She kicked the metal magic dragon away, got some distance, and then started to sing. Her voice sounded even more powerful than before. "Air Machinegun Meteo!" she sang. Countless pockets of tightly compressed air appeared above Filo and rained down on the metal magic dragon.

"How dare you! One of my Four Heavenly Kings daring to turn against me!" the metal magic dragon raged.

"Pathetic copy, they do not belong to you. These are my Four Heavenly Kings," the Demon Dragon replied.

"My only master is my master!" Filo said. She kept getting caught up in these pointless debates, she really did. I felt sorry for her, being dragged into this clash between the two Demon Dragons.

"It's finally time for me to get some action," Sadeena said. She dropped down quickly from the Demon Dragon's back and leapt toward the harpoon guy, quickly suppressing him with her flowing harpoon attacks.

"What?!" he shouted in surprise.

"Here you go! And here too, look. You need to commit more! Oh my. That's where you're going to attack? Really? I don't think you'll like what happens." Sadeena laughed, providing a taunting commentary as they fought. She started with a blunt smash, into a sideswipe, a small thrust and then a big one, a wild spin all around before countering the incoming counter-attack, spinning and weaving as attacks bounced off each other.

"Damn you! Look how cocky you are, just because your stats are a little higher!" the harpoon guy complained.

"That has nothing to do with this. You can't handle the

power of that weapon, can you? I was already reading your attack even when your stats were high," she reminded him. Then she found an opening in his defenses, placing her harpoon against his chest and taking a powerful step forward, thrusting him away. I'd seen that last move back in Zeltoble.

"Enough of this! Whale Hunting Harpoon: Ten . . . and then Brave Fish Blaster: Ten!" The harpoon guy took out a second harpoon and threw it at Sadeena before spinning himself in the air and plunging down toward her. The skill names made them sound like ones Sadeena would definitely want to avoid, but she still had a super-relaxed look on her face.

"Such simple attacks. It doesn't matter how strong you are. You won't hit anyone like this. In fact, I'm getting a bit bored," Sadeena said. She avoided the harpoon vassal weapon holder's wild rush with a few backsteps, then hopped up into the air and came down on her opponent's harpoon. The skill had been a piercing downward strike, which meant Sadeena's careful jump into the air had avoided it completely.

"Damn you! Haaah! Uwah?!" The harpoon vassal weapon holder cancelled the skill and launched a thrust of his own, taking the brunt force of Sadeena's punishing blow.

"You don't know what to do with it, do you? If you swung it around like that in the ocean, you'd never catch any fish," Sadeena bemoaned. A harpoon was essentially a fishing tool, created for hunting fish. Kizuna could use harpoons as weapons, and so could Motoyasu. Sadeena had actually trained with those two quite a bit, proving herself superior. Kizuna was one thing, but Sadeena was good enough to even teach Motoyasu a thing or two.

"The strength of a harpoon lies in attacking swiftly. Like this. Poke, poke. See?" Sadeena rapidly jabbed out with her harpoon, stabbing the harpoon vassal weapon holder numerous times. He moaned. He was still a hero, so he was too tough for that to break the skin, but it definitely seemed to hurt him.

I recalled our undersea adventures prior to coming to this world. There were some pretty big fish-like monsters down there. Sadeena and Shildina had fought them all without backing down a single step. Even under my own powerful enhancement magic, that was still quite the feat. The killer whale was, at least from what I knew back in Japan, the ultimate creature in the sea. That also stood true among therianthropes in the world to which I had been summoned. They were known as the ultimate therianthrope when in the sea.

And here we had one known as a genius even among the killer whale therianthropes—a real genius, too, not the resurrected kind. There was no way one so unexperienced with the harpoon could hope to defeat her.

"Lightning Shock Harpoon: Ten!" the harpoon guy shouted.

"How many times do I have to say it? I can see that

coming," Sadeena told him. "Here you go!" The harpoon guy had spun around rapidly, trying to copy Sadeena, and she had just extended her grip on her harpoon and thrust it into him. His own momentum had pushed him deep onto her weapon, right into his shoulder. I wondered if it would slow him down . . . but he pulled it out right away, blood gushing.

"That hurt! You bitch!" he shouted.

"I am not the bitch in this situation," Sadeena replied. The harpoon guy received a healing ofuda from one of his allies and placed it over his wound. That was a handy item from this world. It acted more directly than potions. Still, the field that the Demon Dragon had created was slowing down the effects of all healing.

"I'm going to kill you!" the harpoon guy roared, eyes open wide in rage as the veins popped on his forehead. I noticed that his harpoon had changed to a pretty nasty-looking one. It was easy to tell what was happening—he'd changed to a cursed weapon.

It wasn't that he'd been underestimating Sadeena until now . . . just that he was finally not going to hold anything back.

"The punishment given to the sinner is that same sentence carried out on the crucified saint. This is holy punishment! Bring judgment to the one before me! Crucifixion!" Something like a black cross appeared behind Sadeena, oozing with black miasma. It extended barbed threads toward her.

"Oh my," she responded, spinning her harpoon to gather all the incoming threads together and then sliding through and away from them as they tried to bind her. She was skilled with a harpoon, I'd give her that.

"Heavenly Wind: Wind Wing Slicer!" Filo unleashed a blade of wind from her wing, cutting in between Sadeena and the threads chasing her and keeping her safe.

"Sadeena, are you okay?" Filo called.

"I'm fine, thank you!" Sadeena called back.

"What a pathetic excuse for an attack! Hah!" The Demon Dragon stamped down on the cursed skill, then bathed it in fire to destroy it completely.

"You destroyed my attack? Impossible!" the harpoon guy raged. Was it really that surprising to him? It looked like the kind of skill that bound a foe and then acted on them, but it was meaningless if it didn't hit—and we weren't going to just stand there, were we? "You also dare to use Kuflika's techniques against me?!" He simply wasn't getting it. The power of Kuflika and all of her techniques belonged originally to the Demon Dragon and had now been given to Filo. Of course, she could use them. He really seemed bent out of shape about it, though.

I'd been mad when my shield was taken, of course, but you used whatever you could get your hands on. The harpoon guy surely had to have stolen things from his enemies in the past. He had killed one of the holy weapon heroes, if I recalled correctly. That meant he had to be making use of that weapon in some capacity. He didn't have a leg to stand on.

"Your pathetic mewling is nothing compared to the Shield Hero and my rage," the Demon Dragon mocked.

"You're joking! I'm far more incredible, obviously!" the harpoon guy roared back. I wasn't about to start comparing personal tragedies with this guy. If that was true, he needed to prove it.

"Whine about it all you like. You can't change the facts," the Demon Dragon said, looking down on the harpoon guy in disgust. I was more impressed with Sadeena dodging all those attacks so easily.

"Sadeena," I called to her.

"Yes, little Naofumi," she replied.

"Are you sure you're not one of the resurrected?" I asked. If she was and was just waiting for an opening to strike at me, I wasn't sure I'd be able to deal with it.

"I can tell you that I definitely don't have any memories of a former life like these resurrected normally do. Shildina can look at me and see the truth too, I'm sure," Sadeena said. The two of them had the ability to see the resurrected, and neither had ever pointed a finger at the other, so it sounded legit. They might have just got their stories straight behind our backs . . . but looking at how Sadeena lived, and what she had done, it was easy to tell that wasn't the case.

If she was a resurrected, she wouldn't listen to anything anyone said and would brag on about being a genius. The resurrected also liked to build a collection of the opposite sex. None of these things really fit with Sadeena.

"Hah! You aren't going to win just because you've got a few harpoon skills! Our Demon Dragon isn't the only one who can use magic!" With that, the harpoon guy took out his own ofuda and made to unleash some magic.

"Oh my! I have some magic skills myself, actually! Jewel Spark!" Sadeena triggered some lightning from her accessory and burnt the ofuda to a crisp.

"What? My ofuda!" the harpoon guy exclaimed.

"Shildina and the others would never let something like that happen. You need to protect yourself better with magic," Sadeena said. It was like she was talking to a child. She had no respect left for this guy at all.

Perhaps having realized Sadeena's qualities, the harpoon vassal weapon started to glow, just like the musical instrument had done with Itsuki. This was the same reaction as when Itsuki got that one. I almost started rubbing my hands. Time to collect a harpoon!

"Now I just need to destroy the accessory on the butt of the harpoon, correct? Little Naofumi, Kizuna?" Sadeena asked.

"That's right," I told her. "That's how Itsuki claimed his weapon."

"That's what I heard. I'll be aiming for it too, so don't worry!" Kizuna turned the hunting tool into a bow and took aim herself.

"I've had enough! I can't take any more games! You rabble! Kill these fools!" the harpoon guy raged at his companions, who all quickly replied in the affirmative. It seemed the harpoon guy had realized that he was going to lose the harpoon if this situation persisted, and that made him even angrier than before.

"What's this? It looks like someone is going to steal away your weapon, and now you decide to leave the fighting to others? I can't believe poor Kuflika would fall for a loser like you," the Demon Dragon said, choosing this moment to put the boot in. The next line out of the harpoon guy's mouth would be, "Shut it! It's fine so long as I win! This weapon is mine! You can't possibly steal it from me!" There it was, just as I predicted. I was getting sick of these cookie-cutter villains.

"Leave this to us!" The harpoon vassal weapon holder's women all dropped down from the ship and quickly surrounded Sadeena and the Demon Dragon.

"Don't get cocky just because you've got a pretty face!" one of them said. "You harlot!"

"How rude. You've actually upset me. Little Naofumi, praise me so I feel better," Sadeena said.

"You aren't upset at all, so don't play the victim. You give off a sexy vibe, anyway—it's sure to give some people the wrong idea," I told her.

"Oh my. That sounds quite sexist," Sadeena said.

"You don't seem very serious most of the time, Sadeena, if I'm being honest. I find Shildina easier to talk to," Raphtalia added for the knockout. Sadeena never really seemed to take anything seriously and had a very flirty attitude. In actual fact, she could get pretty heavy. And when the call to action came, she was always ready.

"Oh yes, praise me more!" she exclaimed.

"I wasn't praising you!" I replied.

"Neither was I!" Raphtalia added. I had to wonder what was going on inside her head sometimes. We'd known each other for a while now, but I still couldn't accept her taking any of that as praise. Did she think treating everything as a joke was some kind of virtue?

"An opening!" The harpoon guy seized what he thought was an opening and Sadeena rammed him with the butt of her harpoon right between the eyes, without even looking.

"Oh my! Did that hit you? I'm so sorry. Even if I close my eyes, I can still tell exactly where you are." She really did have his number. As a killer whale therianthrope, Sadeena had an understanding of the sound waves around her. She could even use them to see through certain types of illusion magic. Surprise attacks were simply never going to surprise her.

"You scum! What are you doing to my master?" the metal magic dragon roared, attempting to aid the harpoon guy in battle.

"You fool! You can't even match my power, and yet you seek to abandon the fight with me?" The Demon Dragon followed this up by whacking the metal magic dragon hard with her tail, eliciting a satisfying grunt. "You can't even block a simple attack like that! In your weakened state, you might be better off just leaving! I guess it would be amusing to see how well you can compete with my magic."

"Hah . . . you can't hope to match my casting! Master! We must remove the debuff and regroup!" the metal magic dragon said.

"Agreed!" the harpoon guy shouted back. "Then this harlot and her Demon Dragon will fall before us with ease!" The Demon Dragon was capable of running incanting interference even against another Demon Dragon, if she got serious about it. In our world, magic of the cooperative class couldn't be blocked, but that would really depend on the quality of the companions of the harpoon guy. I also had a hunch that the Demon Dragon would even be able to interfere with cooperative magic now.

"Time to get serious!" Sadeena raised her harpoon, and the Demon Dragon obligingly clicked her claws. Sadeena's harpoon was immediately wreathed in a mixture of black fire and lightning. "Excellent work, little Demon Dragon," she said.

"You are originally the miko priestess to a dragon. You also share my strong feelings for the Shield Hero. So go ahead and finish off the harpoon guy and his companions!" the Demon Dragon said.

"Take a good long look! For as long as you survive, anyway! This is how the priestess of carnage fights!" Sadeena exclaimed. I was unpleasantly reminded of Sadeena and Shildina conducting all that torture.

"Never!" the harpoon guy shouted, but then he immediately started groaning as Sadeena zapped him with both the lightning and the black fire from her harpoon. That was definitely doing some damage. He just kept on launching himself onto her attacks.

"That skill you tried to use on me . . . is this kind of how it went? Demon Dragon: The Binding Cross!" Sadeena used the magic of the Demon Dragon to make a cross appear behind the harpoon guy, which sucked him toward it like a magnet and held him in place.

"It burns! Owww!" Black smoke started to rise from the back of the harpoon guy, like a steak smoking too long on the grill. Binding the target down and slowly cooking them—quite a nasty piece of magic.

"I'm going to follow up too! Poke, poke!" Sadeena didn't hold anything back, poking at the chest of the harpoon guy. It really was starting to feel like an execution. She seemed to have perfectly replicated the skill her foe had tried to use on her. "And to finish! Let's set that little weapon of yours free, shall we?" Sadeena cooed.

"No way!" Sadeena attacked the harpoon vassal weapon holder's harpoon, but he smashed his way down from the cross and backed away from her, protecting the accessory attached to it. "Hah! You are truly a fool if you think you can steal this!" he shouted.

"That's right! Demon Dragon Freezing Pulsation: Ten! That removes the debuff! Now you can't hope to win!" the metal magic dragon crowed. Rather than using support nullification magic for everyone, she had just used it on herself and the harpoon guy—probably to cut down on incanting time. In any case, our side was putting up a good fight.

They weren't the only ones. Glass and Shildina had just started to pile onto the ofuda guy, both of whom had just been buffed by support magic from the Demon Dragon. Their opponent used his cursed ofuda to summon three creepy looking demon things and fight back. Controlling the demons looked pretty hard, though, because the ofuda guy was suddenly moving a lot slower. Chris pinned one of the demons down while Glass responded to another.

"Laws of Evil: Parasite Poison Curse!" the ofuda guy shouted, causing countless swarming bugs to erupt from an ofuda that made a beeline directly for Glass and the others. It looked like a curse skill, but I was pretty sure my friends could handle it.

"Hah! You seem quite unfamiliar with your weapon. No

matter how strong it is, that's meaningless if you can't land any hits," Glass told him.

"I do have an awareness of not yet mastering the weapon given to me. But I am also not so weak that I need to back down from this fight!" the ofuda guy replied. He used an ofuda to bat away Glass's attacks, while using another to skillfully change the trajectory of Shildina's next attack.

"Hmmm . . . how about this next?" Shildina took out an ofuda while unleashing a monster that looked a bit like a soul eater at her opponent. Then I realized it wasn't a monster—it was a variant on the wind-wreathed water fish that she had used earlier. She shouted as she fired off the attack.

"You are skilled with dark element ofuda," Glass commented.

"I'm starting to enjoy copying skills!" Shildina replied. Just like you could use techniques to copy skills, you could do a similar thing with magic. There was some time lag, but Shildina was good with magic, so she could copy them quickly.

"You copied me?!" the ofuda guy shouted indignantly, even as he avoided the incoming attack. Shildina was strong too, so that probably would have hurt if it had landed.

"Shildina, you really are so skilled," Glass said again.

"I like playing with cards," she replied. I had no idea how many she had with her, but Shildina proceeded to take a bunch of ofuda out from her holder and started to toss them out like playing cards. Each and every one had a magic effect sealed inside, so just throwing them could trigger an effect. They would also interfere with each other, triggering more magic, making them exceptionally suited for Shildina to use. Ofuda were pretty expensive, but that wasn't an issue with L'Arc supplying us. She was also pretty choosey about her materials. I remembered her asking for some blood from the Demon Dragon in order to make ofuda. "This is an exploding ofuda I'm particularly proud of," Shildina said. She lifted a nasty-looking ofuda, imbued it with magic, and then threw it at the ofuda guy. It was one of those that was activated not by incanting to turn it into magic, but by throwing it.

"That won't work on me!" the ofuda guy crowed.

"Watch out! Get down!" someone else shouted, trying to warn him—but he just used one of his own ofuda to try and suppress the incoming attack. As soon as they touched, Shildina's ofuda exploded into black fire. The ofuda guy fell down onto the ground, burning and wailing as he rolled around.

"Oww! Shildina!" Glass called sharply, almost getting hit by the cursed fire herself.

"Wow! Demon Dragon blood is something else! I got sweet Naofumi to give me a little of what the Demon Dragon gave him," Shildina explained.

"That seems a very dangerous substance to make ofuda from! Please be more careful! Are you even listening to me?" Glass shouted.

"This is getting fun!" Shildina replied. She wasn't drinking but was starting to look drunk. Just like her sister, she had the capacity to simply enjoy fighting someone—but I hadn't really seen it in her since her first fight with Sadeena. In fact, she only ever really looked like that when she was fighting Sadeena. That made me question the relationship between the two of them again . . .

Even as I had that thought, the ugly-colored ofuda holy weapon started to release waves of powerful vibrations.

"What now? My ofuda is reacting without me doing anything?!" the ofuda guy said. The ofuda seemed to want to fly toward Shildina, while its current owner was desperately trying to prevent that.

"That looks like . . ." I started, and then a strange vibration also rolled out from the chest area of the metal magic dragon.

"Ugh . . . what now?" she complained as a light emitted from her chest and flew toward the ofuda holy weapon—as though sharing its final power.

"Stop it! Calm down!" the ofuda guy shouted, struggling to control his own weapon. Shildina and Glass looked on, most of the tension drained from them completely. Moments later, something black started to snake out from the accessory, winding around the ofuda. It looked to me like the holy weapon was creating an opening for us to attack—but this wasn't a vassal weapon we were talking about. It couldn't be doing this because it had found a new owner. Holy weapons were awarded to heroes summoned to the world they originated from, and the hero for this weapon was already dead and gone.

"Mr. Naofumi!" Raphtalia shouted to get my attention.

"Master! Do you want to go up?" Filo flew in toward me amid this new distraction. It did seem like a good chance to take out Bitch and her goons.

"Well, well, well." S'yne's sister was still locked in a staring contest with S'yne, who was attacking repeatedly. She had increased her number of familiars to four, allowing for a continued rolling wave of attacks, and she did seem to be gaining a little ground. Dolls that looked like the Demon Dragon were firing off a barrage of magic, pinning her opponent down. She was a real craftswoman, I had to give her that. The chain would fly out every now and then to try and bind S'yne down, but she dodged it smoothly each time.

Our eyes met for a moment, and she seemed to be telling me to go and attack while we could—that she could still handle things here. *Okay then!* Raphtalia and I both raised our hands and Filo swooped in toward us. We grabbed onto her legs and Filo lifted us both into the air, heading for the ship vassal weapon that hovered above us.

"What are you doing? Shoot them down!" Bitch screeched. The cannons blasted toward us, one after the other, but they couldn't do anything about Filo's speed. Bitch and her own goons, along with women from the harpoon guy's allies, all tried to attack us with magic or their weapons, but none of them were anything I couldn't handle with Stardust Mirror.

"Hah! So you've finally decided to pay me the attention I deserve! I'm ready for you!" Bitch was cracking her whip on the bow of the ship, seemingly eager to get this started. "You are such a hard nut to crack—pointlessly hard. But I've got what it takes to crack you now! I've just finished a nice long charge, just for you! Eat this and even you will die, for sure!" That was pretty much what I had been expecting. Motoyasu had a special attack called Brionac, and with all the effects of skill enhancement and other things, his charge time for it was now considerably reduced. The whip seven star weapon had to be thoroughly enhanced, meaning a skill that required a charge as long as this was going to be seriously powerful—perhaps powerful enough to change this entire situation.

I was starting to think their entire plan had just been to buy enough time for Bitch to launch this skill. Things were going pretty badly for them, which was normally the kind of time Bitch would cut and run, but this time she was sticking around.

"You maggots seem to have got the wrong idea about something. You still think destroying the accessories will let you steal the vassal weapons. Haven't you considered that we might have fixed that flaw by now?" Bitch said proudly.

"What?!" I exclaimed. I looked down at S'yne's sister and

she nodded, providing confirmation that this wasn't a bluff.

"That's true. Our R&D guys got quite upset that the goodies we stole were getting stolen back from us, so they've really upped the strength of those little trinkets. They're even stronger than the one we used on the Hunting Hero," S'yne's sister explained. I cursed. If they couldn't be destroyed, that was going to make this a lot more difficult. I still had to have Kizuna try though.

"Brilliant! Lady Malty! Now this fight can finally come to an end! Oh wow! You're so lovely!" Woman B II exalted Bitch with her high-pitched voice. I swore again. I was going to turn her into ash, just like the original Woman B!

"This is the end of our long and sordid relationship, Shield Weakling! Have a taste of Infini—" Bitch raised her arms and prepared to crack the whip again, unleashing her powerful skill.

"Oh yes! Lady Malty!" Woman B II cried. I didn't seem to have any choice but to try and block it with glass shields. Even as I prepared to deploy them—

"Ugah?!" A sword appeared in Bitch's midriff, poking through her from behind. Blood exploded from her mouth. I did a double take. This was completely unexpected. Bitch and her goons had been expecting victory a moment ago, and now they were stunned into silence. Raphtalia and Filo were too. Everyone present was completely shocked by what had just happened.

This could have been our chance, or even a chance for our enemies, but no one could do anything but look on in shock and surprise at what had just happened.

"By which I meant, end with a victory for the Shield Hero, of course."

The primary thing Bitch had done, for her entire existence, was mock others for falling into her traps. If things started to look bad for her, she would pass the buck to someone else and make a run for it. She had rarely suffered any direct consequences of her actions. The most damage to her was perhaps when Raphtalia got close once using stealth and stabbed her. Yet here was that same Bitch, suddenly getting stabbed out of the blue, and by the most unexpected individual.

"Huh . . . huh? Why is there a sword . . . inside me?" Bitch stammered. She didn't seem to understand even this basic fact, trembling, turning around to look at the one who had stabbed her. It was Woman B II.

"Bitch. You have no idea how long I have waited for this moment," Woman B II said coldly, her sword still skewering her target.

Chapter Twelve: Intelligence Operative

"Lyno . . . why . . ." Bitch breathed, an incredulous expression on her face. It sounded like Woman B II's name was Lyno. It was rare for me to learn the name of anyone in her position . . . and I still didn't understand exactly what was going on. Some kind of internal conflict? From the situation that had just been playing out, though, that hadn't really been the moment to turn on Bitch. These gaggling annoyances would do so, certainly, but only when they felt real danger to themselves.

"Why? Because your back was wide open, that's why," Woman B II—Lyno—said, twisting her blade even as it was still stuck through Bitch. That got a scream. Lyno's words and her face displayed a powerful resentment and hate that had clearly been festering for a long time. I was sensitive to it due to the rage curse I was currently under. "Can you fly, Bitch?" Lyno proceeded to extract her sword and then kicked Bitch off the flying ship altogether. Her stomach wound probably stopped her from reacting, and Bitch plummeted head-first to crash into the ground. It looked terrible. Falling from that height without any preventative measures on her part had surely caused massive damage, but the whip seven star weapon had kept her alive.

What the hell was going on?

The other groups of fighters were continuing to fight, but were also aware of the situation with Bitch and Lyno. Our enemies, in particular, couldn't really believe what they were seeing.

"Where did . . . that come from?" Bitch said.

"Is this such a surprise, really?" Lyno countered.

"You won't . . . you won't get away with—" Bitch started to shout.

"That's my line, Bitch!" Lyno cut her off.

"What's going on? Why did you do that?!" The ofuda guy finally snapped back to himself and shouted at Lyno.

"Why? Because this woman knows my real name and still doesn't know who I am!" With that, the woman called Lyno leapt from the flying ship, plunged down through the air with her sword at the ready, and landed right on top of Bitch. That got another impressive scream, her sword piercing Bitch's body a second time as she landed.

I'd heard Bitch screaming a lot in my time, but this was different. There was real desperation this time.

"To you it might be nothing more than a vague recollection, like a meal you ate one night a year ago. But to me, it's something that I'll never forget! I've been waiting for this moment, longing for it to come for so long now!" Lyno dragged her sword out from Bitch's stomach and then plunged it back in again. She repeated this over and over and over, eliciting more screams from Bitch.

"Does that hurt? I'm glad, so glad it hurts. This is nothing compared to the pain you have caused me!" Lyno broke down into maniacal laughter, her crazed peals of joy ringing out across the general vicinity. Bitch spluttered and squealed under the vicious assault, the blade plunging and twisting over and over. It was a product of pure hatred.

"Oh my. That's some serious anger," the Demon Dragon said, looking very pleased with this development. I had to agree with her. This was rage on my own level.

"Ah, of course . . . you aren't worthy of the whip seven star weapon. I'm going to take it from you," Lyno said. She stabbed Bitch in the hand and stole the weapon from her. Then she beat Bitch's face with the whip before shredding the accessories on her clothing.

"Look at all this junk . . . You just love to dress up, don't you? Do you really love accessories so much? The only people they attract are greedy money-grubbers. You're such an idiot," Lyno spat. That comment made me think of Therese for a moment, but she wasn't a money-grubber, just a hardcore, high-quality accessory enthusiast. "Look in the mirror, Bitch! I'm messing up your precious face for you! Suffer, suffer, suffer!" Even as Lyno shouted, Bitch's face started to swell. I could tell Lyno was holding back. Her entire attitude shouted that she wasn't going to let Bitch die easily.

Bitch, however, looked like she had already passed out

from the pain, or maybe a loss of blood. Her eyes were rolled back in her head and she was twitching.

"Huh? It's too soon for you to die! Zweite Heal V!" Lyno still didn't stop cracking her whip, however. Using her accessories to nullify the effect preventing the use of magic, she repeatedly healed Bitch and kept attacking her.

"With the delay on healing, it surely can't keep up with the damage I'm doing—but so what! More pain, more pain for you!" Lyno added black fire to the whip and continued to beat on Bitch. It looked like she was using something like the Whip of Wrath. It had to have some effect to delay healing itself.

The level of violence, of hatred, on display . . . this was not just a falling out among allies. This Lyno woman clearly had hatred close—maybe even equal—to my own for Bitch. Bitch had given hell to so many people by now; there had to be some she had left alive who hated her for it. Lyno must have been a person marked forever by Bitch's actions but whom Bitch herself had completely forgotten. And here she was, enacting retribution—and then I got it.

"You're the spy!" I said. The report from our world had mentioned that someone with a desire for revenge on Bitch was working as a spy. No contact had been made with them since Bitch changed worlds, but the anger we were seeing here definitely suggested that we had found her.

"That's right. That saves a lot of explanation!" she said. It seemed like Lyno really was the spy. Even as she nodded, she was still attacking Bitch—or more like grinding her heel into her face.

"We've got your back! You just carry on beating Bitch into a pulp!" I told her.

"I will! Shield Hero!" Lyno turned her attention back to Bitch. "Suffer! Suffer more!" As she cackled with laughter again, I threw up glass shields all around her, preparing for the enemy attack. Lyno needed to snuff Bitch out as quickly as possible!

"I'm sorry, what?" Raphtalia wasn't keeping up with everything. This was our chance though. We'd never had Bitch on the ropes like this at all.

Then Lyno pointed at the harpoon vassal weapon holder and ofuda guy and said, "Don't worry about their accessories being enhanced either. I switched them out."

"What?!" the harpoon guy shouted.

"What did you say?!" the ofuda guy exclaimed, both of them shouting at the same time. Looking at the way they reacted, it sounded like she was telling the truth.

"Oh my, is that so?" Sadeena said and then quickly smashed her weapon into the harpoon guy's accessory. It shattered into pieces at once, prompting the harpoon guy to give a mighty roar.

"Stop it! Stop fighting me! You are mine! I am the true hero!" he raged. The harpoon vassal weapon was having none of it. It seemed like the accessory really had been the old one.

"Master! No! How dare you resist my master with a mere vassal weapon!" the metal magic dragon shouted.

"I think you're forgetting about me again! Take another one of these!" The Demon Dragon sucked in a big breath and then bathed the metal magic dragon in a second wave of rage fire.

"You stay out of this!" the metal magic dragon screamed back, filled with rage herself even as she lost ground. I clearly needed to get involved in this. The two biggest threats below were S'yne's sister and the metal magic dragon, both of whom could turn the tide back if we let them.

"Kizuna!" I created some Boosted Mirror Fragments and pointed them at the metal magic dragon.

"Okay! Double Lure!" Kizuna's lure struck the metal magic dragon in the same moment as my Boosted Mirror Fragments. I hoped the Demon Dragon didn't waste the chance we were giving her.

"What are you doing?!" the ofuda guy shouted, cowed by Lyon's rage and trying to keep his own wriggling weapon under control. "Hurry up and recover her!" The ship vassal weapon hovering above Bitch moved forward and fired something down at her like a beam from a UFO.

"I'm not letting you get away! You could have lived a little longer, Bitch, but now your allies have caused your premature death! Curse them as you go into the void, Bitch! Gigantic Star X!" Lyno turned the whip into a morning star and brought it crashing down. I guess any close-combat weapon with a string on it counted as a whip.

With a heavy impact and the horrible sound of flesh being packed violently down, blood splattered out from around the head of the weapon. Lyon laughed.

"I've done it! I've finally done it! I've been waiting for this day, for this moment, for so long!" she crowed. I felt like cheering too. Had we finally managed to kill Bitch? Mirth welled up inside me. We'd done it! The Bitch was dead!

There was a dumb grin all over my face, and I felt something hot in my eyes. That resolved my own anger and should help the fallen queen rest in peace.

Then I noticed that the beam of light from the ship was still going.

"We still have time! Protect her soul! We can still save her!" someone was shouting. *She's dead, but there's still time? What does that mean?* Then I recalled that S'yne's sworn enemies had the ability to come back to life so long as their souls remained intact. It sounded like that blessing had been bestowed upon Bitch too!

"Hey! Can you see souls?" I shouted to Lyno, who shook her head with a wild, slightly panicked look on her face.

"Dammit! Raphtalia! Anyone who can! Destroy Bitch's soul and end her! Lyno, use cursed gear, whatever you have that's evil, and just attack all around you! You might hit it!"

"Okay!" she replied. Raphtalia and the others also all snapped back to themselves and started attacking wherever Bitch's soul might be.

"Ah!" Lyno had been standing on Bitch's body to get a leg up. She suddenly tumbled to the ground. I looked down to see that Bitch's body was gone. The ship had recovered it . . . along with her soul!

"You can't get away!" Lyno knew where the body had gone and leapt into the air. Then she swung the whip at the ship above her. It avoided the attack and then opened up with wide-range cannon fire, targeting us all, but it especially focused on Lyno.

"Filo! Get down there! Once we've got Lyno, get up to the ship!" I shouted.

"Okay!" Filo replied. She dropped down at high speed, and I deployed mirrors in front of us to protect Lyno and the others. The incoming volley of fire washed over me. It was powerful, but nothing I couldn't handle.

"Shield Hero! Thank you!" Lyno said.

"No need for that! We have to stop her from getting away!" I shouted.

"Okay! Let's bind her soul and make her suffer even more," Lyno suggested.

"I like the way you think!" We both started to laugh. It looked like we were going to get along just fine. Maybe we should put together a support group for people Bitch had worked over.

"Someone is quickly becoming friendly with Mr. Naofumi! That feels dangerous to me!" I understood where Raphtalia was coming from. She was worried that, rather than overcoming my anger, I would let it consume me.

Still, it really felt like I was going to get along with Lyno. That might also be because of both the rage and compassion inside me.

"The operation has failed! Retreat, retreat at once!" the ofuda guy was shouting.

"Hey! You shut your mouth! If we run away now, what happens to Kuflika? I'm about to lose my weapon too! Help me!" the harpoon guy said.

"What are you talking about?" the ofuda guy replied. "It doesn't matter what happens to you or your little followers. Do not get your priorities confused, understand? You need to protect your weapon for yourself!"

"What?!" the harpoon guy shouted back.

"Now! We must run—stop that!" The ofuda guy tried to escape but was unable to keep the ofuda holy weapon under control.

"You can't escape! Let me show you something else that

ofuda can do that's fun!" Shildina and Glass threw four ofuda at the ofuda guy, who was still struggling with the ofuda holy weapon. I saw some kind of black image on them.

"We've named this attack Moon Cards!" Shildina shouted. The four ofuda started to grow larger in front of the eyes of the ofuda guy, showing images of what looked like the home of Glass's style. Then lights like floating souls appeared around the ofuda guy and all exploded apart. He screamed as he was caught up in the explosion. But the ofuda bound his hands and held him in place so that he couldn't get blown clear. He was little more than a sandbag now.

"What's going on there?" Kizuna asked.

"I linked together some of the ofuda made from the Demon Dragon's blood and turned them into game cards," Shildina explained. It seemed like a cunning way to create magic. Even if you understood the basics of how magic was created, reaching such a high level could still produce some confusing stuff.

"Well, whatever! Here I go! Yaah!" Kizuna turned the hunting tool into a bow and shot through the accessory on the ofuda, which seemed to be begging for Kizuna to shoot it.

"No, no! Not that, no!" the ofuda guy screamed. That was all it took, however, for a soft light to flare up. Then the ofuda holy weapon left his hands, turned into light, and moved over to us.

"Hey! It looks like the corrupted holy weapon has been

released with one shot from Kizuna!" I said. Then light started to swirl around Shildina. Could that be . . . the light that Itsuki said he saw around Shildina when Ethnobalt transported us to this world?

Shildina gasped as her combination with Glass abruptly ended, leaving the two of them looking perplexed. Then Shildina suddenly disappeared completely . . . and reappeared in the spot where the ofuda holy weapon was, now a ball of light itself. In her hand there was a simple object, much like the shield had been for me when I was summoned: just a box for holding ofuda.

"What is this?" Shildina asked.

"Oh my!" said Sadeena. Things were really getting crazy now as a shout rang out from the harpoon guy and the harpoon vassal weapon flew into Sadeena's hand. It looked like it had finally had enough too.

They had been possessing the harpoon by illegitimate means, after all. The weapon seemed to have learned all it needed about the one holding it. But those who had lost the weapons were still going to cry for them back. Both the holy weapons and the vassal weapons had intent of their own from the spirits living inside them. Getting those spirits to accept you as the owner was no easy feat. Considering the current situation, it was perhaps unsurprising that the weapon would seek a new owner. In terms of skill with a harpoon, Sadeena was clearly superior. Sadeena spun the glittering harpoon vassal weapon around and struck a pose, but it felt a little anticlimactic following Shildina getting there first.

"I think Shildina stole my thunder a little there," Sadeena said.

"Don't worry about it. In your case, the vassal weapon definitely came to you, but with Shildina . . . it looked more like the ofuda summoned her," I commented. The holy weapon had pretty clearly selected Shildina and called her over to it. Rather than going into her hand, it had called her to it.

In any case, this meant that we had suddenly obtained two weapons from our enemies—no, three, including the whip taken from Bitch. Shildina took the ofuda out from the box, still looking puzzled about everything that was going on.

"I received that from the greatest authority in existence! It is not something for unworthy hands. It's not for filthy hands like yours to touch! Give it back!" the ofuda guy shouted, trembling with rage. Then he snatched out a sword from . . . somewhere . . . and leapt at Shildina.

Shildina sidestepped the (former) ofuda guy, avoiding his sword by a hair's breadth and then sticking an ofuda on him.

"Formation One: Gale Tag?" she said, the name coming out almost as a question. The response was immediate, however, and the ofuda guy was sent flying away by an incredible impact.

"The holy weapons never actually belonged to you anyway! Stop taking possession of things that aren't yours!" Kizuna shouted, finding just the moment to put the boot in.

"No one is as full of himself as a guilty man," I said, bringing a touch of sage wisdom to the proceedings—so I thought, anyway.

"Our technical department screwed up again. They said the holy weapons were so corrupted there was no way we could lose them. How are they going to explain this?" S'yne's sister said pitifully, still swinging her chain at S'yne. Looking at Shildina, now in possession of the ofuda holy weapon, I recalled the words from the shining tablet in the treasure trove. "—born from—and given life to replace one with duties to perform; who can recreate any technique. You who have run from that role, swimming beyond the worlds in pursuit of freedom. The ofuda holy weapon will surely come to you." While the very start had been illegible, the part about "given life to replace one with duties to perform; who can recreate any technique" was now ringing some bells—Shildina had been born to basically replace Sadeena, after all. "Who can recreate any technique" referred to her oracle powers letting her recreate others' techniques. "You who have run from that role, swimming beyond the worlds in pursuit of freedom" referred to her leaving her role as miko priestess to the water dragon and coming to my village in Melromarc.

"Shildina, if you had left Q'ten Lo before the waves started, I think you would have been summoned to this world then," I said.

"Huh? What do you mean?" she asked. It reminded me of something Atla and Ost had told me in the shield world. It seemed there was a list of possible candidates for holy weapon heroes.

"So they don't only draw from modern Japan," I commented.

"Yes, good point," Kizuna replied. "But from my perspective, the worlds that you and Itsuki came from are different from the Japan that I know," Kizuna said. I mean, it was simply "being summoned to another world." That meant residents of the world to which I had been summoned could themselves be summoned to a world separate from that one.

"Do you think the reason Shildina got dragged along with us, even though she was intending to stay behind, is because of all this?" Sadeena said.

"She got caught up in it because she was a candidate for the Ofuda Hero. Once she started using her powers close to the ofuda holy weapon, it awoke. That sounds likely," I said. Like a special exception to the rule that no more heroes could be summoned until all four current ones had died.

"Oh dear," Shildina said. There was a perplexed look on her face as she checked over the ofuda in her hands. It was true;

Shildina might be suited to be the Ofuda Hero. Just like Kizuna and her fishing suited her to her own role. In any case, these angry idiots had now lost the option to run away.

"We've got the momentum now! Time to finish this! Hurry and capture Bitch's soul!" I shouted.

"Isn't there a better way to phrase that?" Raphtalia complained. It didn't matter—we just needed to pile on!

"You scum! How dare you steal my harpoon! That belongs to me! You've taken everything from me now! I'll never forgive you!" the (former) harpoon guy raged. This guy was getting on my last nerve. Takt and Miyaji had said the same kind of things. These guys were all the same. Inexperience, that was the problem.

The former harpoon guy turned to look at the metal magic dragon for aid—

"Gyah—" she barely managed.

"What's this? You expect something from this pathetic copy? It's too late to find any aid from her," the Demon Dragon said—because she had already crushed the metal magic dragon's head in her jaws. The continued attacks by rage fire, the lingering debuffs even though they had been nominally nullified, and the double-damage dealing skills Kizuna and I had unleashed all combined to allow the Demon Dragon to crush her head completely, metal and all. The metal magic dragon's body was jerking and twitching.

"I just thought I'd give it a try and see if it worked. I was surprised by how soft it was!" the Demon Dragon said, as twisted as ever. As blood spilled from the metal magic dragon, a black chunk from her chest was ejected away and flew toward the ship vassal weapon.

"I don't think so!" the Demon Dragon said as she reached out with her claws to grab the black mass—the corrupted holy weapon—and cling onto it. But even though she tried to use magic, it continued to move away from her.

"This can't be . . . You've taken Kuflika from me and now my Demon Dragon too!" the former harpoon guy screamed.

"I could never belong to worthless scum like you!" the Demon Dragon spat vehemently. "My heart belongs to the Shield Hero!" I just decided to ignore that last part. Instead, I took a closer look at the face of the former harpoon guy. He had pretty good features. He was also glaring at me with the exact same look that Takt, Kyo, and Miyaji had given me when all their silly stuff came crumbling down, and that made me feel good. I could get hooked on people looking at me like that.

"Why do you look so happy, Naofumi?" Kizuna asked.

"You can't tell?" I replied.

"I don't think I want to know," she concluded. She didn't seem to understand what I was feeling.

"That's the right idea," Raphtalia told her.

"You certainly don't want to know," Glass agreed. Business as usual with all the banter then.

"Huh? Is it something nasty? Master was smiling because we're about to win, right?" Filo asked in puzzlement. Filo had been behaving herself recently, but this naive comment hit me right in the feels.

It was wrong. I should accept that . . . and yet I just couldn't stop. I loved to taunt losers like this poor fool here. When I gave it some rational thought . . . I was pretty far gone.

"Enough joking around! Bitch will get away!" Lyno shouted. I looked up at the ship vassal weapon.

"Raphtalia, Filo! Let's see this through to the end! Ignore the rest of these weaklings!" I commanded. They both shouted their agreement. Filo sounded more cheerful she had in a while.

That gave me an idea. The ship was a vassal weapon, meaning Kizuna—and now Shildina—could use their holy weapons to strip the user of their authority to use it or at least maybe slow it down. It looked like the ship was about to make a run for it, but there were still a lot of their allies down on the ground. It was going to take a while for them to retreat. We could use that time to capture Bitch's soul.

Putting that plan in place in my head, I was just about to move into action when . . . the ship vassal weapon blasted away quite literally at light speed.

"Hey! It ran away!" Kizuna was perplexed—and rightly so. It had left a lot of people behind. For Kizuna, fleeing while leaving allies behind was simply not an option.

"Damn! It left all their friends behind!" I couldn't believe it would leave quite so many to an unknown fate facing us. The former harpoon guy was one thing, but I certainly hadn't expected it to leave S'yne's sister and the ofuda guy behind as well.

Chapter Thirteen: Insensitive Individuals

"Hey! What about us?!" the former harpoon guy said.

"Is it just abandoning us completely?" the former ofuda guy cried, both of their faces twisted with anger. The holder of the ship vassal weapon was already far beyond the horizon, however. Then they immediately looked over at S'yne's sister, the only one remaining who looked likely to put up a fight. They were quick to change their tune, just because they no longer had a chance to win!

"Hah. I knew you were all worthless from the start. This is the very time to use your intellect and determine a way to come back from the brink . . . but instead you simply turn to those you see stronger than yourselves," the Demon Dragon spat, abandoning the corpse of the metal magic dragon and chewing out the former harpoon vassal weapon holder and former ofuda holy weapon holder. "Based on your own rules of survival of the fittest, I shall punish you. You should have won!" the Demon Dragon taunted.

"Hah! If you think you can do it, then bring it on! You won't take us down so easily!" the former harpoon vassal weapon holder squawked, his face pale. He knew exactly how much trouble he was in, that much was clear. "Hey, give me that chain! I can use it better than you anyway!"

"Oh . . . I really doubt that," I quipped. There was no way he could handle that thing better than S'yne's sister—or at least, he'd better not be able to. I wondered where that idea came from, that he could do better with it. He had been drubbed soundly by Sadeena when using the harpoon himself. If he thought he could just pick up a random weapon and win, he was underestimating real combat.

"Well, well, well." S'yne's sister gave a sigh. She was clearly pretty pissed off, because even her annoying catchphrase didn't have its normal spark of energy. "I warned you plenty of times; putting together an operation that underestimated your opponents would lead to your downfall. Rather than try and get Kuflika's power back, you should have transferred power to her from somewhere else and at least kept her alive," S'yne's sister said.

"Don't tell me what I should have done! At least Malty lent me her power! Why are you cold and mean? The fact we are about to lose here is all your fault anyway!" the former harpoon guy said.

"That's right! The responsibility for this lies completely with you!" the former ofuda guy said. Now they were completely shifting the blame. S'yne's sister had clearly been against this plan but had tagged along to help out anyway. She'd helped to pin down S'yne, fighting her the whole time to keep her occupied. She was a much more dangerous enemy than these others who did nothing but try to take away our weapons and make us weaker.

They had come for the Demon Dragon but found her both strengthened by my influence and skilled at magic. Their means of nullifying enhancement magic had been taken away and Sadeena had proven to be technically superior with the harpoon. Then our spy, Lyno, had dealt with their accessories, which were meant to prevent the weapons being stolen. The collaborator who actually had their backs, Bitch, had been tricked by Lyno too. Bitch had been attacked by surprise and killed, escaping as just a soul. The string of unexpected events had continued with the ofuda holy weapon choosing a new owner, and then the harpoon too. Blaming all of that on S'yne's sister? That was a bit of a stretch.

Fight on then, if you must, I thought. We would take them down one at a time.

"Well, well, well . . . have you considered the possibility I might leave you here too?" S'yne's sister said.

"What? Do you have any idea what will happen if we don't return?!" the former harpoon guy said.

"You are joking! You will only purchase the wrath of one far greater than yourself!" the former ofuda guy said. He certainly had the hots for someone.

"I'll purchase nothing, I assure you. You must understand. You seem to feel some obligation, but to our great leader you are nothing but an insignificant little bonus. You are not truly a part of the Third Army," S'yne's sister said.

"No! That's not possible!" The former harpoon guy clearly didn't want to believe it, but there was also something on his face suggesting that he did.

I had some like that among my forces too, I was sure. Some of Motoyasu's filolials, for example, had perished during the battle with the Phoenixes. But I'd hardly had any contact with them and had only felt a shallow kind of sadness. I had needed to grieve for them, and wanted to avenge them, but I'd been so full of thoughts of Atla at the time.

It was true. Many who hadn't needed to die had died during that battle. It was so arrogant to feel this now, but my sadness for them, and my rage at Takt, welled up again. The floating mirror responsible for the Shield of Compassion grew in strength a little. It was dependent on my mental state. That much was becoming clear.

Whatever these guys felt about the one they followed, anyway, was of little consequence. They were so removed that their leader would feel nothing when they perished. Their deaths might not even be reported.

"Don't get all full of yourselves just because the technical department gave you a holy weapon. I doubt our leader will even be told of your deaths," S'yne's sister said.

"You lie! You can't trick us like that!" the former harpoon

guy shouted. Bossing around someone that held the power of life and death over you—he really was an idiot.

"Maybe I can help you to resolve this disagreement," the Demon Dragon said, stepping in on the side of S'yne's sister. "These hangers-on are going to be getting in the way of our continued battle, clearly."

"Demon Dragon! I'm not going to allow you to pull anything like yesterday!" Kizuna warned. She was clearly talking about the whole fresh-zombies thing. The Demon Dragon made a noise, as she was pondering something for a moment.

"Very well. I'm in a good mood today. As you wish, Hunting Hero, I shall restrain myself," the Demon Dragon said. Kizuna and Glass looked relieved for a moment, and then—

Faster than either of the girls could move, the Demon Dragon rushed down the former harpoon guy, his party, and the former ofuda guy and chomped into them, crunching them into bloody pieces amid screams and protests that were abruptly cut short. She was eating them while there was fire in her mouth to make sure that none of them would survive. The Demon Dragon was buffed not only by enhancement magic but also transformed into the Wrath Dragon by my rage. Now these guys had lost their holy weapon and vassal weapon and only had middling levels. They were just chaff before the Demon Dragon's flail.

"I didn't just eat their souls, but their bodies too. That suits you better, correct?" the Demon Dragon said.

"That's not what I meant!" Kizuna said.

"I can't believe this! Naofumi!" Glass protested.

"This is my fault?! We're going to get into the same kind of pass-the-buck bickering our enemies were just mired into!" I said. I wanted to prove we were different, not make the same mistakes.

"Very well," Glass said, but she clearly wasn't pleased. "Once this is over, we will circle back around to the topic of how to handle the Demon Dragon."

"I agree with that," I told them. She had already hacked my shield and mirror. I did have a tendency to think the ends generally justified the means, but that wasn't everything.

"Well, well, well. Hasn't today just been full of surprises," S'yne's sister said, sighing heavily . . . and then she swept her chain through the air, wiping out all of S'yne stuffed dolls with a single attack. S'yne had clearly thought she was doing better this time and was stunned at suddenly losing all of her familiars. "In that case, Iwatani, heroes of this world, it looks like I have to fight you alone. Give me your best shot."

"You seem pretty confident," I said.

"I admit, I might get in a little hot water if I don't at least take some information back with me. I don't expect you to hold back. Come at me however you like," S'yne's sister said. I wondered for a moment if she seriously thought she could turn the tide of this battle—but of course she did. Even if we proved ourselves stronger—and I still wasn't sure of that—she had the means to get away from us. We had no ideas at all for stopping her from getting away. How was it that we could be in total control of the battlefield and yet not prevent her escape?

I cursed under my breath, needing some way to strike a decisive blow. We were staring down the barrel of her all-range attack again. It would send us all flying away just like it did last time. We were a little stronger now, and had enhancement magic on us, but we didn't know what other tricks she was hiding either.

"Shield Hero," Lyno said and then tossed me an accessory that she had stolen from Bitch while also indicating she had held one back for herself. "If you have that accessory, you can use as much magic as you like, even with the magic from your world sealed."

"Great!" I said. Gripping the accessory, I focused on incanting magic. It did look like it would work, but something about it felt different. "Okay . . . it will work, but I can't hit anything like Liberation class," I said, sensing that it only allowed use up to Drifa class magic. Trying to use anything stronger than that would destroy it completely.

It was still highly useful, of course. The applications of even lower-class magic were practically infinite. If we could learn the new weapon's power-up methods before S'yne's sister attacked, that would help to form a strategy too.

"Sadeena, Shildina! Tell me your weapons' power-up methods! Look at help, right away! And fall back a bit too. We don't want those weapons getting stolen again," I said.

"Oh my!" Sadeena said.

"Oh dear," Shildina added. Both of them followed my orders and started to move away from S'yne's sister while checking their status and power-up methods.

"Let's see . . ." As Sadeena and Shildina puzzled over their menus, light extended from Kizuna's hunting tool and my mirror and hit the gemstone part of the new holy weapon. "Ah, found it." It didn't sound like the power-up methods were concealed, like they had been with the claws or staff. But someone might have done that to prevent the enemy from learning of the power-up methods.

"I'll go first. Using skills and magic repeatedly makes them stronger," Sadeena reported. So there was some kind of mastery level system for skills and magic. That was a lot like the weapon mastery system from Kizuna's hunting tool—making frequently used skills easier to use and stronger. I guessed it would make sense that some of these power-up methods would start to overlap. The more important one here was Shildina, anyway. She had a holy weapon. That meant it had three times the power-up methods of a vassal weapon.

"Okay . . . I see spending points on magic to enhance it. Then there's . . . raising the rarity of weapons?" As soon as I heard her explanation, I wanted to hold my head for a moment while also clenching my fist. Good news! So enhancing the level of magic came from the ofuda! That did seem suited to the weapon, that was true. The power-up method from the staff seven star weapon was magic enhancement too.

Then there was increasing the rarity of a weapon, one of the sword holy weapon power-up methods that Ren had told us about. I hurriedly started to increase rarity of my mirror. Everyone around me had unfocused eyes too. My weapon started to shine and sparkle.

Then Shildina took a look at the third power-up method. Luckily for us, it was displayed in help, unlike it had been for my shield.

"It says you can sacrifice levels in order to draw out latent abilities and increase status," she said.

"Ah! That's the same as this seven star weapon," Lyno said, holding up the whip that she had stolen from Bitch. I'd known that weapons from different worlds could have the same power-up methods but hadn't expected them to overlap here. It also didn't sound like something that was safe to experiment with in this situation. Magic enhancement was the one we could really use right away.

In any case, an understanding of power-up methods could really boost our current skills and magic.

"Well, well, well, how long do you want to keep me waiting?

I'm about to get bored and attack you!" S'yne's sister said, making a swift swipe with her chain. I cursed, moving a float mirror into the range of her attack and getting her chain tied up with the Mirror of Wrath. The chain made a satisfying clinking sound as it got stuck, but then it started to rotate around where it was caught. What a pain! I grabbed the chain and tried to subdue it, but an incredible force pulled back at me. It looked so light. I was shocked at the strength of it!

"Mr. Naofumi!" Raphtalia shouted.

"Master!" Filo joined her, the two of them rushing to aid me in this new tug of war.

"—!" S'yne wordlessly leapt at her sister, slashing with her scissors. But S'yne's sister used the reverse side of the chain to hit S'yne in the stomach. That was all it took to send S'yne flying off into a wall. She recovered and started to run back toward the action, but she needed a few seconds to do it.

"Shield Hero," the Demon Dragon said to me. "There is another specific reason why I crunched the head of that pitiful copy back there. That is where my fragment was buried. Now I have claimed those memories, which include partial information on the holy weapon power-up methods." Another cause for celebration! "The power-up method for the jewels holy weapon is the same as your shield, Shield Hero: trust. The sharing of power-up methods."

"Well, well, well. We're leaking information like a sinking ship. Handling this scandal could be quite the business," S'yne's sister said. It almost sounded like none of this had anything to do with her—and her confidence that all of this leaking out didn't mean anything really pissed me off too.

This also helped explain why S'yne's sister was so strong though. Thorough implementation of the increase of latent abilities could turn anyone into a monster. Say we were facing an enemy that was level 100, and we were 200. What if that opponent had latent abilities unlocked to the tune of 1000 levels? Even with the same ratio of power-up methods, our stats would be far inferior.

Takt had held the whip, but as one of the resurrected, he had been unable to draw out the true power of the seven star weapon. He hadn't implemented any power-ups at all. But what if he had, I wondered. That was the source of S'yne's sister's confidence and the reason we were currently on the ropes. I wanted to berate S'yne for not more carefully confirming the strength of the people she was picking fights with, but that was for later. She wouldn't like it, but it had to be done.

"What else do we have . . ." the Demon Dragon continued. "Comparing this with your memories, I think this one is like job levels. It says 'profession.' It seems you can choose a profession of some kind." I immediately started to check and saw an option added to the status column. Yes, profession. All sorts of possibilities popped out, including warrior, wizard, monk, ranger . . . no acrobat, but still plenty to choose from. Enhancing them was like the bow power-up method. It involved providing items. The systems were a little different, but it looked like it could work. In any case, I needed to start raising these things at once! I checked around for a more robust conversion function.

"Well, Shield Hero, that's all the knowledge I gained, but it has revealed something important," the Demon Dragon said, even as she sucked in some air to spit fire at S'yne's sister. "We already know the power-up methods for three holy weapons and eight vassal weapons. But our enemies have been performing attacks that aren't covered by the methods that we know. So what must one of the power-up methods in the final holy weapon be?" the Demon Dragon said, like some freaking detective or something. Everyone present who was skilled with their own weapons immediately understood what this meant—the remaining weapon, the blunt instrument holy weapon, had a power-up method for skill levels. This new understanding of the power-up methods made me feel that S'yne's sister had just gotten a little weaker.

"Well, well, well. Very good. You might put up a fight now," S'yne's sister said.

"Spend some points on enhancing magic to raise that up too . . ." I muttered, pretty much ignoring her.

"Well, well, well. You think I'll allow any more of that?" she replied. Probably not, I admitted to myself. She wasn't going to give us a large enough opening to totally upgrade ourselves, and trying to do so could get us wiped out. We had to stay focused when fighting S'yne's sister at her full strength.

"Everyone! Watch out!" Kizuna unleashed Double Lure at S'yne's sister, but she saw it coming with ease and knocked it away with her chain. The range on that thing was insane!

Just like with Attack Support, I had thought that Boosted Mirror Fragments would be a good skill to enhance and tried to put some points into it. But I had been unable to do so. So there were some skills you could enhance and some you couldn't.

Chapter Fourteen: Megido Iron Maiden

"We can't lose any ground!" Glass shouted. "Chris! Lend me a hand! Circle Dance Destruction Formation! Frozen Turtle Carapace Cracker: Ten!"

"I still need to send that Bitch to hell! I can't lose here! Dimension Whip X!" Lyno said, the two of them unleashing skills from outside of S'yne's sister's range. Both of the skills they unleashed were stronger than before. The one that Glass unleashed was traveling along the chain toward S'yne's sister, while the one from Lyno had caused her whip to split into multiple lashes, all of which were now flying for S'yne's sister.

S'yne's sister proceeded to create a chain cage around herself, however, catching the incoming whips.

"Here's a little present!" S'yne's sister retorted. I gasped as the defense-rating combination enhanced skill Glass launched proceeded to come back down the chain toward me.

"Naofumi!" Glass had an apologetic look on her face, but she hadn't needed to worry. The attack entered my body . . . and I gasped again at how strong it was! Almost too strong!

"Raphtalia, Filo! This is dangerous! Everyone, get back!" I shouted. They quickly did so. Then I gathered my life force before stamping down on the ground hard and expelling it outside my body. With a thud, a massive crater was knocked out of the ground, and then the crater instantly froze over. If I hadn't managed to redirect the attack, then I would have been torn to shreds for sure.

"Wow! Just how much stronger are you now?!" Kizuna gasped. Almost everyone there had been caught up to some extent in my sudden terraforming.

"Wow," echoed Filo.

"An attack of such power inside Mr. Naofumi . . . even for a moment . . ." Raphtalia had been scooped up by Filo and was safe too, luckily, while Sadeena and Shildina were safely riding the Demon Dragon's tail. They were as nimble as ever. Kizuna, Glass, S'yne, and newcomer Lyno had all staggered through the sudden earth movement, losing a bit of balance in the process. S'yne's sister looked fine, maybe thanks to her chain.

"Well, well, well. Not very nice of you to try and use such a powerful attack on me," S'yne's sister said.

"What are you talking about? And saying that after you sent it back into me!" I retorted. I could feel some internal damage caused by the energy I couldn't expel. I pushed down the urge to spit up blood and cast some magic . . . Drifa Heal would handle it. I started the incanting and the magic was completed instantly.

"One of my best features," the Demon Dragon said, just inside my head. She had predicted what I was going to do and aided in the completion of the magic. It was a bit like having a parasite inside, and I didn't like it.

"Drifa Heal: Ten," I said. The pronunciation was the same, but it felt different somehow. The pain still faded away, though. The accessory taken from Bitch was helping out.

"Well, well, well. It looks like it'll be quite rude of me if I don't get at least a little serious. Weapon Wearing: Ten!" S'yne's sister wrapped her chain around her body, creating what looked like . . . chain mail.

Chain mail! Why did it have to be chain mail? I cursed. I gave her a thumbs-down, taunting her.

"Don't show me that horrible armor!" I shouted.

"Of course, Naofumi hates chain mail!" Kizuna recalled.

"Yes, you're right!" Raphtalia said. "It's what was stolen from him when the former princess tricked him!"

"Well, well, well," S'yne's sister said with a laugh. *No laughing!* So this was the reason why even just her chain had been pissing me off. She seemed intent on messing with my head . . . but I also might have been getting a little too angry over something so trivial. The more collected part of me called up my status and checked the transformation time on the Mirror of Wrath. There wasn't long left! I was about to get swallowed by rage again! Once it ended, I'd lose various enhancements myself, and so would the Demon Dragon. Did we have any hope to continue the battle under those conditions?

"Raphtalia, Kizuna, everyone, the Demon Dragon and I can't maintain our current state for much longer. We need to pile on and take her down now," I told them. Otherwise, the options would be to take a beating or retreat. Taking a more measured approach might get us some results, but she wasn't going to stick around for a lengthy battle. Regardless of the risks, I didn't want to lose this opportunity, so we were just going to rush her down.

"In that case, Shield Hero, how about we combine my strength with this skill?" the Demon Dragon suggested. She was hacking my status again already and indicating a skill name. It was one that hadn't been converted for me before now, so I hadn't been able to use it. I wasn't sure if I could use it now because of the Demon Dragon's support or because of the Mirror of Wrath.

It didn't matter. I didn't seem to have any other choice. This was the fastest solution.

"I will help you too," Lyno added, starting to incant magic herself. She had the whip, giving her access to some powerful magic.

"As the source of your power, I order you! Let the true way be revealed once more and increase the speed of my allies!" From the incantation, it sounded like support magic. "Drifa Boost X!" That felt good. Our speed was up slightly higher than the support magic from the Demon Dragon.

"Let's go!" I shouted.

"About time! Come at me!" S'yne's sister shouted back.

"We're coming alright! Take this! Mirror Cage: Ten! Into . . . Change Mirror (attack)!" I shouted.

"Well, well—" S'yne's sister started to say as mirrors suddenly appeared around her and boxed her in. Just a few seconds later and the mirror cage started to crack. We had buffed and boosted ourselves considerably—even in just the last few minutes—but it couldn't hold her for long. She must have really been toying with us before!

Change Shield allowed for a Change Mirror (attack). It had a counter effect against S'yne's sister. Then came our moment to really get our hands dirty.

"It's been a while since I used this one!" The Shield of Compassion gave me access to a skill, but it wasn't an easy one to use, so I hadn't really given it the time of day. Right here, right now, it felt like the option. But I'd need some healing immediately after using it. The skill name itself hadn't changed, which meant the conversion might not have been perfect. But so long as I could use it, then that's what I had to do.

"Face a combination skill from the Shield Hero and me!" the Demon Dragon said proudly. "This power is hateful flames of hell, burning even the soul. It's the ultimate magic that can eradicate all! The power to obliterate my foes! The Dragon Emperor, ruler of this world, commands it! Like the flames of the end times themselves, burn this world to ash!"

"The punishment I choose for this foolish evil is to be pierced through by the iron woman. Confined by screams. Roasted by the flames of hatred!" I joined in. "Megido Iron Maiden: Ten!" As the incantation finished, an iron maiden appeared, pitch black, filled with hate, crackling with black flames with a devilish and dragon-like intent wreathed around it. The burning iron maiden opened, displaying an interior that burned with black fire, and then closed again around the mirror cage, skewering it through and turning into a burning pillar of fire.

"Wow! That's really dark!" Kizuna said, looking with concern at the Demon Dragon's and my handiwork. I wasn't sure what else she expected from the Demon Dragon now.

"Stay focused!" I said. "We can't be sure this will even damage her!"

"I know, I know!" Kizuna replied. In the same moment I cautioned her, S'yne's sister appeared from among the dissipating flames, the signs of burns lingering across her body. That was also the moment that my floating mirrors and armor turned back to normal, and the Demon Dragon returned to her baby dragon form. I was out of SP. I'd been using life force . . . EP as well, so I hardly had any of that either.

The rebound from using that skill was also making my bones feel like they were on fire. I needed to get some soul-healing water or healing items quickly, or I wouldn't be able to continue fighting.

"That hurt more than I expected. Is it my turn now—" S'yne's sister started.

"Kizuna, now!" I managed to shout.

"Okay!" she replied. Then she fired an arrow from her Hunting Tool 0, hitting the accessory on the chain vassal weapon S'yne's sister held. With a supremely satisfying sound, the accessory shattered into pieces! While it might not have been a deciding blow, we had at least dealt with her vassal weapon. That should have greatly weakened S'yne's sister! The gemstone on her vassal weapon also turned from cloudy to clear.

"Go!" I shouted. Everyone who could still fight raised their weapons in response, preparing a selection of skills—

"Hydra: Ten!" S'yne's sister shouted, slamming her chain into the ground with a thud. In the next instant, chains raced out toward all of us at incredible speed. If they hit the guys without holy or vassal weapons, it would be over.

I stepped forward to protect everyone, roaring as the attack impacted. I managed to hold my ground, but it was so powerful I couldn't dissipate it completely.

"This again!" I moaned. She attacked so quickly and with such force!

"Master!" Filo grabbed me as I was sent flying away and channeled off the impact.

"Well, well, well. I gave that one everything I've got, and it still didn't kill you. You are developing faster than I expected," S'yne's sister taunted.

"What . . . what was that? That was . . . too fast," Kizuna breathed.

"I can't believe how fast it was," Glass agreed. Both of them had been sent flying, too, and were now barely standing.

"She still seems to be . . . somewhere above us in terms of strength," the Demon Dragon admitted.

"Dammit! We destroyed the accessory controlling the weapon!" I said, unable to keep myself from complaining. I'd been hoping the weapon would turn on the one holding it and leave her behind, not remain in her grasp and start unleashing more skills!

"You make the mistake of thinking that all of the holy and vassal weapons are on your side. If you start to think of yourselves as absolute, as being able to do no wrong, then you become the same as those who terrorize this world," S'yne's sister said. It sounded like . . . it was a vassal weapon that wanted to be with S'yne's sister, fighting for the sake of the waves. I had someone new for my shit list then—the spirit of the chain vassal weapon. At the point that the chain mail had come into this, it had been over.

That said . . . we were looking pretty screwed. We didn't have the power-ups needed to win this. Thorough work on our levels and latent abilities was required.

"We should retreat," the Demon Dragon said, guessing what I was thinking and starting to incant magic.

"Oh, no need to worry about me," S'yne's sister said lightly. "I was just thinking I'd better be getting back myself."

"Is that so?" the Demon Dragon replied. "With us practically lying at your feet? Someone of your strength could play another round or two first, surely."

"Indeed. You seem to have plenty of energy left to spend," Sadeena agreed.

"Yes. We won't drop our guard again," Shildina added.

"Would you accept that I've taken more damage than I expected, and this is all getting a bit much for me? I think I'm cursed too. It's nasty," S'yne's sister said, as laidback as ever. "That skill is powerful and fast, but it takes a long time before I can use it again. You clearly outnumber me, and I don't want another of your special little surprises coming along and making me lose. For example, who knows what those two back there might do with their new weapons," she went on. She really did talk a lot. I disliked her immensely. The "two back there" were Sadeena and Shildina. They did seem the most likely to come up with some kind of cunning plan. We had taken back both a holy weapon and two vassal weapons, so S'yne's sister was right to be wary.

"You also look like you'll grow into someone who will really provide a challenge. You may even prove more pleasing than the opponents we create," S'yne's sister said cryptically. It almost sounded like all this collaboration with Bitch and the others was simply to entertain whoever her boss was. I cursed under my breath. But she continued, "On that score, the harpoon guy did look quite promising too. I didn't expect him to do something as foolish as this."

"What do you mean?" I asked, knowing she would tell us.

"You didn't see it? The ones like him can have strange powers, can't they? In his case, he could place a multiplier on stats when inside his own territory," S'yne's sister dutifully explained. He had been weaker than I expected, but this explained it. His primary ability was about base reinforcement. "It was all a big coincidence, but you really messed up our plans." With Kuflika about to die, he had left behind his home advantage and decided to play a risky away game in order to save her. That allowed us to fight him in a weakened state. "The one you all call 'Bitch' is also a particular favorite of the great one. You harmed her so badly that if I reported killing you, it would be my neck on the line." I could accept that explanation. Bitch knew how to worm her way into someone's heart. "At least, having died once, she might stop being so willfully ignorant." This exchange caused Lyno's anger to bubble over.

"Let your superior know something. Bitch is no virgin. Melromarc is a country of women, with a queen in command. We boast the best membrane reconstitution technology in the world. It will be hard to spot, I assure you," Lyno said. I heard something about "membranes" and zoned out. I didn't need to hear that about the country I was fighting for.

"That is a nice nugget of information. I'll be leaving, anyway." S'yne's sister started spluttering, then looked at the blood on her hand. "Well, well, well." She waved goodbye. She still oozed confidence, but she had clearly taken some damage. Maybe that was why she was running away. It did feel like we had made some progress, at least. "Bye-bye now!" With that, S'yne's sister disappeared. From the sound of it, she had made herself vanish and then ran away at high speed.

"She can run really fast. Giving chase . . . would be dangerous," Raphtalia said, looking in the direction of the retreating noises.

"How much of that do you think was real?" Kizuna asked.

"Good question. I don't think we can draw a clear line yet, but it feels like we're strong enough to threaten her a little, at least," I said—somewhat hopefully. I wasn't sure we would have won if the battle had continued, but I had to believe our first wave of attacks had been strong enough to at least make her consider retreat.

"Hey! We need to get back to L'Arc and the others!" Kizuna exclaimed.

"Right, but first . . ." I turned to look at Lyno. She gave me a salute and then a bow.

"Shield Hero, I am Lyno, an intelligence operative working under orders from the queen. I present to you the reclaimed whip seven star weapon," she said formally.

"Thank you. We made it through this one thanks to you," I said. She had pulled a real deus ex machina for us. I accepted the whip and tried to remove the accessory still attached to it. I took a proper look at the weapon itself. It was the whip that Takt had used. It was kind of a strange shape. I tugged at the accessory for a moment and then it popped right off. The whip seven star weapon regained its glowing light, turning into an orb that circled around me a few times and then vanished. Like the other vassal weapons, it would probably show up again just when we needed it or reveal itself once we got back to our world. I looked at Lyno again. "So you have something against Bitch . . ."

"Yes. That woman and her friends tricked me horribly, plunging me into a living nightmare. I was saved from that by you, Shield Hero, and the queen . . . and after I learned of the evil she was perpetrating, I swore revenge," Lyno explained. So she was another one of Bitch's victims. There were probably fewer stars in the sky. It just turned out Lyno had been the one in the right place, at the right time, to do something about it. Working as a spy, she had found the perfect moment to bring Bitch down.

That had been quite the sight. I was going to sleep soundly for a while after seeing that.

"As best as I could, I have also created a report on their technology and internal structure. I hope you will take a look at it later," Lyno said. She was already proving herself incredibly competent.

"You're hot stuff," I told her. "I'll have to reward you for all this."

"Please, just punish that terrible woman. That is all I desire," Lyno replied.

"No, something other than that. Something that was going to happen anyway isn't much of a reward, now is it?" I said.

"Shield Hero . . ." She breathed with a deeply moved expression on her face. She had already proven it with her actions, but I could tell that she hated Bitch from the bottom of her heart.

"Lyno . . . you're one of my party now," I said.

"Okay!" she agreed.

"Punish the Bitch!" we both said together. She looked up and I gripped her hand tightly.

"She's ingratiating herself with Mr. Naofumi at an incredible pace! This is like Ruft all over again . . . As Mr. Naofumi would say, she is Ruft II!" Raphtalia sounded confused by what was happening and had already given Lyno a strange nickname!

"Yeah, you're right. Looks like someone who is really going to get along with him," Kizuna agreed.

"Kizuna, you should stay away from her," Glass cautioned. "We don't need you falling to the dark side."

"What's wrong with that?" the Demon Dragon asked, genuinely puzzled.

"You stay out of this!" Glass shot back.

"Naofumi! We need to move!" Kizuna insisted.

"I know. Let's hurry back and see how L'Arc and the others are doing," I replied. The normal banter had started up again, but there would be time for the comedy routine after this was all resolved. We treated our wounds and then moved to the port town.

Chapter Fifteen: Defense of the Port

"Death Dancing!"

We arrived in the port, left Kizuna's house, and rushed to where the fighting seemed the harshest to find L'Arc happily swinging his scythe through a horde of enemy soldiers.

"Hey! Kiddo! You took your time," L'Arc shouted gleefully.

"Raph!" said Raph-chan, leaping down from L'Arc's back and rushing over to us.

"Your shikigami kept me informed of what was happening with you, but things were bad here too," L'Arc said. These guys showed up with what looked like unknown vassal weapons. It was crazy.

"Looks a lot less crazy now," I commented.

"Yeah. They got the order to retreat just before you showed up, and they all just started running away. The ones left are those I decided should . . . hang around for a bit," L'Arc joked. Maybe kicking the crap out of Bitch—thanks again to Lyno—and making the ship vassal weapon holder retreat had caused them to retreat here too. Realizing their plan had failed, they made a run for it. "Just need to take care of this . . ." L'Arc made a signal with his thumb toward the back—or more like the edge—of the battlefield. A ring of people appeared there with Therese standing in the center. She had what looked like a shining halo over her head. The entire circle was comprised of jewels, and they seemed to be praying to Therese, almost . . .

"The jewels involved in the attack saw Therese and were captivated at once. They started praying to her and then attacked their former allies . . . it all caused quite a confusion," L'Arc explained.

"Ah! Over there we have the Master Craftsman himself, the one who's divine talents forged this accessory!" Therese said. Her ring of onlookers all erupted into cries of wonder and joy. Some of them immediately started begging me to make something similar for them. I popped out Stardust Mirror without a second thought, at a full ten, making sure none of them could get close.

"Filo, fly!" I ordered. "Keep them away from me!"

"Okay!" Filo turned into her monster form. I climbed onto her back and we quickly got some distance from the horde of jewels trampling toward me. Raphtalia and some others tagged along with me, while Kizuna and Glass would stay with L'Arc's party to operate with him for a while.

"I'm not sure what to say," Glass commented.

"Incredible, isn't it? It just seems like a joke to me," Kizuna replied.

"Jewels are pretty intense too . . ." Glass agreed. Both of them had exasperated looks on their faces.

"Dammit! This is the guy I'm up against?!" L'Arc raged. It was not the time for comments like that!

Then I felt a massive vibration in the direction of the port.

"Filo, get going," I ordered.

"Okay!" she replied.

"Kizuna, you handle things here," I told her.

"I don't like the responsibility, but no problem!" she replied. Then we headed off for the port. From up in the sky, it was easy to see what was going on. The violence had ended in our victory, and the mysterious vassal weapon holders had all completed their escape.

"Acho! Bring it on!" the old lady shouted.

"You're good! Haah!" the old man shouted too. The area they defended, their students, and the library rabbits seemed not to have taken much damage at all. There were plenty of fallen enemies scattered around though.

"Who's that up there . . . hey!" Yomogi shouted.

"Everything is okay here now!" Tsugumi added, both of them waving up at us. There were what looked like hostile women tied up around them, likely their former comrades. It was as they had expected, then.

"You fed us something horrible, but it actually really helped out. Thank you," Yomogi added.

"We would have been in trouble without it. That's the only concession I will make!" Tsugumi said. It sounded like they were going to hold the Demon Dragon blood pudding against me for a while longer.

The other three heavenly kings spotted us flying with the Demon Dragon and each gave a salute.

"Good. They seem to have been pulling their weight. Shield Hero, when I was transformed by your power, the Four Heavenly Kings were also powered up through me," the Demon Dragon commented.

"You got stronger too, didn't you, Filo?" I said.

"Boo!" she replied.

"I think this battle has truly displayed to the Four Heavenly Kings and my other minions just how important you are to our forces, Shield Hero," the Demon Dragon said.

"You come out with that after basically stealing Mr. Naofumi's power from him!" Raphtalia said.

"And look how well things worked out for us. You should be grateful," the Demon Dragon said. I just gave a sigh—it was all far too exhausting to deal with right now.

"Musical Vulcan! Shock Music!" I heard Itsuki's voice—accompanied by screams from his target—and looked in that direction next to see Itsuki landing the finishing blow on Armor. The big suit of metal was down on the floor, perhaps paralyzed. Itsuki had one foot on him, like a big-game hunter, and his violin musical instrument was pointed at his armored face. It looked like Armor's axe had been completely shattered. So it hadn't been the seven star weapon this time.

"That settles this. You lose, Mald," Itsuki said.

"Bah! You infidel from another world! My axe! If I had my seven star weapon, then this would never have happened! Giving me that hunk of junk! It's all their fault, and now my justice is in the dust—" Armor complained, until Itsuki stamped down hard on him.

"So it was your weapon's fault. And if you had a better weapon, what would you blame it on then? I'm sick of hearing it," Itsuki said.

"Fehhh," said Rishia. I wasn't sure why, but I rarely was.

"It sounds like you lost the weapon because of your own misdeeds. I'm not sure you have anyone to blame but yourself," Ethnobalt said, a troubled expression on his face. It looked like they had everything under control here too, anyway. Some damage had been caused, but nothing catastrophic.

"Someone save me! If no one appears to save me now, what is the meaning of my justice?!" Armor shouted.

"It means your justice is meaningless, of course, Mald," Itsuki said, his voice cold and quiet but filled with raw anger. Then he noticed me closing in.

"Hey, Naofumi. You missed all the fun," he said.

"We bumped into the harpoon vassal weapon holder and Bitch," I told him.

"Mald let their plans slip already . . . It seems you were able to handle things on your side," Itsuki said.

"Lyno! What are you doing here? Quick, save us!" Armor suddenly cried. Of course, he knew her.

"Whatever are you talking about?" Lyno replied, a smile of victory spreading across her face. "I am your enemy. It was I who crushed Bitch's plans."

"Boy . . . that face Bitch made, that was a real sight! I want to see that face again!" I started laughing along with Lyno. The Demon Dragon joined in too, but I just ignored her.

"That laughter sounds so evil," Raphtalia said, worried, but I paid her no mind.

"What! You monster! You were evil all along?!" Armor exclaimed.

"You're making a nice face right now too," Lyno continued. "I've always hated you, Bitch, and all of you. So this feels so good."

"You traitor! You'll pay for this! All of you, you'll all pay dearly for this!" Armor raged.

"I'm not paying you anything," I said. It looked like Armor had lost the axe seven star weapon and been forced to take part in this operation. He was a man, after all, so he didn't have access to the same wiles as Bitch. After the incident last time, it was no surprise he had been demoted.

"One thing has been bothering me, Mald, so let me ask it here," Itsuki said, trampling down on armor again. "Back before Naofumi's name was cleared, someone stole the reward for a quest that I completed. That thief . . . was you, wasn't it?" I recalled the incident in question myself. He had accused me of the crime. Itsuki was really going back into the past now.

"No!" Armor said immediately, to which Itsuki fired a musical note from his musical instrument right past Armor's cheek.

"The next one goes into your brainpan. Answer me," I said.

"Justice will not bend to any form of torture!" Armor answered.

"I see. Deadly Poison Music," Itsuki said quietly. This time the note struck Armor on the shoulder. His face turned red and started to swell up, and he screamed.

"It hurts! It's like my body is burning!" His screaming intensified.

"I have caused the status effect deadly poison. If you don't wish to die, admit the truth. You were the thief!" Itsuki said, not backing down.

"Fehhh! Itsuki, enough, please!" Rishia said, trying to stop him—but he was having none of it.

"Yes, yes!" Armor managed between screams. "We took the reward and drank it away in the tavern! Please, just save me!" That didn't take long after all. Rather than fear death, he seemed to just dislike pain. He wasn't going to last under torture.

"Oh my . . ." Even Rishia was surprised at how quickly he gave up. That was the sum total of his justice.

"I knew it. Detox Rondo!" Just as promised—but still somewhat grudgingly—Itsuki played a new note and removed the poison from Armor. "You are still our prisoner, of course."

"Hah! Don't get too pleased with yourselves just because you captured me! Justice cannot lose! Rojeel will come to save me! When that happens, our justice will prevail!" Oh no, I thought. Even when we removed Armor from play, there were still others out there. What a pain.

"Mald, you seem to have the wrong idea. I was trained in torture by the executioners of Zeltoble, and I'm just getting started on you. You're going to sing to my music like a songbird when I'm finished. If Rojeel does show up . . . we'll be ready for him, I promise."

"Wh—" Armor started, then froze in terror at the shaded look on Itsuki's face. It was partly this guy's fault that Itsuki had gotten so broken. Now he just had to pay the price.

Rishia looked pretty terrified too.

"That said, I don't have the time to deal with you today. Just get some sleep," Itsuki continued, smashing his musical instrument into Armor's stomach and knocking him out. I could only hope that Itsuki wasn't going to awaken to some kind of curse.

"That seems like the end of the battle," I said.

The fighting had died down, and everyone gathered to check on the damage and report the results of their efforts. It wasn't a case of all's well that ends well, not really. But we had managed to take out the harpoon guy and his goons without any major losses. And we had acquired a reasonable amount of fresh intel along the way, so it seemed like a win to me.

"What's the next move? Attack the harpoon vassal weapon holder's country right away?" L'Arc asked cheerfully.

"No. I think S'yne's sister and her lot are probably still there. We'll need to prepare more before we attack," I replied.

"You bet!" the king replied.

We spent the rest of the day helping put the port town back into order. Once night fell, we threw our classic victory celebration. Everyone shared the joy in how much easier things looked going forward. However, I was also reminded starkly of the need for further training, due to the latent ability's power-up method.

Epilogue: A Visitor Late at Night

After the celebrations died down, I had a chance to learn more about our enemies from Lyno. Now I needed to take some time and collate all the information. I still needed to look at them properly, but it seemed we had collected all the weapon power-up methods here before we even achieved that back on our world. I wasn't sure how I felt about that. It was strange to think we were stronger on Kizuna's world. I guess I was just overthinking things again.

I stretched and gave a yawn. The celebrations were over and everyone had headed off to rest. I was preparing breakfast for tomorrow. I could have left this to someone else, tonight of all nights, but I was still a bit hyped up and couldn't get to sleep. I'd made Raphtalia go on and go to bed. S'yne was still with me, but she was sleeping in a corner of the dining hall. Today had been a pretty packed one, after all. With that Demon Dragon blood pudding, I'm pretty sure I would have collapsed myself.

"I thought as much . . . She had the adjustments for the energy transfer all wrong. That's why everything she said was skipping like that." I spun around at the voice to see S'yne's sister standing there waving to make sure I spotted her. She had just put a blanket carefully over S'yne. I thought she had repaired her familiar and had him on watch . . . but it wasn't moving, returned to nothing but a stuffed doll.

"You!" I shouted, the first thing that came to my mind.

"Well, well, well. Why don't we let S'yne continue to rest?" S'yne's sister said.

"What have you done to her?" I asked.

"Well, well, well. That makes me sound so nasty!" S'yne's sister objected. "I haven't done anything. I just don't want her to wake up, so I've dulled her senses a little."

"So why are you here?!" I shouted. I couldn't see why she would do this. We were on high alert. There didn't seem to be anything she could achieve. I decided to wake up Raph-chan, who was also sleeping, and have her tell Raphtalia and the others what was going on. I just needed to buy a little time and we could launch a unified attack all at once.

"Hmmm, that's such a complicated question. So I have one for you first. Before we talk any more, tell me how much S'yne has told you," S'yne's sister said.

"What do you mean? With all the sound skipping, we can hardly understand anything she says," I replied. She could hardly talk to us at all anymore. I was starting to think that she might be easier to talk to if her vassal weapon was finally destroyed completely.

"Well, well, well. It isn't only due to the broken vassal weapon," S'yne's sister explained. "I think it's also because anyone she has told about herself in the past, well . . . they all died." It was some kind of jinx that caused anyone she shared such information with to die. If that was the case, her silence had been to protect us.

No, that sounded crazy.

"First things first, Iwatani, you should really give some thought to exactly why S'yne is so fixated on you," S'yne's sister said.

"To say how much she hates you, maybe you know something about her fixations," I replied.

"No need to worry about me," S'yne's sister said deprecatingly. "If S'yne told you everything and you didn't believe her, it would break her little heart. I'm sure she's worried about you, you know, dying."

Worried about me not believing her, and worried about me dying . . . I gave it some thought and couldn't really think of anything I had done for S'yne that would warrant such devotion from her. I had promised to aid with her revenge, but she had already been protective of me before that. "I'll give you a hint. Have you seen S'yne with what looked like a small holy weapon core?"

"Yes, I have." When I was close to death, she had healed me using an item that looked like that.

"That is the compressed energy from one of the holy weapon power-up methods in our—now-destroyed—world. It can lend that strength to others," S'yne's sister explained.

"Okay . . ." I wondered why she had been able to heal me using it. More mysteries here to throw them on the pile.

"I don't want to interfere with S'yne's policy for dealing with you, so I'd better not tell you anything more than that," S'yne's sister said.

"So what do you want to say? There has to be something in this for you, a chatterbox coming all the way here," I said.

"Maybe," S'yne's sister replied, giving a small cough, and then answered normally. "To put it plainly, everyone you've seen from us so far—apart from the hangers-on we acquired locally—are part of the Third Army. I'm talking grunts, military worker ants here. We can lose as many as you can wipe out, and it doesn't hurt us. They basically exist to test out the prototypes that are created by the technical department."

"All of this is just some kind of experiment to you?!" I shouted. If the forces attacking this world were just the lab rats, that meant the boss had to still be far removed from them. Considering all the fighting we had come through so far and we'd caused no damage to them at all, it made me sick to hear it.

"So yes, we use the holy weapons, the vassal weapons, and all sorts of toys, but we aren't the main force. This is just another of the numerous worlds that the Third Army has attacked. The main force is off on some other world some-where trying to track down and win over a certain young girl," S'yne's sister said. I didn't need to hear that. "Taking this world is proving more difficult than anticipated, so you are being put on the back burner for a while. They are going to flash the holy weapons around a little to keep you on the hook in this world, making it easier for them to take their next target." Those holy weapons being the jewels, blunt instrument, and ship vassal weapon. It did feel like the battle here wasn't over yet. "Iwatani, they are heading to the world you came from next. All because you killed Bitch for the time being."

"Is Bitch really that important?" I asked. That would explain why S'yne's sister had been trying to hamper Bitch's efforts and made her fail though. But I was sure S'yne's sister had more authority than Bitch anyway.

"My point is, if you spend too long collecting holy and vassal weapons in this world, your own world is going to fall. That's what I came to warn you about," S'yne's sister said. If Ren and Motoyasu were killed by a wave while Itsuki and I were away, leaving the world without heroes, it could indeed be wiped out. That was bad, of course . . . but it also raised another big question.

"Why are you here explaining all this?" I asked.

"Well, well, well, I thought you might have worked it out," S'yne's sister said. "Things are complicated over here too. We need to please our leader, and some among us think that means providing a challenge."

"Okay then." I shook my head. So their leader liked to fight. I could understand that impulse, perhaps, but it was a pain in the ass right now. What was with these people using entire worlds like their playthings!

"Well then, Iwatani. Next time we meet, it will be in your world. That is all I came to say. Bye-bye!" With that, S'yne's sister vanished. Immediately afterward S'yne leapt up, turning her weapon into scissors and standing ready.

"Just now! Was my sister here?" S'yne asked. That was odd—her voice wasn't skipping. The movements of her familiars looked to have improved too.

"Yes, she was here," I replied. "She said they're coming to our world next." It was some nasty information from an almost one-sided conversation, and then she left again. In any case, right now I needed to talk to S'yne.

"S'yne, your sister said something else—that if you talk about yourself, everyone you tell will die," I said. S'yne gave a start at my words and looked away. Wow, so it seemed to be a real thing. S'yne's sister had been telling the truth. "No need to worry about that now. We don't need any more surprises, do we?" I reasoned with her.

"No . . . you simply don't need to know. My world is gone. My sister is nothing but a traitor, and I want nothing but to defeat her. You don't need to probe too deeply, Naofumi. You will be fine without any of my knowledge—you saw me fight

her, and I couldn't win. If knowing will kill you, then not knowing will produce the better result." Once she started talking, she talked a lot.

"Then I'm not going to help you out," I said, trying a different approach.

"I'm still going with you. What I can tell you is that this enemy is so strong you will need to become much stronger yourself. Even with all the holy weapon and vassal weapon power-up methods, and raising your level super high, I'm not sure if you can win or not," S'yne told me. She was stubborn, I'd give her that.

"Just tell me one thing. Why me?" I asked. It could have been any of the holy weapon holders, surely, so long as she eventually got a shot at her sister. Rather than a twisted weirdo like me, she would have been far better off with a tried-and-tested hero type like Kizuna. Or maybe she had already tried lots of other times and just come to me last.

"That's because . . . you're Naofumi," S'yne replied.

"Huh?" I said, puzzled, but she offered nothing more—even going so far as to squeeze her mouth shut. She really was stubborn. Even if she thought she was protecting me from this death-jinx business.

I also realized she had used my first name. No "Mr." or anything.

A few moments later Raphtalia and the others charged in

and the castle descended into a brief moment of uproar. That soon passed, but we were left with a very sticky situation indeed.

Somewhere, right then, I was sure I could hear S'yne's sister laughing.

The Rising of the Shield Hero Vol. 19
(TATE NO YUUSHA NO NARIAGARI Vol.19)
© Aneko Yusagi 2018
First published in Japan in 2018 by KADOKAWA CORPORATION, Tokyo.
English translation rights arranged with KADOKAWA CORPORATION, Tokyo.

ISBN: 978-1-64273-104-0

Written by Aneko Yusagi
Character Design Minami Seira
English Edition Published by One Peace Books 2020

Printed in Canada
1 2 3 4 5 6 7 8 9 10

One Peace Books
43-32 22nd Street STE 204 Long Island City New York 11101
www.onepeacebooks.com